A.E. NALLE

**EVERNIGHT PUBLISHING ®**

**www.evernightpublishing.com**

**A.E. NALLE**

# DEDICATION

This one is for all of my mom bitches.
Thank you for being the best hype group and always
supporting me.
"Okay, love you, bye!"

# A.E. NALLE

## WICKEDLY TRAPPED

### *The Wicked Series, 1*

**A.E. Nalle**

**Copyright © 2022**

❮•••◆•••❯

### Chapter One

"Come on, Kate, just one more shot!" Jill had been relentless tonight with her need to celebrate my move away from Georgia to the sandy beaches of Florida. She'd been trying, and failing, for years to get me down to Pensacola. Turns out, all it would take for me to leave the place I had built my life for the last nineteen years was a cheating husband and a high school grad who wanted to move across state borders for college.

If anyone would have told me when I had Lindsey that I'd be starting over just after watching my baby get her diploma, I would have laughed in their faces. If I was being honest with myself, I probably should have started over a lot sooner than I had.

I thought my marriage to Tom had been just fine, if not a little boring. I assumed that was normal. You never hear of married couples keeping the same passion they had when they were young and fumbling around in the backseat of a car. I thought Tom and I had just grown up and didn't require all the frills we used to have. As it happened, he was finding his frills somewhere else— mainly he found them in his much younger blonde bimbo of an assistant.

I was shocked to find out about his unfaithfulness, but if I was being completely honest, it didn't hurt as much as it probably should've. I'd been feeling trapped for years and just couldn't admit it.

So, here I was, sitting at The Sand Dollar with my best friend since third grade, trying to not seem as miserable as I felt. After all, a recently divorced mother following her daughter to a college town didn't exactly scream *winning*.

"I really shouldn't. I have my job interview in the morning, and I don't think it would make the best first impression to show up with a hangover."

Jill stared at me like I had a third eye. "Kathrine Hart, what part of *you already have the job* do you not understand? Samantha works under me, and I get the final say in who gets the job. You don't even have to show up to get it," she said with a smirk.

Ever since we were kids, Jill Brookes knew how to get what she wanted. She was beautiful with her long copper hair and stunning blue eyes you could just fall into. She was what every girl wished they could be. Obviously a walking bombshell with soft curves most would kill for, but she was also one of the smartest people I knew. She also had confidence in droves.

She owned the publishing firm where my interview was. I wasn't allowed to work when I was married, so my résumé wasn't exactly stellar. Tom preferred to be the sole provider. All that accomplished was making sure I had no skills to fall back on when shit hit the fan.

I tried to make her see reason. "I still have to do the interview, Jill. How little would people think of me if they knew I only got the job because I'm best friends with the owner?"

Jill rolled her eyes, brushing me off. "Come on, Kate. Please? You know as well as I do that a divorce from Tommy boy is more than enough to celebrate. Especially now that you can find some hot young thing to give you all the orgasms you've been missing out on all these years," she said behind a playful smile.

My cheeks flared. "Jill! You don't have to announce it to the whole bar!"

She giggled, then said in a sing-song voice, "Do some more shots with me and I promise I won't embarrass you anymore."

I rolled my eyes and smiled. "All right, but only one more and I have to go!" I hopped down from my stool at our high-top, leaving Jill grinning while happily clapping her hands together as I walked my way to the main bar.

We were seated at the back of the upscale bar. There wasn't anything nearly as nice as this place in our small hometown. Looking around, I took in the swanky establishment. To the left of us were all the VIP booths with rich black leather seating and maroon-colored clothed tables. The dim lighting offered a certain feeling of intimacy to those who occupied them. They had their own private bar with bottle service and an assigned waitress. We regular folk had to wait for one of the other waitresses buzzing around or walk across the dance floor to the front of the building to get our drinks.

I supposed it was set up this way to get people on the dance floor. Right now, it served as an annoyance. Trying to avoid all the gyrating bodies was a feat in itself. I had no choice but to shove my way through them as best as I could.

"Hey, what's your name?" The question pressed right against my ear.

I swiftly turned around to tell him I wasn't interested. He took that as an invitation to start grinding on me like if he showed me how much he could hump me now, it would somehow get me into his bed later. I didn't understand how most men's minds worked.

I pushed his chest to get away from the smell of beer and cigarettes assaulting my nose. Using my best authoritative voice, I said, "I am not interested in being used as a stripper pole tonight, thank you."

He wasn't letting go. "What about a blow-up doll? I can make you feel real good," he slurred as he ran his hands down my hips.

Just the thought of this man touching my body made my skin crawl. I finally got a good look at him. His hair was greasy, and he wore a tropical button-down in desperate need of a wash. "I said no, and I meant it. Now stop touching me!" I yelled over the roaring music.

He rolled his heavily glazed eyes but finally dropped his hands. "Fucking cock tease!" He spat his volatile words at me.

I didn't care what he called me, I was just happy that he stalked away. What was it with most men? When they didn't get their way with a woman, they immediately had to act like women were the ones who led them to the path of temptation?

I turned away from Creepy Charlie and headed to the bar again. The bar was way busier than I thought it should be for a Tuesday night. A lot of it probably had to do with it being close to finals week at the college. Students were flooding the bars trying to blow off some steam.

While this place let minors in, they had to wear a

bright yellow wristband so the staff knew not to serve them alcohol. It was nice that they allowed them entry, offering a place for all to come and escape from reality for a bit. I was surprised Lindsey and her friends weren't here as well. Last time I talked to her, she said her classes were getting brutal.

I never had a college experience. Yet another one of Tom's ways of keeping me at home and under his thumb. He convinced me that I didn't need to be educated in order to raise our daughter, especially since he was going to be our provider. He was convinced he would inherit his dad's car dealership and I wouldn't be required to make my own income.

That plan worked out fine until he started fucking Vivian in the showroom cars after hours. Maybe one day I would check out the local community college and look into some classes. For now, I needed to focus on getting my shit together.

I finally pushed through the crowd and made it to the bar. Getting the bartender's attention was going to be another story altogether. I tried to wait patiently, but he kept moving around to other customers, completely ignoring me. A waitress brought out some food from the kitchen and walked right past me. I closed my eyes and took a deep breath. Whatever she was carrying smelled amazing, and my mouth watered.

I needed to calm down my inner fat girl and figure out how to get this bartender's attention. I laughed at myself. Who was I kidding, I didn't have an inner fat girl, I *was* the inner fat girl. Sighing to myself, I turned back to face the bar.

Some girl standing next to me ordered beers. While she was turned around talking to her girlfriend, the bartender put two of the beers down behind her. As if it happened in slow motion, she turned back around, knocked her elbow into the beers, and sent it flying right at me. Before I had time to react, my blouse was drenched. I tried to move as fast as I could to catch the now-empty glass before it fell and shattered. Quickly leaning over the bar, I caught it.

"Hey!" was all I heard as I stood back up.

I looked up just in time to come face to face with a black t-shirt stretched across a very impressive chest. My gaze traveled up from there. From his chest to his broad shoulders, to his hard jaw with the sexiest amount of black stubble spread around his sensual lips. The kind of lips that made all my forgotten girl parts clench. His jaw was all masculine angles and squared, and his wavy, jet-black hair reached the nape of his neck, curling slightly.

My fingers itched with the need to run through that hair. *Is it as soft as it looks?* I finally made it up to his emerald-green eyes, and my breath caught in my throat. It took me a beat or two to realize he was scowling at me.

He scolded me, "What the fuck do you think you're doing?"

I flinched and looked around to see if he was talking to someone behind me. When I concluded that he was indeed talking to me, I stumbled over my words. "Wh–What do you mean?"

"If you can't wait like everyone else here, then you need to get the fuck out of my bar," he said behind clenched teeth. Someone had definitely pissed in this man's Cheerios this morning.

"What?" I was only getting more confused by the second. That was the moment he pointed to my outstretched hand. I hadn't even realized I was still holding the glass, and it did look like I was trying to reach across the bar to get my own drink.

"Oh, I—"

"Save it! I know what you're doing. You can't wait a couple of minutes for someone to help you, so you decide to help yourself. If you haven't noticed, we are a little swamped right now. From the looks of you, you've had enough anyway," he said with an exasperated huff. "I think it's best if you pack it in for the night. I'll call you a cab right after I have security to escort you out." Aggravated, he turned his back to me and reached for the phone.

I felt my face going cherry red from not only embarrassment but also anger. "Excuse me, asshole!" I waited for him to turn and look at me. Satisfied at the surprise I saw on his face, I continued. "If you would stop trying to talk over me for two seconds, you will see that I'm not trying to get a free drink."

Pointing to my right, I said, "She spilled her drink, and I was trying to catch it. You would have known that if you bothered to ask the other bartender who gave her the drinks."

Said bartender came jogging through the kitchen door with fresh towels in hand. He abruptly stopped, seeming a little confused about the heated argument he'd just walked in on.

"But no, you jumped to conclusions and assumed I was trying to steal." At this point, his scowl seemed to be softening in realization, but I didn't care. I was so fed up with self-righteous pricks. "Don't bother calling security. I'll find my own way out of your precious bar."

I slammed the glass down on the bar and took off toward the nearest *exit* sign. I could feel everyone who had been huddled around the bar area staring at me now. Embarrassment flooded me again as I picked up my speed to get away from the looks. I needed to get Jill, but I had to get some fresh air before I completely fell apart.

How pathetic must I look right now? I was probably one of the oldest women in this place, covered in beer, and to top it all off, I just got yelled at by the most gorgeous man I had ever seen.

I came to the door that would lead me to my freedom and pushed it open. As the door closed behind me, I was left with the muffled sounds of music from the bar. In my rush to get outside, I must have gone out one of the side doors because I stood in a dark alleyway.

It had cooled off quite a bit since the sun went down, but the crisp air felt good on my overheated skin. I leaned against the cool brick wall of the building and shook my head.

"What a jerk," I mumbled. I was so done with this night. All I wanted to do was go home and take a hot shower to get the smell of beer out of my hair. I would bet if I checked a mirror, I would look just as miserable as I felt.

I reached into my bag and dug to find my phone so I could give Jill a brief rundown of what happened and tell her I was headed home. Suddenly, I saw a flame from a lighter spark.

"Did you decide you wanted to play after all?"

## Chapter Two

Creepy Charlie stood ten feet away, sneering at me behind his cigarette.

"Look, dude, I'm really not in the mood for more bullshit tonight. Just leave me alone."

He took a long drag off his cigarette and blew the smoke out as he prowled toward me. "You weren't being very nice in there while I was just trying to let you know how sexy you look. Why don't you come over here and make it up to me?" He grabbed himself in a vulgar display.

My drinks of the night were about to make another appearance. From the look in his eyes, this man had to be on some kind of drug. Getting a little nervous, I backed away. "I think I'll pass."

I turned around and walked away. Before I could get more than a few steps, he rushed up and grabbed me from behind. "Now, now that's not very nice either." He chuckled next to my cheek before inhaling deeply. Then he ran his nose up the side of my neck, making my adrenaline spike and a shiver run down my spine.

Panic now squeezing my throat, I tried to squirm away from him, but that seemed to make him more excited. Before I could do anything else, he had a fist full of my hair and cranked my neck back so there was no room for escape. Pain crackled along my scalp. His other arm had snaked around my waist and held me so tight it was hard to get a full breath.

"You need to learn some manners. I think we will start with my cock in your mouth. I'll teach you how to accept a compliment when given one." The smell of his breath invaded my senses, and I gagged. Panic settled in as I wildly searched for a way out of his grasp.

I was about to scream when there was a grunt behind me. All of a sudden, Charlie was gone. I turned around in time to see my attacker on his back with the Greek god of a bartender sitting on top of him and slamming his fist into his face. He was so vicious in his attack that it should have frightened me. It should have, but it didn't scare me in the least.

Charlie kicked out and tried to buck him off. His face was a bloody mess. My defender wrapped his big hand around his throat and squeezed until I thought Charlie's eyes were going to pop out of his head.

"If you ever think to come back here and put your hands on a woman that clearly does not want you, I will kill you myself." He let go of his neck, and the man took an audible gasp of air. Charlie scrambled out from underneath my champion and half-ran, half-fell his way out of the alley.

I got my first real look at this man who just saved me from a certain tragedy and had to search for the right words. He stood and wiped his hand down the front of his jeans, glancing at his knuckles. Then he took a couple of big strides toward me, and I had to look up to make eye contact as he studied me for any damage.

"Are you okay? I've seen that guy prowling around the past couple of weeks and just knew he was going to start some trouble." His eyes searched mine.

God, he was beautiful. The way his hair fell onto his forehead when he was looking down at me took my breath away. He was so much taller than me, and I couldn't help but wonder what it would be like to be held against him.

He grinned slightly as he stared at me, clearly waiting for me to say something.

I stumbled to find the right words. "I, uh, well, now I regret calling you an asshole."

It was his turn to look embarrassed as his cheeks flushed slightly and broke eye contact. "I need to apologize for my behavior inside. After you walked away, Joe confirmed your story. It was all a big misunderstanding. I'm sorry for being a dick."

*Well, thank you, Joe.* He must have been the other bartender. I nodded. "Thanks for the apology." Not sure what else to say, I fell silent.

He stuck his hands in his pockets and looked down at his feet, the move making him appear even more handsome. He faced me again. "Look, I can't leave you alone out here after what just happened. Do you want to come back in, and I can get you a drink? On the house, of course." He gave me a sheepish smile, revealing his dimples. If I thought he was sexy before, it was nothing compared to how sexy he was when he smiled.

He was almost acting a little nervous now that we were alone. I really couldn't imagine what would make him nervous. If I didn't know any better, I would say this man was looking at me with a spark of attraction in his eyes.

It wasn't like I was some great beauty. With my plain, dirty-blonde hair and brown eyes, I was as average as they came. If you put me beside Jill, it would be a landslide on who would win that particular beauty contest. The only thing I had going for me was a round ass and medium-to-large breasts. Although they sagged a little from having a child, they were still nice in the right bra. I always carried an extra twenty pounds that wouldn't come off no matter what fad diet I tried.

"I was just getting ready to head home. I have an important interview in the morning. Thank you for the offer though," I said with a small smile.

A look of disappointment crossed his face. "Okay, let me at least get you that cab," he offered.

I stopped him as he reached for his cell phone. "Actually, I just live around the corner, so I'm just going to walk."

His eyes lit up at that for some reason. "Well, let me walk you, just to make sure you don't have any more problems tonight."

"Oh, I couldn't keep you. I don't want you to get into trouble with your boss."

He was full-on smiling now as if he found something funny. "I think I can get away for a few minutes."

I didn't know what it was about this man. I shouldn't be as trusting as I was most of the time. Especially after my brief encounter with Charlie. But I couldn't find a reason to tell him no. I nodded in agreement before I could talk some sense into myself.

I pulled out my phone and sent a text to Jill, telling her I was headed out and I would explain everything tomorrow. Then I put my phone back in my bag and walked with my Greek god. "My name is Kathrine, by the way. But everyone calls me Kate," I said with a blushing smile.

He grinned, holding out his hand for me to shake. "Heath Gillup."

I put my hand in his, shocked when he pulled it up and kissed the back of it. I felt a flush creep across my cheeks as I stared at my hand.

We walked in silence for a couple of minutes before he spoke. "So, are you new to town? I don't think I've seen you before."

I, for one, would remember meeting him, so I could say the same thing. "I just moved here about a month ago from my hometown in Georgia. I needed a fresh start."

He looked at me with those endless green eyes

like he was trying to figure out a puzzle. "So, Kate, are you running from something then?"

I liked the way my name rolled off his tongue. "I wouldn't exactly say I'm running. I woke up one day and decided I wasn't happy with the person I had become. I had poured my soul into raising my child and trying to keep my wayward husband happy, and I realized somewhere down the line I lost the girl I used to be. It was past time to go searching for her." I didn't know why I was telling this to a perfect stranger, but for some reason, Heath was very easy to talk to.

"Don't take this the wrong way, but you definitely don't look like someone's mom, let alone someone's wife," he said.

I laughed out loud. "Believe me, Tom didn't think I looked like a wife either. He started fucking his assistant years ago as a way out of our marriage." I winced when I realized how bitter that sounded.

Heath shook his head and didn't say anything else. Before I knew it, we had made it to my apartment complex. I dug through my bag to find the key for the front door. I swore and scolded myself for buying such a big bag. I was forever losing my keys in the endless thing.

I looked up to tell Heath that he could just head on back and he didn't have to wait for me when I saw him pull a key out of his pocket and open the door. I was stunned. Only tenants of this building were supposed to have a key to open the front door. Suddenly, his smile from earlier made all the more sense. "You live in this building, don't you?"

He gave me a full smile that made me go a little dizzy. "Sixth floor. You?" he asked.

"Me too." Seeing as there were only two apartments on each floor, my guess was that we shared a wall. "Small world," I mumbled with a grin.

He gestured for me to walk into the building first. I got up to the door and turned to thank him, not expecting him to be right behind me. He was so close that when I turned, our noses just about touched.

Jerking back, I lost my footing and started to fall. My brain stopped working as he held my waist to steady me, and I grabbed his forearms for balance. I sucked in my breath at the feel of his warm hands wrapped around me, making me feel petite. It would be just like me to fall on my ass in front of this man. He held me, staring at my lips. I swallowed around the lump in my throat and puffed out a small breath. His unique scent surrounded me, making me stifle my sigh of satisfaction.

His gaze finally left my lips as he mumbled, "My shift was over thirty minutes ago, and I was on my way home anyway." His sweet-smelling breath fanned across my face. It wouldn't take much to lean in the extra few inches and seal my lips with his. "I can go if I'm making you uncomfortable."

*Uncomfortable* wasn't the term I would have used. *Unsteady, wanting, needy.* Those were words I would use to describe how I was feeling. The question popped into my head and out of my mouth before I could even stop it. "How old are you?"

He let out a burst of air that ended in a chuckle. "That's a very random question, sweetheart. I'm twenty-six. Can I ask your age, too?" He smiled like I was one of the most amusing things he had seen in a while.

I blushed at the term of endearment. I was breathless when I told him. "Old enough to have a daughter in college," I murmured. I forced myself to turn around and headed toward the elevator with him hot on my heels. How was I supposed to share an elevator with him when I could barely stand next to him without losing my balance?

As we entered the elevator, both of our fingers reached for the number six. He chuckled and gestured for me to go ahead. I pushed the button and held my breath as the doors closed.

I tried to ignore it, I really did. The tension built higher and higher. I could feel the air sizzling, getting ready to pop. I kept my eyes straight ahead, afraid to look over at him. I could feel his gaze roaming over me. If looks could burn, I would have been on fire.

I glanced at his hands that were shoved in his pockets, like he was trying to hold himself back. I let my gaze trail up his strong arms, to his shoulders and chest, then to his face. We made eye contact and held for what felt like minutes. I felt like there was an audible crack in the air when the tension broke.

Heath mumbled a curse as he lunged for me, pushing me against the wall and trapping me. He sank his hands into my hair and held me still as his lips crashed down on mine. His tongue practically begged for entry, and he groaned as I opened under him. With his body flush against mine, I could feel how much he wanted me.

I moaned and brought one of my legs up around his hip. He quickly caught it and ground down on my sex as he kept kissing me as if his life depended on it. His other hand left my hair and made its way to my breast. I could feel my nipple tighten as his fingers dragged across it, and I nearly squealed as he seductively pinched it through the fabric. I expected pain but was surprised when it was heat that zapped right to my core. I had never felt like this before.

My hands found their way into his hair, tugging. It was as silky as I thought it would be. He rewarded me with another groan into my mouth. "You taste so fucking sweet," he murmured against my lips. A fresh wave of arousal rushed to my pussy as he ground his erection against me.

I pulled away long enough to push my hand between us. I needed to feel him. I could feel how hard he was under the fabric, but I needed more.

I looked back up at him as I tugged the hem of his shirt up, exposing the slightest amount of warm skin. He took my mouth again as my hands made contact with his hard abs. He groaned as if my touch pleased him before he fumbled with the button on my jeans.

I hadn't been kissed like this since … ever. I have never in my life wanted someone to put their hands on me as much as I wanted Heath to. I felt him get the button released, and his fingers brushed the top of my panties. Then he let his fingers graze just below the seam, and I sucked in a harsh breath against his mouth.

Somewhere in the back of my mind, warning bells rang. I'd just met this man, and I was letting him fuck me in the elevator. I ignored all those bells as Heath pushed his fingers just a little further down.

My breath hitched as he got closer and closer to where I needed him. I nearly convulsed on the spot as his finger dragged right along my engorged clitoris. "Fuck, you're so wet, sweetheart." He groaned as he circled the nub lightly.

The ding barely registered in my lust-filled brain as we made it to the sixth floor. I was so consumed with Heath that I didn't realize someone was standing at the door until they cleared their throat. "Looks like I should probably take the stairs."

## Chapter Three

My eyes popped open, and I tried to push Heath away. He seemed to come out of our lust bubble to scowl at our visitor. He still took his time removing his hand from my panties and lowering my leg. I was sure my face was fifty shades of red as I tried to catch my breath. I looked up at our visitor, trying to hide my embarrassment as well as I could.

If Heath was a Greek god, then this man was a Viking. He was taller than Heath but just as muscular. Where Heath seemed to be bulkier, this man was lean. I had no doubt he would be able to hold his own though.

He was smiling down at me as if I looked like a particularly juicy steak. His amber eyes almost seemed to pull me in. His hair was just about as long as Heath's but a very light blond. He had the start of a beard that covered a very sharp-looking jawline. I couldn't help the thought of what that beard would feel like against my naked skin. Standing there in his ripped blue jeans and leather jacket, he looked like sin on a stick.

"Sorry to interrupt the party, Heath," he said, not taking his eyes off me.

I pulled away and tried to shrink into the corner of the elevator.

Heath looked at our intruder, cleared his throat, and said, "Reid, I thought you had to work early and were turning in for the night."

Reid finally took those scolding eyes off me and looked at Heath. "Greg called in, so I have the graveyard shift. Looks like I'll be missing out on some fun though," he said with a pout as he turned his attention back to me.

I didn't quite understand what he meant by that, but I let it go.

Heath grunted at his friend, accepting his answer. Then he turned back to me. "Kate, this is my roommate, Reid Hudson. Reid, this is our next-door neighbor, Kate." He said the latter with a small smirk.

Reid still had me trapped with his stare. "Well, that's interesting. She looks like a little bunny, snared in your trap with those big brown eyes of hers. It's nice to meet you, Kate. I wish I could stick around, as this seems infinitely more interesting, but I really do have to go." He looked me up and down, licking his lips.

Yeah, that did something for me too. Then he said in a smooth-as-silk voice, "Maybe another time, Heath?"

The boys exchanged a look that I couldn't quite understand, and Heath nodded. "Most definitely," he mumbled as he looked back down at me.

I had to get out of here. Reid thought I looked like a bunny caught in a trap. Well, I definitely felt like one. I ducked out of the elevator with a backward glance at the boys. Heath followed me while Reid got in and pushed the button for the lobby. He gave me a wink as the doors closed.

As I stepped up to my door, I dug my keys out of my bag while I could feel Heath's breath on the back of my neck. Each breath sent another electric jolt down to my core.

I finally got the door unlocked and I turned around. Heath put his hands above me and grabbed my door frame. There was the sexiest little peek of tattoo wrapping around his bicep I hadn't noticed until now. My fingers itched with the need to run along the smooth black lines. The sight was enough to make me melt into a puddle on the floor.

Heath reached out, tucked some stray hair behind my ear, and leaned forward like he was going to kiss me again. I closed my eyes and gave in to the sensation. I waited for that kiss to come, and when it landed on my cheek instead of my lips, I was a little disappointed.

"It was really nice to meet you, Kate. I'll be seeing you."

His hands left me as he turned and headed to his door. I stood there in my stupor for probably too long, trying to gather my wits. I finally turned around and entered my apartment, shutting and locking the door behind me.

I leaned against the door, trying to process what just happened. I was a thirty-five-year-old woman who just had the make-out session of her life with a twenty-six-year-old she didn't even know. Until now, the riskiest thing I'd ever done was drive ten miles over the speed limit. I giggled at the craziness of it all.

I shook my head to clear it and made my way to my bathroom. No matter how much I wanted to go across the hall and finish what we started, I needed to be logical about this. Heath was so young, and he had his whole life still ahead of him. He didn't want to be with someone like me. A man like him could be sleeping with supermodels. He wouldn't want an overweight mom warming his bed. According to my ex, I was the most boring person, in and out of the bedroom. I had nothing to offer a guy like that. How could I start a relationship with someone when I didn't even know who I was?

After taking a quick shower to get the smell of beer off of me, I got ready for bed. Turning out the light, I slipped into bed. As I lay in the dark, I couldn't help my thoughts as they wandered back to the man I shared a wall with. I wondered if his bedroom wall was also my bedroom wall. That thought alone got me more aroused than it should have. I could see a date with my battery-operated boyfriend in the near future.

Getting involved with someone like Heath would

be trouble, but damn, wouldn't it be wild if I could just let myself go for once and do something just for me. My eyes started to droop as sleep took me. I couldn't stop the dreams that came of emerald and amber eyes.

****

"Oh, my God!" Jill squealed from behind her desk. I already regretted the decision to tell her about last night. "I can't believe you have been in town for a month and didn't know you lived next to that hottie! I am so proud of you for hittin' that, girl!"

I felt color bloom across my cheeks. When Jill got excited about something, everyone heard. She was good at a lot of things, but discretion was not one of them.

"So, when are you going to see him again?" she asked with a big grin.

I hadn't told her yet that it was a one-time thing. The more I thought about it, the more I talked myself out of it. My life was such a mess right now. There was no way I could bring someone new into the fold to watch this trainwreck.

The last thing I needed was to try to start a relationship with my next-door neighbor. If we did end up taking it further, what would happen when one of us wanted out? The whole situation spelled disaster. "It was fun, but I don't see it happening again. I bet he woke up this morning and regretted kissing an overweight old lady," I said with a self-deprecating smile.

Jill's mouth hung open and she looked at me like I'd lost my mind. "You've got to be kidding me! You act like you have one foot in the grave, Kate. You need a serious morale boost. I don't know if you have looked in the mirror lately, but you have a bangin' body. You're a total MILF. It might come as a shock to you, but most men dig the older chick thing. And they also like a girl with curves. I don't know very many men who want to sleep with a stick."

She made the face she normally got when she was annoyed with me. "You need to get out there and do some experimenting. Then you need to tell me all about it so I can live vicariously through you." A smooth smile stretched over her lips and she waggled her eyebrows. I couldn't help the giggle that bubbled up.

She definitely didn't need to live vicariously through me when she was out living for herself most nights. We both knew that Jill had gotten around a lot. She had gone a little wild in our younger years, but I couldn't blame her. She had some past trauma she didn't like to talk about, but I knew that one of the ways she had gained control over her life again was through sex. It probably wasn't the healthiest way to deal with trauma, but as long as she was safe, I couldn't fault her. Some people changed their hair as a way to cope with the loss of control, and Jill simply changed her sexual partners. Though she had slowed the one-night stands over the last few years, she still indulged from time to time.

My sex life, or lack thereof, was something I didn't want to talk about right now. "So, did Samantha say anything to you about how my interview went? I have a pretty good feeling about it. After all, how hard can answering phones and making appointments really be?" I tried not to grimace at my own lame attempt at changing the subject.

Jill rolled her eyes, indicating she knew what I was trying to do. "Don't think that this conversation is over. She told me that she has a couple more people she needs to talk with, but she thinks you will be a good match for the job."

I couldn't help the excitement that rolled through me at the thought of getting my first job. Jill looked at me out of the corner of her eye. "You know I just want you to be happy, right?" Her voice was filled with sympathy.

I tried to stop the embarrassment that washed over me after seeing the pity in her eyes. "I think you just need to get out of your head for a little while, ya know? Maybe have some fun. You have spent most of your life taking care of someone else. Now it's time to take care of Kate."

As I left the office building and went to my car, I couldn't help replaying Jill's words in my head. Maybe she was right. Maybe I did need to get out of my head and just think of myself for once. After starting my car, I headed home.

Truth be told, I was getting tired of being sad. I had been in a slump for a long time and just couldn't admit it to myself. I had trouble finding my passion in anything and chose to throw myself into taking care of Lindsey and ignoring everything else. I'd always accepted everything that was thrown into my lap. Never asking any questions or fighting for what I needed. I didn't know when exactly it happened, but I had become an onlooker to my own life.

"Stop being so pathetic," I said to myself as I drove the busy streets leading to my apartment. It was far past time I stopped wallowing in self-pity and did something for myself. Jill was a saint for putting up with my sad-sack ass for so many years. I needed to open my eyes and see that my life didn't have to be so miserable. So Tom left me for a younger woman. My marriage was over long before he even told me he didn't want me anymore. I deserved to be happy for once.

Heath sure acted like he was into me last night, so why shouldn't I go for this? Even if it all blew up in my face, at least I could say that I tried. I couldn't help but think the sex would be enough to make it all worth it.

I pulled into my assigned parking spot and exited the car. Locking it behind me, I marched up the stairs with new determination. I hopped on the elevator, hitting six with a plan. I was going straight to Heath's door and asking him on a date. If he decided he didn't want me anymore, then I would deal with it after. It was past time to move on and try again because I was done being lonely. It was time to start taking some risks.

I looked at the wall he had pushed me against last night and blushed, remembering the way he had kissed me like he was drowning and I was his last breath of fresh air. If I closed my eyes, I could almost feel his hands as they roamed my body.

The loud *ding* of the elevator jolted me from my daydream, and I took a deep, fortifying breath. I was going to do this. After getting off the elevator, I marched right up to his door. Fist up, ready to knock, I paused.

Those thoughts of not being good enough crept back in. I could almost hear Tom's voice as he told me I wasn't good enough. I was too overweight. I was too boring.

*Enough*, I thought to myself. When I moved, I promised myself I would try to find the person I was meant to be, and this might be the first step to doing just that. *Fears aside, for better or worse, here we go.*

I knocked and wiped my sweaty palms down my jean-clad thighs. It felt like forever until I heard shuffling on the other side of the door. As the knob turned, I steeled myself. Only I was not met by Heath. I sucked in my breath as I came face to face with the ruggedly sexy Viking from last night.

## Chapter Four

"Reid," I breathed. At first, he looked a little confused, and then recognition sparked in those amber eyes.

"Bunny." A smooth smile slid across his lips as I flushed at the endearment. "I didn't think I would get to see you so soon. To what do I owe this pleasure?" he asked as he leaned against the door frame.

I looked him up and down. He wasn't wearing any socks or shoes, telling me he had been relaxing when I interrupted him. I didn't know why, but the sight of his naked feet turned me on more than I would've liked to admit. Taking in the low-slung faded blue jeans covering strong legs, I swallowed hard as I looked past his tapered waist. I bet he had that sexy $V$ that led to the promised land. My gaze traveled up to his dark-blue shirt with the sleeves rolled up, revealing his forearms.

Like Heath, Reid also had a tattoo. Only this one wrapped around his forearm and disappeared underneath the fabric. I wondered how far up the tattoo went. It probably ran up the entire length of his arm and wound around his shoulder.

I dragged my gaze to his chest that stretched the fabric of his shirt. There was an emblem on his left pec that led me to believe Reid was a first responder of some sort. My gaze finally made its way back to his face, where a lock of hair had fallen onto his forehead, partially covering my view of his eye in the sexiest way. I made eye contact and found him staring at me too, waiting.

I blinked and tried to swallow with my suddenly dry mouth. He'd asked me a question and I should've answered—if only I could remember what he'd said.

I flushed. "I'm sorry. What did you say?"

I braced myself, figuring he would get the same look of annoyance that Tom used to get when he realized I wasn't listening.

Reid chuckled. "Oh, bunny. What are we going to do with you?"

It felt like he put a little emphasis on the *we* part. I shook my head to clear all the intrusive thoughts. I swallowed again. "Is Heath home?"

Reid shook his head in the negative. "No, he had to run to the bar to do inventory early this evening. The trouble with owning a bar is that you don't have much free time."

I was a little taken aback by his words. I had just figured Heath worked at The Sand Dollar, I didn't think he owned it. I was a little impressed by the fact that someone at his age owned such a successful business. So, that was why he laughed at me when I said he would get into trouble for leaving work early. *Can't get into trouble for leaving work when you're the boss.*

I felt like an idiot for assuming he was only a bartender because of his age. I blushed as if Reid could read my thoughts. He continued to study me like he was trying to figure out a particularly difficult puzzle. "He should be back any minute if you want to come in and wait."

That was a really bad idea. I was here to ask his roommate out, yet I was dumbstruck like a pre-teen pining after the high school quarterback. Yes, it would definitely be an awful idea to follow this man into his empty apartment where we would be alone for who knew how long. So why did I find myself nodding and following him through the door?

Once inside, I looked around. The layout of the apartment was a mirror of mine. For two bachelors living together, it was a lot cleaner than one would expect. They had a big U-shaped sectional that covered one of the walls, facing a big TV in the main room. The overstuffed cushions just begged for someone to sink into them. Being that the floor plan was the same as my apartment, I knew down the hallway would be two bedrooms and a shared bathroom with the same oversized shower I had. I was right in my late-night contemplations. From the looks of it, my bedroom did, in fact, share a wall with one of theirs. I wondered whose.

"Would you like anything to drink? I think we have tea, water, or beer." Reid looked at me with humor in his eyes.

"Sure, I'll have a beer," I said in a too-shaky voice.

Maybe a little liquid courage would calm my nerves. He headed toward the kitchen. Hearing him digging in the fridge, I found myself being drawn to the pictures hanging on the wall.

Most of the pictures looked like they were from the boys' younger years. From the looks of it, they had been friends for a long time. The pictures spanned from two boys with toothless grins to what looked like high school graduation. *Good to know they have always been this attractive.* It really wasn't fair to all of womankind for these two to be so good-looking.

I felt, rather than saw, Reid come up and stand next to me.

"Heath and I have been friends our entire lives. Our moms were best friends in school, so we were pretty much raised together."

I nodded. "That's awesome that you two have each other. Life is always easier when you have someone to go through it with."

Reid regarded me almost seriously as he handed

me my beer. "So, tell me about yourself. Health said you're new to town."

*Heath talked about me?* A giddy feeling surged through me at the thought of these two talking about me. Tamping down my thrill, I took a swig of my beer. I watched Reid's hooded eyes follow the movement as I brought the bottle to my lips and swallowed.

I felt a rush of nervousness as I cleared my throat. "There isn't much to know. I'm quite boring. I got pregnant in high school, got married, got cheated on, got divorced. Kid left for college and now here I am. I know, real exciting stuff." I let out a shaky laugh.

I took another sip of my beer before I continued. "I've led a very bland life. Don't get me wrong, I love being a mother and wouldn't take it back for anything. I just wish I hadn't given so much of myself up in the process. I moved here to sort of find myself again, ya know? I need to see if I really am as dull as my ex likes to say I am."

When did I start deciding to share my whole life story with strangers? For some reason, Reid was super easy to talk to, the same as Heath.

Reid was studying me again. "You look anything but dull, bunny. Tell me more about this ex of yours. Is he blind or just an idiot?"

I tried to hold back the laugh that escaped. "No, he isn't blind. We started dating sophomore year and got pregnant with our daughter in the backseat of his mom's car. He did what he thought was right and married me. We were married for nineteen years, but it only came out recently that he was unfaithful for half of that."

I had the irrevocable need to open up to this man. "He didn't even tell me like a man. I walked in on him and Vivian at work one day. I felt bad he had to work so late and I decided to bring him supper. You can imagine how surprised I was when I walked in and he had her bent over his desk. After that, he confessed to how long it had been happening. He told me that I had gotten fat and he couldn't stand to look at me anymore. That I was the reason he cheated and if I hadn't been so boring, maybe he would have cared enough to stay with me." The laugh that escaped me held no humor.

"He even dared to act like I was the reason he couldn't satisfy me. Saying something was wrong with me because I could never..." I trailed off and looked away, shaking my head as my eyes started to burn. What was I doing telling Reid all of this? My face blazed as embarrassment washed over me. I had overshared.

I opened my mouth to make an excuse to leave when Reid took hold of my chin and raised my face so I was forced to look at him. If I didn't know any better, I would say there was anger in his eyes.

"Your ex sounds like a limp-dick fucker who wouldn't know how to satisfy a woman even if someone gave him a playbook." His gaze roamed all over my face before landing on my lips as he said, "I'm sorry if nobody has ever told you this before, but you are beautiful. Anyone who says otherwise is a fucking idiot. I don't understand what your ex was thinking, stepping out on someone with a body like yours."

Reid's other hand took the beer from me, bringing it up to his lips for a taste. The sight of his mouth against the same place my mouth had been moments ago caused a wave of arousal to flood between my legs. I watched his tongue lap up the remaining liquid on his lips before he placed the bottle to the side.

Then he brought his hand back and settled it on my hip. His thumb made slow, maddening circles, dipping under the waist of my jeans. He slid his other hand past my cheek, settling behind my head and digging his fingers into my hair at my nape.

I loved the way I was forced to make eye contact. His gaze bounced between my lips and my eyes as he said, "If you were mine, you wouldn't be able to walk away without a reminder that I had been inside you."

It was as if his words had a direct link to all my girl parts. I couldn't stop the moan from escaping as he crashed his lips to mine. He was intoxicating. Unlike the gentle coaxing from Heath, this was a full-on assault on my senses.

Holding the back of my neck, he moved me the way he wanted me, forcing my mouth to open so his tongue to enter. His tongue's fucking motions in my mouth were enough to make my panties increasingly wet, and the roughness of his short beard rubbing against my skin only lit me up further.

Reid released the back of my neck in favor of grabbing the curve of my ass to pick me up. Never releasing my mouth, he carried me toward the couch. He tore his lips from mine long enough to drop me on my back.

I looked up at him with lust-glazed eyes. He looked downright savage standing above me. I found my gaze glued to the front of his jeans, where it was obvious he wasn't unaffected by our kisses. His hard length strained against his zipper. In a moment of boldness, I reached up to rub my hand on the bulge, but he caught my hand before I could.

He tsked. "Oh, bunny. Try to make another move like that and I'll have your hands tied up before you can even protest. You take what I give you." Then he lowered himself on top of me, making room for himself between my legs.

His words should have sent warning bells ringing, but all they did was make my core clench and burn as arousal flooded my entire body. It was like he'd added gasoline to an open flame. My body was on fire. This was one of the hottest experiences of my life, the other being my elevator encounter with Heath.

Reid leaned back down and devoured my mouth once again, and his cock pressed against my sex. I cursed our jeans for stopping his hardness from meeting my softness, and I moaned as he ground down on me.

He pulled his mouth away in favor of traveling lower. "Heath was right. You are so fucking sweet, baby." His mouth came to the top of my blouse and kissed the swells of my breasts that poked out. With deft fingers, he unbuttoned the buttons.

I mentally thanked myself for putting on one of my nicer bras this morning. It was black lace with just a slight push-up to it. It made the girls look fabulous despite their age.

"Did you know your bra is see-through? I can see those pink nipples through the lace. They are poking up, just begging for some attention." He growled.

I gave a little shout when his hot mouth came down on my right nipple. I looked down long enough to make eye contact as he flicked his tongue over the tight bud. The movement went straight to my pussy. "You're so fucking responsive, bunny. I wonder how you would react if I licked other places too," he said with a wicked grin.

With quick fingers, he pulled the cups of my bra down and out of the way. No sooner had the cool air caressed my breasts, than his mouth was back down working the kind of magic I wouldn't have been able to imagine even in the deepest recesses of my mind.

He sucked my nipple into his mouth while his fingers gave my other one the same attention. He pinched one while lightly nibbling the other. His facial hair against my breast added to all the sensations, and his demanding mouth made me arch my back, seeking more. "Does the little bunny like it when I am rough with her?" he teased against my skin.

"Reid, please!" I begged with a moan. I felt something building that I didn't think was possible without the help of a couple of AA batteries, and I was desperate to see where this feeling led.

"Please what, baby? Please keep sucking your pretty tits? Tell me what you need, Kate."

He knew exactly what he was doing. "Please, t-touch me," I whined. I could feel the sweat gathering at my brow.

Reid put his big hand under my breast, lifting it so I could see what he was doing. He flicked his tongue across my nipple once more and said, "I am touching you, baby. You're going to have to be more specific than that." He laughed deep in his chest. Bastard, he was going to make me say it.

Reid pulled my nipple back into his mouth and nipped harder this time, making me cry out as I arched up for more. "Tell me what you want, bunny," he rasped as he stared up at me.

I whimpered. "I want you to touch me lower."

He chuckled against my skin as I writhed in frustration. One hand traveled to my hip, and I thought for a moment he would give me what I wanted. "Is this where you want me?" Reid's husky voice raked across me like a gentle caress.

I groaned a frustrated sound. He knew where I wanted him to touch, but he was hell-bent on making me say it. I looked down at him with a scowl, and he had the nerve to smirk at me. "You are going to have to be more detailed with what you want, bunny," he said right before he latched back on to my nipple with that hot mouth. I almost screamed when he bit down and sucked hard.

His fingers dug into the flesh at my hip. I wanted him to touch me so badly that I trembled.

Trying not to feel embarrassed, I looked him in the eyes and said with all the conviction that I felt, "Please touch my … my." I paused as I felt a deep heat stain my cheeks. "My pussy." I nearly choked on the word. "I have never felt anything this good." I tried to squash the urge to look away from him.

I panted when his eyes flared. The dark look he sent me made me shiver. If I was a smart woman, I would have shrunk back from the look in those amber eyes.

"That's my good girl," he praised and I felt an unknown emotion flutter in my stomach.

He sat up, taking his heat with him. I almost whimpered at the loss of contact until he unbuttoned my jeans. "You have no idea how you look right now. You look like a wanton female ready for a good fuck. I wish I could sink into your wet cunt right now, but I have to wait. So this will have to do for now."

He pulled my pants and panties down in one fast yank. After tossing them to the side, he grabbed my knees, bringing them up and spreading them.

I didn't know what he meant by not being able to fuck me yet. What was stopping him? I was obviously willing. I let the thought go as I brought myself back to the moment.

He was staring down between my legs at my most intimate part, and I could feel the heat flushing across my face anew. I'd had a baby with everyone in the room looking at my vagina, but this encounter made me feel so much more vulnerable.

"Would you look at that." Reid growled as he ran a finger down my center, gathering the arousal he found there. "This is the prettiest pussy I've ever seen, and it's so fucking wet, just for me."

He inhaled deeply through the nose, and his eyes flared when he opened them again. "You smell so fucking delicious, Kate. I can't wait to see if you taste as sweet as you smell. But for now, I will give you this." He leaned back down and captured my lips again. His hand blazed a trail from my breast down to my pussy.

His fingers found my clit and made small circles. I trembled uncontrollably, and he slid further down until he plunged a finger into my hot channel and I nearly screamed. "Oh, bunny, you're squeezing my finger with that greedy cunt. God, you're going to feel so amazing wrapped around my cock."

His dirty words drove me higher and higher. He added another finger and moved his thumb methodically around and around my clit.

I felt like a champagne bottle that had been shaken, and I was about to blow my cork. He kept moving that thumb faster and faster while driving his fingers deeper and harder. "That's it, baby, let go and fucking come for me."

His words were my undoing. I exploded around his fingers with a scream, feeling a new flood of arousal coat his fingers. My vision went dark around the corners, and I feared I would pass out. I had never in my life experienced an orgasm that rocked me to my core the way this one had. I slowly came back down as his fingers slowed. He removed his hand and held my stare as he brought that hand up to his mouth and licked his fingers clean with a deep groan.

I should have been grossed out or even embarrassed, but that was the most erotic thing I'd ever seen in my life.

"Mmm, just like I thought. Sweet as pie," Reid

mumbled. "Don't even think I am done with you yet, baby. I have to ask. Has anyone ever kissed this sweet pussy before? My bet would be no."

He didn't wait for my reply as he lowered himself, settling his shoulders between my thighs. I arched my back as I felt his breath brush across my wet flesh. Then he lowered his mouth to touch me, and I nearly came on the spot as he swiped his tongue against me in a long lick.

He groaned long and hard like he was getting pleasure from what he was doing. The sound sent the vibrations straight up my clit. I dug my fingers into his hair, pulling him closer. I was just about to tell him not to stop when I heard the front door close and a familiar voice said, "Damn, I always miss the good stuff."

## Chapter Five

I jackknifed straight up, grabbing the blanket on the back of the couch. Before I could cover up, I made eye contact with the man I came here to see in the first place.

Heath and I stared at one another. I was a little shocked to see a wide smile crack across his handsome face. If I walked in on the person I'd made out with the night before in this situation with my best friend, I might be a little upset.

I struggled to find the right words because I'd never been in a situation like this before. I felt like I'd been caught with my hand in the cookie jar. Still not sure what the hell had come over me in the first place, I scrambled to find something to say.

Before I could open my mouth, Reid broke the silence. "Heath, you remember Kate?"

I shot him a look that I hoped said *Really, that's what you come up with!* I stayed silent as Heath walked forward, staring at me. He bent down and picked up my discarded jeans and panties. Then he stood back up to his full height and, to my mortification, pulled my lacy panties out of my jeans, holding them up to inspect them.

Heat rushed across my skin as I watched him rub his thumb and forefinger along the material. His dark gaze drank me in. "How could I forget?" he responded with a husky voice.

How was I going to get out of this with as much dignity as I could? I tried to swallow and speak, but my voice came out a broken mess. "Heath, I, ah, was looking for you." I winced at my words. My inner voice mocked me as it replayed my words in my head. *Yeah, Heath, I was looking for you in your roommate's mouth.* I didn't think I could have sounded any more like an idiot. I wished the floor would just open up and swallow me whole.

Heath chuckled darkly and exchanged a look with Reid. They both looked like they would erupt into laughter at any moment, which only heightened my embarrassment. Heath finally took pity on me and handed me my clothes, holding on for a moment longer than necessary before releasing my panties.

As best as I could, I put them on under the blanket, trying to keep what dignity I had left intact. I spoke to both of them when I stood up, buttoning my pants. "I'm so sorry, this was obviously a huge mistake." I needed to get the hell out of here. I didn't know how I was ever going to show my face around these two again.

Reid stood up and grabbed me before I could make it more than a couple of steps. He pulled me, placing my back against his front. There was no space between us at all, I could feel that he was still excited from our earlier activities.

I gasped as he rubbed his erection against my behind. I couldn't believe he was still ready to go after Heath walked in on us. "This was a lot of things, enlightening being one of those things," he whispered against my ear. "But a mistake is not one of them." Nipping my earlobe, he nearly made me moan.

I was so distracted by Reid touching me that I didn't realize Heath had come to stand in front of me. He grabbed my chin, tilting my head to face him. He flexed his jaw, the look of restraint crossing his beautiful features.

I was trapped between two men I barely knew. The thought alone should make me run for the hills, but I felt myself getting aroused all over again. What was wrong with me?

Heath licked his lips, and I found my eyes following the movement. "What was it you needed, Kate?"

*Someone to pinch me.* That was what I needed. I tried to speak, but when I opened my mouth, a low groan came out instead as Reid ran his tongue against the shell of my ear with a chuckle. He was playing with me, and I was going to lose this game.

I finally managed to speak, but it came out breathier than I intended. "I was going to see if you wanted to maybe get a drink with me sometime, maybe a bite to eat?" Swallowing hard. I expected Reid would back off, but it seemed to do the opposite as he moved his hands from my hips, climbing back to my breasts. That was when I realized my blouse was still partially undone. My bra was on full display, revealing the top swells of my breasts.

I watched Heath's eyes follow those hands, looking a little glazed. I sucked in a breath as I grabbed Reid's wrists, halting their upward motion as I managed to speak again. "I don't know if that's such a good idea anymore."

Heath brought his eyes back up to my face, seeming to search for something as he spoke. "I was actually going to attempt to ask you out tonight when I got home. I was knocking on your door when I heard some … sounds coming from here." He gave me a devious grin.

Reid, who had been quiet through this embarrassing conversation, finally spoke. His breath brushed over my ear, leaving me to shiver. "I think that is a great idea, Heath. Why don't you take our little bunny out and then we can all meet back here for a movie? We can get to know each other a little better."

I could hear the smile in his words.

A thought broke through my lust-filled brain that had me pulling away from Reid. This whole conversion was confusing. Why wasn't anyone angry? It was so weird to be asking one guy out while the other one was all but fucking me from behind.

I needed to get out of here now before I made more of a fool of myself. I opened my mouth to speak, but a shrill ringtone cut me off. My phone was ringing. Reid bent down and retrieved it from between the couch cushions. It must have gotten wedged in there when we were fooling around. My face reddened again at the thought.

Reid smirked and held his hand out for me to grab my phone. I looked at the caller ID and knew without a doubt I needed to answer it. If I didn't, he would just keep calling. I looked between both boys and told them I needed to take the call.

I practically sprinted to the door and quickly exited. I rushed to my door and yanked it open before slamming it behind me. Taking a deep breath, I prepared myself as I slid my finger across the screen.

Holding the phone to my ear, I answered with a chipped tone. "What do you want, Tom?" If I was having trouble getting my libido to calm down before, I certainly wasn't now.

"Sugar." He drawled my old pet name, making my lips twist in disgust. "When are you coming home? I miss you something terrible." He was slurring his words.

"Are you drunk, Tom? Where is Vivian?" I could practically smell the cheap whiskey across the phone.

"She fucking left me for some prick who drives a Porsche, gold-digging cunt." He hiccupped.

"Tom, I really don't have the patience for this conversation. I'm sorry your mistress left you, but these phone calls need to stop. You need help."

"Oh, now come on, sugar. You remember how good it was between us? Do you remember when we spent the weekend in that honeymoon suite at that bed-and-breakfast by the lake? I remember how sweet you were when you sucked my cock."

He and I remembered that time very differently. I remembered being completely sexually frustrated because he thought going down on me was distasteful. He sure was willing to receive though. The thought churned my stomach. I had just received more pleasure in the last ten minutes with Reid than I ever had in the last nineteen years with Tom.

"I know what you're doing. I'm not coming back no matter what you have to say. I sure as shit am not willing to replay our greatest hits. You need to lose my number," I seethed.

I'd been receiving these phone calls for the last couple of weeks. Normally, I would let him say what he wanted to say and politely ask him to stop calling me. Something about being with Reid had lit a fire under me though. I didn't want to put up with this shit anymore.

"You know what, you're just like the rest of them! You no-good fucking cow. I'm the best thing that ever happened to you and you leave me?" He spat with righteous indignation.

"You cheated on me for six years, Tom, on top of refusing to let me work. You made me completely reliant on you and then you took it all away. My lawyer suggested I take you for all you have, but I didn't. I just want you to leave me alone. I left a nineteen-year marriage with nothing just to get away from you! You have no right to blame me for any of this. You did this, Tom, not me!"

"You wanna know why I cheated on you, Kate? It's because you are the most boring person I have ever met. You remember the end when I wasn't fucking you at all? It's because you weren't even doing it for me anymore. Just one thought about your fat ass had my dick soft. I only called to make you this offer so you would feel better about yourself. You'll never find anyone willing to put up with you like I did!" *Click.*

I was left staring at my phone, eyes burning. I hated that I cried when I got really mad. I wasn't about to shed one more tear over that man. I would never understand what happened to him. He was so sweet when we were first together, but somewhere down the line, he turned into this nasty person.

Tom and I got pregnant with Lindsey when I was sixteen, and he was only two years older. He did what he thought was right and married me before we even graduated high school.

To a sixteen-year-old, the idea of marriage was like a fairytale. The dream of having my small little family together was all I wanted. To the thirty-five-year-old I am now, the idea of marriage left a nasty taste in my mouth. Our marriage was more like a really good roommate agreement with the occasional half-hearted booty call thrown in. Even those had stopped years before we had gotten a divorce. Not to mention touching me at all. I couldn't even remember the last time he had even so much as held my hand despite my endless effort to attract his attention.

What he had said to me on the phone only served to drag up those old insecurities. Had I really been the one that drove him to find comfort in another woman's arms?

I shoved away from the door and went down the hall to my bathroom. Feeling like I was on autopilot, I turned the shower on and undressed. After having my world rocked to its core by Reid, the weird encounter with Heath, and the conversation with Tom, I felt a little raw.

The shower's hot spray burned my skin as I stepped in, but it would help drag me out of my head. I tried to tell myself that Tom's issues were just that, his issues. So what if he couldn't get it hard for me? Heath and Reid didn't seem to have the same problem. Some of what Tom said had sunk in, though. What if I wouldn't be able to find someone to put up with me? Was I really boring? I didn't feel boring ten minutes ago.

I washed my hair methodically, wishing the thoughts would go down the drain too. After washing off, I dried myself. I didn't stop myself from thinking about Reid's hands on me. He had left a trail of fire everywhere he touched, and I couldn't help wondering if it would be the same with Heath.

I sighed heavily. I needed to stop thinking about them. I had a pint of ice cream in the freezer with my name on it and a Netflix show to binge-watch. I would hunker down for the rest of the evening and shut down my brain. Tomorrow was a new day, and I would deal with everything then.

Hopefully, I would hear from Samantha sooner rather than later. Having a job would make it easier to get out of my head. I would try my damnedest to avoid the boys because I might die from embarrassment the next time I saw them.

## Chapter Six

I was going to die. It had been two days of trying to avoid the boys. Two days looking through my peephole before I would sprint to the elevator and hope to God nobody would exit that damned apartment. I even thought I got away with pretending to not be home when Heath had knocked, trying to get me to come out.

I had time to come out of my head space and started to feel a little better. I'd needed that blow-up with Tom to happen. It was almost therapeutic in a way. I had been nothing but polite through the whole divorce, trying to keep it as civil as possible. It felt good to finally let a little bitchiness out.

I woke up the next morning feeling refreshed and a little sore from the prior night's activities. When your girl parts went from being severely neglected one day to having a mind-blowing orgasm the next, things got a little achy.

Shortly after getting up, my phone rang. It was Samantha with the job offer. I, of course, took the offer, and she asked if I could come in that day.

Then I spent the next two days completely immersed in learning the ins and outs of the company, and I was completely hooked. Samantha had told me that my position was an entry-level position, but there were always advancement opportunities if I was willing to put in the work. It felt so good to be needed again and to be doing something productive.

The days flew by so fast that I hadn't even realized it was Saturday until I woke up this morning in a panic because my alarm hadn't alerted me. I decided it was far past time for me to get out and get to know this city I was calling home. I decided I needed to explore a beach or two while I was at it, too. I'd been in town for about a month now, and I hadn't even seen the ocean yet.

I packed all the stuff I would need for the outing and put on my swimsuit under my cutoff overalls. After putting my hair up in a messy bun and completely foregoing makeup, I was ready to march out the door.

I stopped at the peephole and looked out. Although I was feeling better, I still wasn't ready to face the boys yet, having not recovered from my embarrassment. I still couldn't figure out what their deal was. Why hadn't Heath gotten mad after catching me with Reid? I could believe that he wouldn't think he had a claim on me because we had only had one moment in the elevator. But even if that was the case, wouldn't he still be slightly upset? The whole situation left me confused.

It looked like the coast was clear, so I rushed out my door as quietly as I could. Pushing the button for the elevator, I kept my eyes trained on their door. If it opened, I might be able to make it back inside before they saw me. The elevator dinged as it stopped on my floor, and I let out a breath I hadn't realized I was holding.

Just when I thought I was in the clear, the doors opened, revealing the very men I had been trying to avoid. Hence my impending death. Death by embarrassment was a thing, right?

Heath had been in the middle of a sentence, cut off when they noticed me standing there. They both caught me in their stares. Reid kept his eyes on me as a grin spread across his face. I could feel the heat left behind as his gaze trailed down my body while he played his tongue across his teeth.

The sight made me cinch my thighs together as arousal flooded my veins. He reminded me of a hungry lion, and I felt like the prey. All the color drained from my face as I stole a glance at Heath. The darkness I found in his eyes was enough to make my breath catch. I guessed he was mad after all. How was I going to get out of this?

Before I could come up with an excuse to go back to my apartment, Reid cut me off. "Hey, Kate, long time no see." There was amusement in his voice. His gaze still traveled over my body, from my flip-flops, and up to the top of my bun. Soaking in all of my details with hungry eyes.

"Uh, yeah. I-uh, started my new job so I have been kinda busy." God, that sounded so lame.

Heath held me with his hard eyes as Reid spoke. "Huh. See, Heath? I told you she wasn't avoiding us. She was just busy." He tried to hide his smirk by dragging his hand across his mouth. "So, is that where you're headed now? Work?" He put a little emphasis on the *K*.

"Uh, no, actually. I figured I would head to the beach. I haven't been yet, so I thought today was the day to see what I've been missing out on."

I was sure I sounded like an idiot. Reid looked at Heath, who still wouldn't take his eyes off me. "You know what, we haven't been to the beach in ages. Have we, Heath?" It didn't sound like a question. "What do you say to a little company? We could show you the best beach then take you to the boardwalk for some grub."

I opened my mouth to say that probably wasn't a good idea when he cut me off again. "Great! I'll go get our trunks if you guys want to hold the elevator," he said with a shit-eating grin as he brushed past me.

I was left alone with Heath in the elevator once again. We just stared at each other for what felt like hours. The silence stretched, getting louder. The overwhelming need to speak took charge. "So what have you been—"

He cut me off. "You never let me answer your question the other night."

Okay, he wasn't beating around the bush, was he? "Oh, I guess you're right. I just— I just figured after walking in on ... you know, you wouldn't want to go out with me." I could feel a flush climbing up my neck.

He stepped forward and crowded me. "So you just thought you would take the choice away from me by avoiding me?" He growled.

I flinched. Was he mad at me? It seemed like he was mad at me. "No, I—"

"Because let me make it perfectly clear. I don't like being ignored, Kate. Me walking in on you and Reid did nothing to cool my feelings for you. And you would know that if you had answered the door when I knocked the last couple of days." He was full-on scowling now.

Guilt panged through my system. I didn't want to upset him, but I just needed to breathe for a minute. I guessed I could see where he was coming from. If someone had avoided me like the plague after the encounter we had, I was sure that would hurt.

I stared at my hands like they held the secret to life itself. "I'm sorry, Heath, I really didn't mean to hurt you. You and Reid are just so intense, I didn't know how to deal with everything I was feeling. It won't happen again, I promise."

His face softened. He stepped forward and grabbed my chin, tilting it up and forcing me to meet his eyes. "You're forgiven, sweetheart," he said with that drop-dead smile, showcasing those dimples that made my knees weak. "And you can pick me up tomorrow for our date."

I choked on a laugh at his sudden turn in mood. Was it really that easy? In the past, whenever I had pissed off Tom, he would bull up for days, laying on the guilt trips so thick that I was drowning in them. "You still want to go out with me?" I asked.

He looked at me like I was crazy. "Of course, I do. But don't think you are out of the doghouse just yet. I expect flowers and don't even think I put out on the first date. I'm not that type of girl." He teased with a playful grin.

I laughed out loud, tears coming to my eyes. "All right, I will try to remember that." I grinned up at him.

Still giving me that hundred-watt smile, he pulled me in for a kiss. His hand moved to my hair, giving it a light tug that had me leaning in for more. Then he pulled me back long enough to look at me with serious eyes. "Don't ever think that you can't talk to me about how you're feeling," he said before leaning in to take my lips again.

Before the kiss could get too deep, Reid came waltzing back up to us with his swim trunks slung low on his hips and a cutoff shirt showing that sexy tattoo winding up his arm and disappearing beneath the fabric. He threw Heath his trunks and grabbed me away from him. Pulling me to his side, we all stepped into the elevator.

As I stood between the boys, Heath pushed the lobby button and we started our descent. I looked up at Reid, and he gave me that panty-dropping smile. When I glanced at Heath, he winked at me. I swallowed the lump in my throat and focused on the lights on the panel. I was in so much trouble.

****

"You cannot be serious," I said to Heath, humor in my voice. I had been smiling and laughing so much that my cheeks were starting to ache. This was probably one of the best days I'd had in years.

We had left the apartment complex in Reid's truck. They convinced me that it would be silly to take two different vehicles if we were all going to the same place.

They'd placed me in the middle, and I tried to keep my hands in my lap as we started the forty-five-minute drive from the mainland to Pensacola Beach. I feared it would be one of those long drives made awkward by the silence in the cab. But to my surprise, it was pleasant.

Heath grabbed my hand five minutes in, raking his thumb across mine in a soothing motion. I dumbly looked at our hands for long moments. I'd almost forgotten what it felt like to have a man hold my hand. There was something about the pure innocence of it that made butterflies take flight in my belly.

Reid spent the drive pointing out places of interest to me as he drove with confident precision, I relaxed more with each mile that passed. Every now and again, when we hit a bump, I would feel Reid's thigh rub against mine. By the smirk on his face, I would've bet he was trying to hit every pothole he could.

When we got to the beach, the boys found us a nice spot with a few loungers and a big blue umbrella. I contemplated keeping my overalls on, worrying about what they would think of my body. Even though Reid had expressed how much he liked the way I looked, I was still self-conscious.

I watched as they stripped their shirts off, revealing two sets of lickable abs and impressive pecs. I almost drooled as my eyes traced their happy trails before they disappeared under those low-slung trunks. By the time I stopped ogling them, they were looking at me expectantly, smirks on their faces.

I turned away from them and took a deep breath.

With shaking hands, I stripped out of my cutoffs, revealing my simple black tankini. I placed my clothes in the lounger before facing the boys again.

I always covered as much as possible, but there was only so much a bathing suit could keep contained. It was like a second skin and probably showed an indecent amount of my ass. When I looked up, both men were staring at me. The heat in their gazes was enough to make me want to cover back up.

We spent all morning and most of the afternoon playing in the ocean with each other and lazing about. It felt particularly nice when Heath took me out until the water was just about to my breasts and held me. He had taken his time, kissing me softly, nipping at my bottom lip every so often. I was in such a daze when he came up for air that I hadn't even felt Reid come up behind me.

He grabbed my hips below the water, and with a deep rumble, pressed against my ear as he asked if I was getting hungry. I was ravenous, but not for food. It was like I had no control over my body as I leaned back into his embrace. I managed to nod. Heath grinned and vouched that he would go get us all burgers from a nearby food truck.

As Heath waded through the water, I started to follow him until Reid grabbed my wrist and spun me around to make me face him. I let out a shocked breath before I looked back at Heath to see him still moving forward, paying us no mind.

I felt slightly uneasy when Reid turned my face up to his. "Have I told you how sexy you look in this?" he asked as he ran his finger between my top strap and the swell of my breast.

Just like that, I melted under his touch. Unable to form any words. I shook my head. He grinned and said, "Well, let me make it up to you." He knelt down, taking my mouth in a rough show of dominance. Where Heath was soft and loving, Reid was firm and demanding. It was an intoxicating combo.

I didn't know how long it was until he broke the kiss, grabbed my hand, and led me back to the beach. It should have felt wrong kissing two different guys within minutes of one another, shouldn't it? Having still not figured out what this was with us three, I kept waiting for the other shoe to drop.

The boys told me story upon story of them growing up. From some of the tales they told, I felt bad for their mothers. They had been mischievous, doing all sorts of dangerous acts that would have put gray hair on any adult that was responsible for keeping them alive.

I found myself laughing so much that my throat was a little raw. I didn't think I'd ever felt that carefree or alive. Watching them laugh and poke fun at each other made me see how special their bond was. They might have just been friends, but they were brothers at heart.

We spent the rest of the afternoon swimming, joking, napping, and sunbathing. When it started to cool off, they thought it was a good idea to take me to the pier to watch the sunset.

That was where I was now, as Heath retold the story of when Reid had dared him to jump off this very pier. I stared up at him with a look of bewilderment. "And you just jumped? I'm surprised you didn't kill yourself," I exclaimed.

He looked down at me with humor twinkling in his eyes. "Of course, I jumped. Twenty bucks is twenty bucks. Besides if I hadn't, that asshole"—he pointed at Reid—"would have held it over my head for years. It was totally worth the broken arm I got."

I shook my head, looking at Reid. "Well, some friend you are. That could have gone so much worse than it did," I scolded.

Reid really could look innocent when he wanted to. "You can't blame it all on me. If I remember correctly, you were trying to impress Becca, remember?" he gloated.

We made it to the end of the pier where there was a bench for us to sit on. Heath laughed as he pulled me down and tucked me into his side, Reid taking up the other side sliding his hand across my thigh. "Well, it was still worth it. That girl did this amazing thing with her tongue," Heath replied with a look of nostalgia crossing his face.

I smacked him across the chest, causing him to grunt. "You are such a deviant!" I said around a laugh.

He looked at me with a playful light in his eyes. "If you think that's bad, just ask Reid what he did to get in her pants."

Reid pointed at him, ready to defend himself. "That was one time, dude, and it didn't even total the car." They both dissolved into a fit of laughter while I was left reeling.

I realized it was a habitual thing for these two to sleep with the same woman. Was this a game to them? A competition to see who could get me to sleep with them first? At first, I hadn't realized they were using me as some sort of prize to be gained.

I felt myself flush with shame for not seeing it sooner. Of course, they didn't want to spend time with me because they actually liked me. I was an easy target. Feeling stupid, I tried to get up, but they just pulled me back down.

"What's wrong, bunny? Are you upset because we are talking about other women? Becca happened years ago, we haven't seen her since she left for a job in Colorado six years ago," Reid assured, concern written all over his face.

I didn't know what came over me at that moment. Maybe I was still carrying some residual anger left over from my conversation with Tom the other night.

I snapped my head in his direction, narrowing my eyes. "I'm not upset, I'm pissed off! What? Did you think it would be easy to fuck with the sad, fat, old lady next door? See who could get me in bed first? Bet you were pretty happy with yourself for getting as far as you did, huh?"

Huffing, I tried to stand up again only to have Reid grab me and pull me into his lap. I tried squirming away from him, but all that led to was me rubbing my ass against his crotch.

He grunted as he held me tighter. "Keep rubbing yourself against me like that and it won't be a mystery as to who is going to be fucking you first, bunny. Hold still," he commanded firmly against my ear. "I understand you're angry right now, but if I ever hear you talk about yourself like that again, I'm going to take you over my knee and spank that attitude right out of your juicy ass."

That got me to stop fighting him. I pushed my hair out of my face. When I opened my mouth to say something snarky about where he could shove that attitude, Heath grabbed my chin, making me face him. "Is that what you think this is, Kate? A game?" he asked.

Tears pricked the back of my eyes. I wouldn't cry in front of them, further making a fool of myself. "Well, it sure seems that way to me. I didn't realize you guys liked to try to fuck the same woman, like some sort of competition. I've been confused about this whole situation from the beginning. Now I just feel so stupid for not figuring it out sooner." How could I just let them keep taking turns kissing me? What was I thinking?

A look of confusion crossed Heath's face, and then he looked up at Reid. I could feel Reid chuckling against me as Heath started to smile. That just pissed me off further. I squirmed again, trying to get up. "You guys don't have to be so cruel. Let me go so I can call an Uber and start looking for a new apartment."

I knew I should have just steered clear of them. Now I had to find a new place to live where I wouldn't feel shame every time I walked past their door.

Reid pushed his face into my neck, and I hated the way I wanted to lean in to keep the contact. "If you think I'm going to let you go, you can just forget it. And you are most definitely not moving," he rasped as he ground his erection on my ass.

The tears pricking my eyes were about to spill over now. My voice wobbled when I spoke again. "I don't understand any of this."

Heath reached for my cheek, rubbing away a stray tear with his thumb. "Don't cry, sweetheart. We should have told you sooner. We kinda just assumed you knew what was going on here. But now I can see how new you are to all of this." He gestured between the three of us. "Reid and I don't compete for the same woman." His stare turned molten now. "We like to share."

I was taken aback for a moment. "Share? As in I split my time with both of you? I don't know if that's a good idea, Heath. What if someone gets jealous? I would hate to come between you guys like that."

Reid turned my head, making me look at him. "That's exactly what we want you to do, bunny, come between us," he said with a wicked smile that had me going soft for him.

Heath drew my attention back to him when he said, "What Reid means is that we like to fuck our women..." Pausing, he looked at Reid and then back at me. "Together, at the same time."

I sat there, unable to move and stunned into silence. Only a singular thought ran through my head. *I am so fucked.*

## Chapter Seven

The truck ride home was a quiet one. The boys must have known I needed the silence to think about the bomb they'd just dropped. I could feel Heath looking over at me every so often, almost like it was killing him not to ask me if I was okay.

I was relieved they didn't view me as a game, but what was I supposed to say? I would've been lying if I said the idea didn't make me all hot and soft in a certain part of my anatomy. What was wrong with me? This was completely ridiculous. I'd only had sex with one person in my entire life, and there was no kink involved at all.

Just the idea of Tom trying to be kinky had me giggling like a lunatic. I tried to stop laughing, but it just kept coming. By the time I looked up, both men were staring at me like I had lost my damn mind. That just made me laugh harder to the point where I was crying.

Reid looked at Heath with wide eyes and said, "Dude, I think we may have broken her."

I finally gathered myself, squelching the rest of my laughs. I cleared my throat and wiped my eyes. "I'm sorry, it's clearly been a really long day, and I think I just might have gotten too much sun to the brain."

Reid pulled into his spot in the parking lot. As soon as Heath let me out of the truck, I made a B-line to the building like my ass was on fire. A lot of good it did me as their long legs ate up the distance. Before I could run to the open elevator and go up without them, Reid grabbed my hand and pulled me back to stand between them.

The thought entered my brain and exited my mouth before I could stop it. "This is why you guys are constantly putting me between you." I rolled my eyes.

"Goddamn, I truly am that oblivious," I murmured with a shake of my head.

The elevator started to go up, and I felt my anxiety go down a little bit with each floor we passed. A couple more levels, and I was home free. I went through my mental checklist as I stood there.

I'd start looking for a new apartment in the morning, and I would have to find someone to sublet this place. I had just signed a six-month lease and there was no way out of that. Maybe Jill would know someone who needed a place. I'd call her in the morning too.

Reid was openly staring at me now. "Look, Heath, she's thinking about running." He grabbed me and brought me flush to his front. "I told you I wasn't going to let you move, and I meant it, bunny."

Heath came up behind me, putting his hand in my hair and pulling so I looked back and up at him. I had to bite back my moan as pleasure raked across my scalp.

"Will you at least talk to us about this?" Heath asked.

I pushed out of Reid's embrace and turned to face Heath. "I'm not this girl, Heath. I'm not kinky. I wouldn't even know how to handle one of you, let alone both of you."

Reid pulled me back to him and drew his hand around my waist, pushing his hand into the open slit of my overalls. I sucked in a breath when his fingers found the edge of my swimsuit bottom. "You sure knew how to handle me the other day," he whispered into my ear.

Heath stepped closer, fully trapping me between them. He reached over and pressed the *stop* button on the panel, making us jolt to a halt. "I think you could handle both of us just fine, baby. I know you've thought about it. You know it would be fucking hot between us. Look at you now. Reid is barely touching you, and I bet your pussy is wet and ready."

Reid took that as his cue to push his fingers into my bottoms, grazing over my clitoris and going further down to dip inside. He groaned as he pulled them back up, rubbing my wetness around my swollen bud. "Oh, yeah, she's fucking drenched."

This time, I couldn't stop the moan as it ripped from my throat. The rest of my resolve melted away as I tilted my head and laid it against Reid's chest. My knees buckled as he pinched and played. Heath held me steady as he got down on his knees, making himself eye level with my breasts. "You wanna talk about making me jealous, baby. Reid has already had a taste of these sweet tits and played with that pussy. All I got were a couple of kisses," he said the last with a pout.

I lifted my head long enough to watch him unhook the straps of my overalls, letting them fall past my hips. Now I could see Reid's hand playing beneath my bottoms. The sight made me even more aroused.

With heated eyes, Heath also watched what Reid was doing. He clicked his tongue, tsking like he was disappointed. "Now, that just won't do. I want to see what he is doing to that pretty cunt." He pulled my bottoms down to reveal Reid playing in my slick folds. Then Heath lifted my ankle to have me step one leg out of the fabric, making it clear he didn't have the patience to take them fully off. Just the view I got of him staring at what we were doing had me gasping softly.

He reached up and pinched my hardened nipples above my top, making me arch into the touch. Reid pulled his hand away, revealing some very wet fingers. I protested the withdrawal, but before I could voice my disdain, Reid held up his hand. "Here, man. Taste her and tell me she's not the sweetest fucking thing you have ever tasted."

Holding my gaze, Heath took the offered fingers and sucked them into his mouth. The sight was the most erotic thing I had ever seen. His dark eyes flared as he licked my juices off Reid's fingers.

Heath released his fingers and said, "Let's make her come. Give her a taste of what she could have with us."

Reid trailed his fingers back down to my lonely nub and pushed his cock against my ass to let me know he wasn't unaffected by what we were doing. He used his other hand to grab my throat and squeezed. Not enough to cut off my air but enough to let me know who was in control. I almost screamed when he shoved his fingers into me and rubbed my clit with his palm. I wasn't going to last much longer.

Heath looked at my breasts and slowly lowered my top until the brisk air brushed across my aching nipples. He pushed his hand under them, bringing his mouth to the peak. "Oh, goddamn, sweetheart. I am going to fuck these perfect tits soon. But for now, I want to feast on these while Reid fucks you with his fingers."

His words made me quake with need. When his hot tongue slid across my nipple, it was almost my undoing. Heath grabbed my thigh and raised my leg up and to the side. Holding me open, he pulled away to look at me. I was spread wide for them. Reid's fingers found some magic spot inside of me as he finger-fucked with the vigor of a man on a mission. Something explosive was building inside of me. Heath groaned as he leaned back in to tease my sensitive nipples again.

My hips started to move on their own accord, grinding into the hand fucking me and the cock lying against my ass. I was alternating both of their names in between moans.

"That's it, baby, take what you need. You're so

hot, riding my hand while Heath sucks on those pretty tits. He didn't get to see you last time. You look him in the eyes when you come this time. Come for us, Kate," he said between clenched teeth.

Looking Heath in the eyes, I screamed my release and felt Reid's hand getting soaked with my orgasm. I almost felt the embarrassment rising at the mess I made until Reid gave me a groaning, *"Fuck,"* behind me. Heath pulled away and shoved Reid's hand out of the way.

Before I could protest, his mouth descended on me with the hunger of a starving man. He pulled my bent leg up and over his shoulder, bringing me closer to him. I screamed as he shoved his fingers inside of me and thrust in and out, fast and hard. He sucked my clit into his mouth as Reid used his now free hand to pinch my nipple while he continued to squeeze my throat with his other hand.

I thrust my hands onto Heath's hair to hold him to me so he wouldn't stop as I came again. Reid harshly whispered in my ear as I screamed my release. "That's a good fucking girl. You like the way Heath eats that pussy, don't you?"

Heath licked me now in long lazy licks, making me jump with aftershocks. When he stood up, he took my mouth, shoving his tongue in, like my kiss was his rightful payment. I delighted in the taboo flavor of me coating his tongue.

Before I wanted him to, he ended the kiss. "We have to stop or I'm going to fuck you in this elevator. I don't want to do that until you have had time to think about this. Because believe me, baby, when you say yes, we don't plan on letting you go," he promised.

He turned away, released the *stop* button, and we continued our ascent. Reid righted my top before he bent down to help me pull up my bottoms. He pulled my cutoffs back up, replacing the straps, and turned me to face him. He had his hands in my hair and his mouth on me before I could blink.

I didn't know if it was the recent orgasms that made me bold, but I reached between us to rub against him. He thrust into my hand with a grunt. "You know what they say about playing with fire don't you, bunny? You better stop before you get burned," he threatened playfully.

I gave him a sultry grin and flicked my tongue against his lower lip. His eyes flared, and he looked like he was about to pounce. Before he could do anything of the sort, Heath grabbed me and led me to my door.

Stopping, he grabbed my key from me and unlocked my apartment. Then he handed me back my key and took my phone, putting his and Reid's numbers in my contacts.

Regarding me seriously, he said, "We are completely serious about this, Kate. If you agree to be ours, that's it, you're ours. We won't share you with other guys and we won't fuck any other women. This is a committed relationship for us, and we're all in." He brought his head down like he was going to kiss me again but just brushed his lips across mine ever so lightly. "I will give you a couple of days to think it over, but I won't wait forever before I come knocking. I want this, Kate. We want this. Say yes."

He opened my door for me and waited until I got inside to head to his apartment. I was still trying to compute what just happened. This was all so surreal. Being between those two was the best sexual experience I could have ever hoped for. So, what was holding me back? It wasn't normal, that was one thing.

I didn't even want to imagine trying to explain to Lindsey what kind of relationship I was in. Jill would lose her fucking mind, but she would be the one to offer to stand in the corner with pom poms and cheer me on.

I headed to the bathroom to wash the beach off me. I contemplated not showering just so I could smell them on me for a little longer. I decided on the less stalkery thing to do and walked under the hot stream. What was I going to do?

I believed they would take this very seriously if I did decide to do this. Was I ready to jump into another serious relationship so fast after my divorce? Wasn't there some waiting period for this type of thing?

I toweled off and headed to bed. Forgoing my usual PJs, I decided to sleep nude tonight. The fewer things touching my overheated skin, the better.

Whatever I decided, I realized the answer wouldn't come tonight. I was exhausted from the day and my earlier orgasms. I shut my light off and lay down. I was out when my head hit the pillow.

## Chapter Eight

After a week, I still didn't know what I was going to do. Both Heath and Reid stayed true to their word and gave me time to think. It was odd that I hadn't run into them at all this last week, but I just figured they were both busy.

I told myself it was a good thing I hadn't seen them, but now I was starting to miss them. I had even stooped so low as to rush to the door and look out my peephole just to try to catch glimpses of them when I had heard the elevator ding.

The fact that neither of them had knocked on my door had me worried that they'd changed their minds. I tried to make a decision this last week, but I was still reeling over what to do. I was as uncertain now as I had been last week.

So, here I was, lying in bed on a Sunday morning and throwing myself a little pity party. Sighing to myself, I got up and went about my morning ritual of making my bed, dressing, and brushing my teeth. I needed to get away for the day without the boys. I needed room to think, and I couldn't do that with them living twenty feet away. Deciding I needed to have some mother/daughter time, I called Lindsey. She answered on the second ring.

"Hey, Mom!" Her bright voice came over the line.

"Hey honey, how are you doing? It's been forever since you last called." I tried not to sound like I was nagging too much.

"I know, finals have started and I am just so stressed out. I've been cramming every night." She sounded so tired it made my heart squeeze.

"Well, that's kind of what I was calling for. What

do you think about taking a break? We could meet up for lunch and do some shopping?"

"O-M-G yes!! You should call Aunt Jill and see if she wants to come with," she practically yelled into the phone.

We agreed on what restaurant to meet at and said our goodbyes. I sent a text to Jill, and she immediately sent back her response, saying she couldn't wait. I needed to put on a little makeup and do my hair. While I was getting ready, my mind wandered back to the boys.

Why was this such a hard decision? The obvious thing to do would be to stop this before it got any further. I had a dreadful, sinking feeling in my gut that I would be left heartbroken when shit hit the fan. And it would hit the fan, wouldn't it? Relationships like this couldn't be built to last. God, wouldn't it be wonderful if they were, though? Being loved and doted on by two men sounded like a dream come true.

I had no examples to go off of. Maybe I could ask Jill in a non-conspicuous way if she knew of anyone in this type of relationship. Maybe she could introduce me.

I giggled at the thought. "Hi, I know you just met me, but could you tell me, in depth, how you carry a healthy relationship with three people being involved? Also, could you tell me if the sex is as mind-blowing as I think it would be?" I said to myself.

Finished with my hair and makeup, I stared at myself in the mirror. I couldn't figure out what Health and Reid saw when they looked at me. I wasn't ugly by any means, but I was just kind of plain. If I was up against some of their exes, I was sure I paled in comparison. That same suspicion from last week crept back in. Maybe I was just an easy target.

I shook the thought off. Whatever I decided, I needed to do so without tearing down my fragile self-esteem. I exited the bathroom and made my way to the front door.

After grabbing my keys and purse, I looked through the peephole to see if anyone was out there. I wasn't avoiding them, per se, but I would rather not see them until I had my answer.

I huffed at myself for being a coward and yanked my door open, then shut it behind me. The coast was clear the whole way to my car. I released a breath I hadn't realized I was holding.

Driving to the restaurant, I contemplated for the hundredth time telling Jill about my situation and decided that was still a terrible idea. The whole town would know in a matter of minutes if I did that. I loved the girl to death, but she had a big mouth.

A pang of guilt went through me at the thought of not telling Jill. She was my best friend, and keeping this from her was hard. Every time I had seen her this last week, I had to bite my tongue so I wouldn't blurt it out. I had the irrational fear that she would think less of me if I decided to do this.

Traffic was thick today, so I knew it would take a while to get to the restaurant. My mind wandered back to last Saturday. I genuinely had such a good day with them. I couldn't remember a time when I had felt so good. It was a nice change of pace, going from sad and lonely to joyful and carefree.

There was something about being around them that made me forget about all the other crap I had to deal with. I was more relaxed around them than I had ever been. I honestly liked the person I was around them too. I usually never stuck up for myself, preferring to be non-confrontational. But when I was around them and one of them pissed me off, I voiced it. And then, of course, there was the sexual chemistry that was off the charts.

Every time I was around one of them, I went soft and needy. It felt so damn good to be between those two in the elevator. Would it be so bad to find out what it would be like to be caught between them again?

Before I knew it, the restaurant came into my view. I pulled into the parking lot, seeing Lindsey and Jill already seated outside. Lindsey beamed at me, making me forget about everything else. She ran up to me and gathered me in a fierce hug. I vowed I would put my problems on the back burner for now. I settled into my seat, letting everything else fall from my mind.

****

We sat at that table for so long that I thought our waiter was going to kick us out. It had been so long since I'd gotten to see Lindsey. We talked about everything from her classes to boys. She proved to be my child when she blushed and looked away shyly. Of course, Jill, ever the one to poke fun, teased her relentlessly.

We left our waiter a hefty tip when we exited three hours later in favor of getting some shopping done. We picked that particular restaurant for its location. It was within walking distance of a small strip mall.

All three of us walked arm in arm past the stores, stopping in a few. I told Lindsey to get what she needed and we would just put it on my credit card. Seeing the joy on her face was enough to make that bill worth it. We stopped in one of her favorite stores and browsed the racks. She picked out a couple of outfits she wanted to try, so we made our way back to the fitting rooms.

The store was one of those posh upscale boutiques. It was well decorated with a boho theme that made you feel nice and cozy when you walked in.

The fitting rooms were at the back of the store and provided privacy for a group of people to chat while trying on clothes. There was a waiting area outside the room with a nice plush, cream-colored couch that Jill and I sank into. I placed the bags we had already gotten on the floor in front of me. "Go ahead, try them on and come out so we can see," I said, shooing Lindsey on.

As she locked the door behind her, Jill turned my way, pinning me with her stare. I gave her the side-eye, trying to ignore her. I knew what she wanted.

"You're really going to try to ignore me? Let me know how that works out for you," she said with a chuckle.

I grinned and looked at her. "I don't know what you're talking about."

She rolled her eyes. "Oh, puh-lease, you think you're fooling anyone? I know when you're keeping something from me. You forget I was there when you tried to keep your pregnancy test results from your dad. You can't lie for shit, and I assume something has happened with your hot neighbor. Now spill it," she demanded.

I sighed. There was no way I was going to get around it. "Well, things have ... progressed and gotten a little more serious."

She twisted her body, bending her leg in front of her and fully facing me now. "I knew it! Tell me everything. How's the sex? Is he packing? I bet he is. He probably has one of those cocks that reaches right up to his belly button." She said the latter with a waggle of her eyebrows. Sometimes I thought Jill said stuff like that just to see me blush. She truly did have no shame at all.

I shushed her, looking back at the dressing room. "Keep it down. I don't want to have to explain to Lindsey that her mother is sexually active," I whispered harshly.

Jill picked up on one thing I said, and one thing only. "Oh, so you are getting laid then, nice! I knew there was something different about you. You look like a well-fucked woman." She giggled.

Lindsey chose that moment to come out, showing us a cute pink mini skirt and strappy sequined top she had picked. "What do you think? Does this top make me look frumpy?" She spun around with her arms out to her sides.

"Honey, you could never look frumpy. I think it's a nice outfit," I said with a smile, silently thanking God that she didn't hear what Jill had said. She beamed at me, reminding me how beautiful she was.

She was built like me and she had my smile. She got Tom's dark brown curly hair and gray eyes though. I may not have done a whole lot right in my life, but I undoubtedly made pretty babies.

She shut the door behind her, and I turned back to Jill, smacking her arm. "I haven't slept with him!" I hissed quietly.

Jill looked at me suspiciously. "Well, then I'm confused because you definitely look more relaxed than usual. That kind of look only comes with a couple of really good orgasms." She sat back with a satisfied look.

Feeling my face go red, I tried to look away. She was having none of that as she grabbed my arm, forcing me to look at her. "Why are you so reluctant to share with me today? You were always so quick to tell me about how terrible Tom was. You always used to say he couldn't find your G-spot if you drew him a map. What gives?"

She forgot to mention that I was usually a few wine glasses in when I shared those stories with her. But she did have a point. We had always shared everything growing up. That was what best friends did. We used each other as a sounding board when we were having a hard time with something. It was an unspoken agreement that we always helped each other. I knew I needed to give her something, otherwise, she wouldn't drop it.

"All right fine, I'll talk, but you have to keep it down. I don't want my Lyns involved in this," I whispered.

She nodded her head vigorously, making the zipper movement across her mouth with her fingers.

I took a deep breath. "He's amazing, Jill. He is the sweetest guy I've ever met, and I lose my mind when I'm around him. I can't concentrate, and I end up being a puddle on the floor by the time the encounter is through." I practically swooned.

Jill grinned at me and got that dreamy look in her eyes. "A guy who knows what he's doing downstairs will do that to you, girl."

I found myself spilling now, unable to stop. "You have no idea!" My thoughts wandered back to last week. I bit my lip as I felt myself sinking into the memory. "Heath is amazing, I can tell he has some experience pleasuring a woman. The things he did with his tongue, oh." I closed my eyes and leaned back against the couch, having vivid flashbacks.

Visions of being between them, Reid touching me before holding me still while Heath devoured me. "And I mean, Reid. God, he's just as good at playing me like a finely tuned instrument. I can't help but think it would be fantastic to be betw—"

Jill's sharp gasp brought me back to reality. I slapped my hand over my mouth when I realized what I'd said. I winced and looked at Jill. Maybe she didn't hear me.

Her eyes were huge, and her mouth hung open. *Shit! Shit! Shit! What do I say now?* "Oh, fuck," I said behind my hand. "Jill, don't freak out."

I heard Lindsey as she came back out of the

dressing room. I jerked back and looked at her with a little panic in my eyes.

"I like this dress, Mom. I think it brings out the color of my eyes. What do you think?" she asked with a sweet smile.

Without even thinking about how the dress looked, I nodded maybe a little too quickly and cleared my throat. "Yes, sweetie, that dress is really pretty. Go show me another one," I said with what I hoped was an encouraging smile.

Lindsey looked at me and then Jill, squinting her eyes. "Is she okay?" She pointed at Jill.

Jill was still open-mouthed, staring at me and clearly in shock. I smacked her lightly on the leg to snap her out of it.

She shook her head and looked over at my girl. "Y-yes, I'm fine, Lyns. Your mom just told me something I hadn't been expecting. Go on and try on the next one."

Lindsey looked between the both of us suspiciously and walked back to the dressing room. As soon as she shut the door, Jill snapped her head back to me so fast I was sure she got whiplash. Before I could say anything, she punched me in the shoulder.

"Ouch!" I exclaimed, rubbing the offended arm.

"You bitch! Why didn't you tell me you were shacking up with two different guys? I'm trying not to let it hurt my feelings that you didn't feel the need to share with me, Kate!" Anger was plain in her voice.

"I'm not shacking up with anyone. There was only one incident with both of them in the elevator last week, I swear." I winced again. "Well, that and the time with just Reid at their apartment. But that was it!" I tried to reply more calmly than I felt.

I knew immediately that I fucked up again when

Jill jerked back from me and screeched. "Both of them!"

I slapped my hand across her mouth, practically climbing on top of her in the process. "Shhhh!" I hushed her. I looked back at the dressing room, thanking God that Lindsey wasn't standing there.

Jill shook me off and gapped at me. "What do you mean by both of them? Like both of them at separate times or..."

I rubbed my hands across my face and mumbled my answer. "Like, together..." I braced myself, expecting her to whoop and holler, alerting the whole store to my almost threesome.

To my surprise, she was quiet, smiling at me. Giggling, she pushed my shoulder and said, "You lucky slut!"

I flinched in surprise. "You don't think it's weird? They took me to the beach last Saturday where they told me that they wanted to share me, like, at the same time, monogamously. I didn't even know those types of relationships were a thing."

She calmed her voice when she spoke this time. "Why would I think it's weird? Girl, you have been living in the dark ages with Tom for far too long. That type of relationship isn't as uncommon as you think. People are a lot more accepting of those types of kinks these days, babe. If Reid is half as hot as Heath and you don't want them, then send them my way," she said with a sultry smile.

I couldn't help the laugh that escaped. Leave it up to her to make a joke. "And you called me a slut?" I teased.

She relaxed back on the couch. Grinning at me, she replied, "I'm not going to apologize for liking sex, and neither should you. It's past time you start letting yourself feel the finer things in life. Mainly, feeling what it would be like between those two." She winked at me.

I sighed heavily, feeling relief run through my body. I hadn't realized how much I'd needed to talk to her about this. It was stupid of me to try to keep her out of this. She was my rock, and I felt ashamed trying to keep a secret from her.

Someone cleared their throat in front of us. I snapped my head in the direction to find Lindsey staring at us. We had been so consumed by our talk that I didn't even know how long she had been standing there. "Shit, how long have you been here, Lyns?" I started to stand.

"Long enough to hear that you have a couple of love interests," she said with a small smile.

This was not happening to me. I stepped toward my daughter and grabbed her shoulders. "I'm so sorry, honey. You weren't supposed to hear any of that. Do you want to talk about it? I know I haven't been with anyone other than your father, and I don't want you to think that I didn't respect what we had." I grimaced. This was so awkward. "If you aren't ready for me to date, then you can tell me and I won't cross that line," I promised.

I couldn't fault her if she didn't like the idea of me being with someone other than her father. Even though she was all grown up, I would never intentionally make her uncomfortable.

Lindsey surprised me by laughing. "Fuck Dad. He was such a shit to you, Mom. You literally did everything for him and he repaid you by sleeping with *Vivian*." She said her name like it left a bad taste in her mouth. She looked at me seriously. "I would never tell you not to date. I want you to be happy, and you deserve someone to treat you like you're precious for a change"—she paused—"or multiple someones."

She gave me an encouraging smile, and I let her words sink in.

"Are they good to you, Mom?" she asked.

I thought about it. I hadn't known them for very long but... "I think they will be."

She grabbed me, pulling me in for a hug. "Then that is all that matters," she whispered.

Tears pricked my eyes. She pulled away and looked at me seriously again. "Now, if you're the one with two hotties chasing you, then why are we shopping for me? You're the one we should be dressing up."

Jill jumped up, clapping her hands together and squealing happily. "Yes! I have been wanting to dress up your curves for years now!"

I tried to shake my head and plant my feet, but they were having none of that. They dragged me from store to store, making me try on things I never would have tried myself. After trying on their choices, I finally conceded that maybe they were on to something. I looked in the mirror and was shocked at what I saw staring back at me.

They had forced me to try on a form-fitting black strappy dress. The back was completely open, dipping down until it reached just above my bottom. The front of the dress had a swooping neckline and built-in cups for the girls that kept them from sagging too much. Paired with nude pumps Jill made me shove my feet into, I was looking hot.

I purchased the dresses and heels, along with some skimpy thongs Jill strong-armed me into getting.

I hugged Lindsey before she got in her Uber with a promise to text me when she got back to her dorm. Then I looked at Jill and had the overwhelming urge to hug her too.

"Thank you for listening to me and not judging. I promise to not keep anything from you again," I assured her.

She pulled back and pointed at me. "Make sure that you don't. Remember, whatever you decide to do with those hunks, I'll support you no matter what."

I truly didn't deserve this girl.

After starting my car, I headed home. I felt better than I had in days. I didn't know what I was thinking trying to keep all my feelings bottled up.

The drive home was shorter than I expected. As I pulled into my spot, I smiled to myself, wondering if the boys were home. Should I knock on their door and give them my answer tonight?

As I brought all my bags with me inside, I figured I should wait. Maybe make them sweat it out for a couple of days. I was thinking when I said yes I should wear one of the knockout dresses I just bought.

Smiling to myself, I made my plan. As I made it through my front door, I decided I would wait until tomorrow evening to go see them. I had to be up early for work in the morning, and I had a feeling the boys would want to take their time with me. I would go to them straight after work tomorrow.

Decision made, I settled in for the rest of the night, daydreaming about what was to come.

## Chapter Nine

I awoke with a start, sitting straight up in bed. I looked around wildly, clearing the haze left behind by sleep. Spying the clock next to my bed, I read the time and lay back down with a huff.

It was only two in the morning. I had only just fallen asleep a couple of hours prior, unable to get comfortable. I had shed my PJs to see if it would help. Sleeping nude always seemed to do the trick. I was uncomfortable, but I was mostly giddy about talking to the boys.

Once I had decided to say yes, I couldn't stop thinking about them. It had been from pure exhaustion that I had even fallen asleep at all. Now I was just annoyed that I had woken up. I looked around, trying to figure out what had woken me.

I shifted my legs under the blankets and then I felt it. I let my hand snake under the sheet, pressing it right on my throbbing sex, the pressure ripping a deep groan from my chest.

I was so aroused and aching. In a flash, I remembered the dream. It must have gotten so intense that it woke me up from a dead sleep. Grasping at the thread that would lead me back, my hand started to rub in slow circles as I brought the dream back.

Heath was on top of me, kissing me with a mighty passion. He was gloriously nude with his big cock poised at my opening. I gasped at the fantasy before I opened my eyes long enough to reach into the top drawer on my nightstand.

Though I didn't use it often, my vibrator had been the only man I relied on to bring me pleasure for years. I clicked it on and placed it on my needy nub. The steady hum filled the room, and I moaned my pleasure. Recalling the dream, I envisioned Heath as he grabbed his cock and rubbed himself through my wetness. I ramped up the vibrations and pushed down harder on my clit. I was working myself up into such a frenzy, and I couldn't be quiet as I mewled out loud.

I closed my eyes and remembered looking down between us as Heath grasped himself with a tight fist. He slid it from his bulbous head, down to the base of his shaft. Just watching him play with himself in my mind's eye was enough to make me moan again.

He looked down with hooded eyes and started to thrust himself inside of me. I could feel my muscles tightening as I got ready to come. Heath started to say something deliciously dirty. But when he opened his mouth, all I heard was a distant pounding. He seemed confused, opening his mouth to try again. Again, the pounding came, only getting louder this time.

My eyes flew open as I realized the pounding was actually happening. I threw the blanket off of me, tossing my vibrator to the bed before grabbing my robe.

I tied a hasty knot around my waist and bolted to my front door. Panic replaced my excitement. My first thought was that it was Lindsey trying to get into my apartment because something had happened. I almost slammed into the door in my rush to get there. My hair flew back from my face as I threw it open, but the eyes I found waiting weren't those of my daughter.

Instead, I found myself staring at a very pissed-off, black-haired, Greek god of a neighbor of mine. A very pissed-off and shirtless neighbor.

"Heath," I breathed in a rush. "What are you doing here? You nearly gave me a heart attack." I tried to swallow, bringing moisture back to my suddenly dry mouth.

I took in the view. His hair was mussed in the sexiest way that told me he had been asleep not too long ago. I resisted the urge to run my fingers through the silky strands to smooth them.

My gaze traveled further south, down his drool-worthy body, and my hands itched with the need to rake them across the ridges of his abs. He had a light dusting of hair that spanned his chest, and I wondered what it would feel like when it rubbed against my bare nipples.

Further down, I could see an impressive bulge tenting his low-slung pajama pants. I was willing to bet that he was going commando underneath if the outline of his cock was any indication. The sight was enough to make me squeeze my thighs together to ease some of the ache. I forcefully shook myself and met his eyes as I flushed.

He continued to glare as he prowled toward me. "Who's here with you, Kate?" he practically growled my way. I started to back away further into the apartment. He didn't take his eyes away from me as he reached behind him, shutting and locking the door.

I tried to swallow past the lump in my throat. "I don't know what you mean, it's just me here. I was sleeping until you woke me up, pounding on my door like a crazy person."

He was still stalking me like I was his prey when he cocked his head to the side and grinned at me. "If you were sleeping, then why did I get woken up to the sound of your moans coming through my bedroom wall, sweetheart?"

I felt my whole body burn. Well, that answered that question. I shared a wall with his bedroom, not Reid's. I couldn't tell him I had been masturbating to the thought of him fucking me. I hadn't realized I had backed up clear into my kitchen until I bumped into my island.

Heath stood right in front of me, trapping me. He looked down at my robe-clad form, reminding me I was naked underneath. He fingered the sash, making my breath hitch. I wondered if he would make that one tiny pull, exposing me to him. The idea made my core clench in excitement.

"Are you going to answer me, or are you gonna make me find out the hard way, baby? If I reach under this robe and touch you, am I going to find that pussy wet and ready to fuck? I swear if I find out you have someone in your room, you're not going to like what happens." He glared at me.

I was stuck. I didn't want to tell him I was playing with myself, but I also didn't want him to think I was messing around with someone else. I opened my mouth but then closed it, shaking my head.

His eyes darkened as he grabbed the bottom of my robe, flipping it open enough to expose me. "That's the wrong answer, sweetheart." That was all the warning I got as he thrust his hand between my legs.

I had to grab on to the counter to stop myself from crumpling to the floor. I inhaled sharply, trying to keep the orgasm at bay that was so close to the surface. Heath's eyes darkened further at the evidence that he found between my legs before he ripped his hand away as if I had burned him.

Before I could comprehend what was happening, he brushed past me. His legs ate up the distance between me and my bedroom. I panicked and ran after him, but I was too late.

I wasn't fast enough to stop him as he turned my light on and was stuck standing in place. He stared at my bed, where he found my rumpled blankets and my vibrator sitting in the middle of it all. I felt my whole body flush with embarrassment when I noticed there was even a small wet spot where I had been lying.

He turned around to face me with surprise written across his face. I started to bring up my hands to hide my inflamed face when he lunged for me.

He had me flat on my back with him wedged between my legs faster than I could take a breath. A startled squeal crossed my lips, and he took the opportunity to crash those luscious lips down on mine. He rubbed his tongue against the seam of my lips, begging for entry. I obliged while grabbing his ass, pushing him down onto me and causing him to emit a deep groan.

He reached between us and undid the sash to my robe, exposing my naked flesh. Then he broke the kiss long enough to look down at my body in appreciation. When his eyes met mine again, they were filled with need. "Did I hear you playing with your little pussy, baby? God, that's fucking hot." He thrust his pelvis. "Show me," he demanded with dark eyes.

He sat up just enough to look down at me, and I felt myself wanting to hide again. It must have been all over my face because Heath took pity on me. "It's okay, sweetheart, you have nothing to be embarrassed about. You want to know a secret?"

I nodded, and he smiled. "I've jacked my cock almost every night since we met. Thinking of you gets me so worked up. When I shower, I pretend my fist is that tight pussy of yours."

That did something for me. Sometimes I thought I could come just from listening to him and Reid talk dirty to me.

"Show me, baby, and I'll show you too." He stood up beside the bed and proved me right. He was completely commando underneath his PJs. He pulled them down until his impressive cock sprang over the edge. I squeezed my thighs together and tried not to reach out to it.

He was long and thick. Just like Jill guessed, he curved up, nearly touching his belly button. This was easily the biggest dick I had ever seen. A pearl of pre-cum wept from the head, and I desperately wanted to swipe it with my tongue. I had never enjoyed the act of giving oral sex, but I found myself wanting to try again with this man.

"You keep looking at me like that and this will be over before it starts," Heath ground out between clenched teeth.

He reached down and tweaked one of my nipples, extracting a squeal that turned into a moan as a delicious heat went straight to my pussy. He wrapped his other hand around his length and started to pump his fist. After he threw his head back with a long moan, he looked down at me expectantly.

He wouldn't wait forever, and my embarrassment faded with each stroke he gave himself. I let my legs fall apart and reached down. As soon as my fingers raked across my clit, I arched my back. I hadn't realized how close I was to the edge until right now. This was definitely not going to last long.

"Fuck, Kate, that is so fucking hot. Put those little fingers in that cunt and feel how wet you are," he commanded softly.

I did as I was told. Watching his strokes get faster egged me on. I started to finger-fuck myself with vigor now. The fact that Heath was turned on by the sight I was making served to bring me closer to release. The only sounds in the room were our heavy breathing and the sinful wet noise my fingers made as they fucked in and out of me.

I felt myself arching into my own touch, and I knew I was about there until Heath grabbed my arm and moved it away. I muttered a curse before he climbed back onto the bed and replaced my hand with his mouth. I nearly screamed as he sucked my clit into his mouth and flicked his tongue across it wildly. He pulled his arm down and pushed two fingers inside of me, making a *come here* motion. Then he hit that magic spot inside of me that I didn't even know existed until recently, and I went flying.

I screamed his name as I came, and that encouraged him to keep going. He didn't even give me a chance to come down from the first orgasm before he hummed, causing his mouth to vibrate over my core.

The second time I came was so intense that I felt every muscle in my body contract and fight to release. He removed his fingers and started to lightly lap at my pussy, sending aftershocks through my body. Then he finally gave my poor clit a kiss and made his way up my body to settle his pelvis between my open legs. I could feel his still naked hard length against my swollen, wet flesh.

"I'm sorry, I couldn't let you finish yourself, sweetheart. I have been thinking about tasting you again since last week, and I couldn't resist. I think I could watch you come all day," he said in a husky tone.

I didn't care that he had finished me off. I had only experienced someone's mouth down there with him and Reid, and I was afraid I might be addicted now. Even though my body was completely spent, I rocked my hips up, trying to get his cock where I wanted it. "Heath, I need you so bad right now," I begged.

Heath closed his eyes and thrust forward just the tiniest bit, making the head of his cock breach my entrance. He stilled my churning hips with his big hands, and I whimpered my protest. Though he didn't take himself out, he didn't move further forward either.

"I'm not going to fuck you yet, sweetheart. Reid would have my balls if I took you without him. Even though all I want to do right now is watch your face as I sink into your heat, I can't. We start as we mean to finish, together."

He brought his forehead down to mine and kissed my nose sweetly. I almost broke right then and there, wanting to tell him I had made my choice. But I closed my lips, unwilling to ruin my plan.

He pushed up and away from me, taking his heat with him. He stood next to the bed and started to pull his pants back over what had to have been a very painful erection.

Before I could think about what I was doing, I scrambled up and slid down to the floor in front of him, not bothering to close my robe. His eyes flared as he looked down at me "What are you doing, Kate?" he rasped.

I stared into his eyes as I reached up and grabbed hold of his cock, extracting a hiss from him. "You and Reid have made me come more in one week than I have in my entire life. I would like to return the favor for once."

I swiped my thumb across his weeping head, causing him to jerk in my hand. He looked down at me with need in his eyes. "You don't have to do that, sweetheart. We both enjoy watching you lose control for us. We don't expect anything in return."

I hoped my expression was letting him know how much I truly needed this. "I know that, but for the first time in my life, the thought of giving someone pleasure with my mouth is turning me on. I want to see you lose control too." I didn't wait for a response as I leaned forward and swiped my tongue against him, lapping up the liquid I found there. I was rewarded with a masculine groan.

I sucked the head into my mouth, flicking my tongue on the little V underneath.

"Fuck, baby, your mouth is so hot it's burning me. I should make you stop, but I don't think I can." He breathed heavily above me.

He threaded his fingers into my hair and tugged, causing fresh arousal to flood down my thighs. I pulled him further into my mouth and sucked hard. He started to pump his hips forward in time with my sucking as he looked down at me, his chest heaving fiercely. "You want this, sweetheart? Then take it. Take it all, suck me hard," he ordered.

His words drove me higher. I sucked hard, swirling my tongue around with each pull. I was getting more of him in my mouth with each swipe. I could never take him all the way to his root. He was too big, but I could get close. Using my hand to stroke what my mouth couldn't reach, I looked up at him.

He closed his eyes. "Baby, I'm trying to let you do what you need, but I need to fuck that mouth of yours. Tap my thigh if it's too much." He put his other hand in my hair, grabbed two handfuls, and pulled, lighting my scalp up. It was on the right side of pain, and I moaned around his cock, sending the vibration up. *"Fuck."* He hissed. Holding my head still now, he fucked his way into my mouth. He was ruthless with his thrusts, and I focused on my breathing the best I could and sucked as if my life depended on it.

His movements became erratic as he neared his release. He was panting as he growled. "You feel too good. I'm gonna come. If you don't want to swallow me down, you better pull away now and I'll finish this."

I had always hated this part the most with Tom, but with Heath, I found myself grabbing the back of his thighs and urging him on. The movement wasn't lost on him, and he was going wild now. I took a deep breath and relaxed my throat while pulling him closer. As soon as he touched the soft spot in the back of my throat, he held himself still and shouted his release. I swallowed around him, not wanting to lose a single drop.

He slowly pulled out and released my hair. Then I looked up at him, licking my lips, and I could've sworn I saw his cock twitch with new life. He knelt down, picking me up as if I weighed nothing, and carried me to the bathroom. After setting me on the counter, he turned and flipped the shower on. Once he came back to me, he wrapped my legs around him and kissed me sweetly.

Discarding his PJs and my robe on the bathroom floor, he then carried me into the shower and under the hot stream. He pulled away from me long enough to grab my lavender-scented body wash before he started to wash me with his bare hands. He paid special attention to my breasts, pinching my tight nipples before moving down. All while he told me how beautiful I was and how perfect I had been with his cock in my mouth. Telling me how much he appreciated what I had done for him. His appreciation made pride flow through my body.

I felt myself getting achy all over again as he turned me around, pressing his hard length against the seam of my ass. His hand wandered lower, and he showed me again how much he appreciated me while whispering praises in my ear. This time when I came, his name was a broken plea from my lips.

When the water ran cold, we reluctantly exited and Heath toweled me off, taking extra care of my more delicate parts. He carried me back to my bed and tucked me in.

After he leaned down to kiss me, I stopped him. "Stay? Please." I watched his face soften as he nodded. He turned the light out and climbed into bed, bringing my back to his front.

He ran his hand up my side, finally coming to a stop under my breast. I was completely wrung dry, but I still found myself pushing back into his groin. He chuckled and kissed my neck. "Sleep, sweetheart."

I grinned into the dark. I wasn't sure how I was supposed to sleep pressed up against this naked man, but it wasn't long before my eyelids drooped and oblivion took me.

## Chapter Ten

I woke the next morning wrapped in warmth. I tried to roll over but was unable to move. Raising my head to look down at myself, I saw the reason why. Heath and I were face-to-face. He had his arm slung over my side, and our legs were tangled together.

Looking up at the clock, I saw that my alarm would be going off in a couple of minutes. It was time for me to get up and get ready for work, but I didn't want to move.

Heath looked so peaceful in his sleep. I reached up to run my fingers across his sensual lips, his stubble tickling me. He truly was gorgeous, which begged the question of what the hell he saw in me. He had the body and face of a man who could get any woman he wanted, and yet he had latched on to me.

I took this time to do a little more exploring. Sometime during the night, we must have kicked the blanket off in favor of using our body heat to keep warm. He was just as impressive asleep as he was awake. His arms were a testament to how much he took care of his body. His tattoo looked to be some type of tribal design with a Celtic background, running from just above his elbow all the way up to his shoulder. As I traced the lines with awe, I made a mental note to ask him what it meant.

Lightly putting my hand to his chest, I found myself loving the feel of his dusting of hair against my palm. I never thought I'd be a woman who could find body hair appealing, but Heath made it sexy. Letting my fingers run between his pecs, I followed the line of his abs to his belly button. The trail I found there leading down was almost too tempting not to follow.

Moving away from temptation, I let myself revel

along that sexy *V* his hips made instead. He hadn't even touched me, and I could feel myself softening, getting ready for him.

I looked further down to look at his cock, which happened to be growing, getting harder with each passing second. It lay heavily against the curve of my stomach now. My gaze flew up to his face to see him staring at me with a sleepy smile on his face. I tried to jerk my hand away, but he caught it.

"Doing a little exploring this morning, are we?" he rumbled, his voice thick with sleep. He took my hand and moved me to grab his hard length. The movement made my core clench in desire.

He groaned as I moved my hand in soft strokes. "If you wanted to cop a feel, all you had to do was ask, sweetheart." He grinned down at me.

I opened my mouth to defend myself when he rolled over to where he was half on me, half on the bed. He brought his mouth to mine, and I opened under him, allowing his tongue to plunder. His kiss was sweet and almost loving. Feeling myself softening further under him, I squeezed my hand around his length to convey my intentions without words.

His intake of breath was sharp against my lips as he pulled away to say, "Are you wanting to play this morning, sweetheart? I figured you would still be worn out from last night, but I'm always willing to please," he teased.

He started to leave a trail of goosebumps as he slowly dragged his hand down my torso. His slow advance was killing me with anticipation. I started squirming against my own will while he stared down at me, watching my eyes. My breath became more ragged with each inch he gained. He finally got to my mound and started to slide his fingers through my labia.

And that was when my alarm decided to go off. He looked down at me, startled for a second before he started laughing. His laughter was contagious, and I found myself giggling under him. I rolled out of his embrace and turned the offending noise off. He was still smiling at me when I settled back down.

"Well, it sounds like we'll have to continue this later." Bringing his hand up, he brushed my hair behind my ear, leaving his hand against my jaw. He leaned in for one more soft kiss.

The way he was so gentle with me made me simply melt. He pulled away. "Reid and I both have late shifts tonight, but I know he's gonna want to see you soon. What do you say we all get together tomorrow night? Maybe we can answer any questions you may have?"

I could feel my chest deflate, but I forced a smile anyway. I had planned on telling them what I wanted tonight. Waiting another day wasn't what I wanted to do, but I nodded my acceptance, because what else could I do?

Heath bounded up from my bed and went on a search for his pants, giving me the most delicious view of his backside. I leaned up on one elbow, watching him.

He grinned at me as he turned back around. I couldn't help but stare at his cock now. He was still long and hard. Apparently, he liked his view too. He grabbed himself, giving it a couple of long strokes that had my breath hitching.

"Enjoying the show, are we?" He winked at me before he pulled his pants on. "You keep looking at me like that and you'll be late to work."

I tried not to pout as he took away my fun. Leaning down, he kissed me again and promised to see me tomorrow.

As I got ready for work, I let my mind wander back to last night, smiling like an idiot. Wouldn't it be wonderful if every night could be like last night? Well, except I wanted to have some super-hot sex too. Sex had almost always been a thing to endure in the past, but now I was excited at the prospect. I knew, without a doubt, Heath and Reid would make it worthwhile.

I only wished that we could get together tonight. I didn't know when I had become so insatiable. Something about these men made me want to do things I never knew I could want. Sighing as I walked out the door, I told myself good things would come to those who wait.

****

Work flew by in a blur of activity. No sooner had I sat down at my desk to check the weekend's emails, Samantha was up and out the door needing me. She had a list of things that needed to be done before she met with a new author.

I didn't get a chance to breathe with everything that she needed from me today. I loved absolutely every minute of it too. I had never felt this type of accomplishment before.

Sure, I had accomplished raising a human being, but this was different. This was all for me, and it felt great. Samantha had even given me some new manuscripts to read over and give her my thoughts. I had always loved reading. It was always a nice escape from my life.

She told me to take them home and start on them tonight but not to worry about finishing until Friday. I came straight home with takeout from a local Chinese restaurant and was currently poring over the first manuscript with my box of noodles.

This was a romantic comedy book with some pretty spicy scenes throughout. According to Samantha, this was a new author the firm was considering taking on. I was no expert, but I could clearly see that she had promise. This was a very well-written book, and I found myself laughing often.

I was just getting ready to open my fortune cookie when someone knocked on my door. Looking at the time, I wondered who it could be so late in the evening. I had been reading for hours, and it was already after ten.

I put the script down on my coffee table and threw my soft sherpa blanket to the side. I got a little excited when I thought maybe it was one of the boys. I was hoping it was Reid. After being with Heath last night and him being so sweet, I was craving a little of Reid's dominance.

Looking down at myself, I wondered if I should try to change. I had shucked the bra as soon as I got home and I had traded my slacks and blouse for short cotton shorts and a tank top. I smiled and decided it didn't matter. Both of them had already seen me naked and they didn't seem to care that my breasts hung lower than a twenty-one-year-old's.

Without checking the peephole, I opened the door, still smiling like a goon while daydreaming of the gorgeous Viking on the other side. I started to say something sultry when I took a shocked step back from the door. Instead of Reid's sinful smile, I came face to face with someone I'd hoped to never have to see again.

He looked me up and down, making my skin crawl with every drag of his eyes. Still staring at my breasts, he smiled, swaying a bit. The gesture reminded me of a weasel.

I crossed my arms in front of my chest in an attempt to hide myself. "What are you doing here, Tom?" I asked in what I hoped was a stern voice.

His gaze finally came to my face with a look of disappointment in it. "After our last conversation on the phone, I figured I needed to apologize," he slurred. "I have to say, sugar, I love the outfit. Why didn't you ever wear anything like that when we were married?"

Looking at him now, I felt embarrassed I had spent nineteen years with this man. He was the exact opposite of Reid and Heath. He was tall but reminded me of a beanpole except for his beer belly. His hair was thinning on top, and he had taken to the comb-over technique to cover his bald spot. All of these things wouldn't have been bad if he at least had a good personality.

Truth was, he had always been slightly misogynistic, and it had only gotten worse with age. He was truly one of those men who thought they were God's gift to women. It was one thing when he had an athletic physique to go with that complex, but now it was just sad.

I felt my chicken lo mein fight to stay in my stomach. I was sure my face was a mask of disgust. "I did and you just never noticed. How did you get past the front door? You can't get in without a key."

He waved me away like I asked a stupid question, staggering a little. "I just followed one of the other tenets. All I had to say was I lost my key and this sweet old lady let me in." He looked around my apartment from the entryway with a long whistle. "Damn, this is your new place? My money from the divorce has treated you well."

I rolled my eyes. "What the hell are you talking about? I didn't take any of your money. I could afford this from my own savings."

I didn't mention that I had a little extra help. My dad never did like Tom. Dad had all but begged me years ago to leave him, and I believed him when he said he would have helped me raise Lyns. I was just too stubborn for my own good and wanted to make my marriage work.

I was his only child, and he'd raised me alone when my mom ran off with another man, leaving us both in her rearview mirror. When he passed, he made sure to leave everything to me in a separate account that Tom couldn't access. Tom never knew about the account, and I never took any money out of it until the divorce. Even from the grave, my dad made sure I had everything I needed to leave Tom.

Something dark flashed in Tom's eyes, and I realized my mistake when he took a step toward me. I should have slammed the door in his face the moment I discovered it was him. Instead, like an idiot, I had taken a step back, retreating from my ex like a wimp.

All too late, I tried to stand my ground. "Y-you need to leave. If you came to apologize, then I accept it. Now go."

That was clearly the wrong thing to say. His eyes dilated and he prowled toward me. I backed up another step.

"You saved that money when we were together. If it hadn't been for me paying the bills and keeping a roof over your head, you would have never saved anything. So I suggest you stop being such a bitch and move out of my way." He didn't wait for me to move. He shoved me hard, and I landed flat on my ass.

Surprise drowned out the pain in my hip as I registered the shock on my face. Through all the years we had been together, Tom had never been violent with me. We may have had our little arguments, but most of the time, he had just dropped the subject like he hadn't particularly cared enough to fight with me. This Tom that stood above me with his fist clenched was a completely different person.

I hated the fact that I scooted further away from him. He stepped forward and kneeled down next to my face. I flinched when the smell of liquor fanned over my face as he spoke.

"Are you happy now? You made me push you. If you would have just let me in, I wouldn't have had to do that. I don't know what's gotten into you all of a sudden. You never used to backtalk me," he snarled before his eyes softened. "I'm sorry, sugar. You just make me so crazy sometimes. When you left, things started to go to shit, and I just want you back."

I jerked away as he tried to touch my face in a loving gesture.

I saw now how bloodshot his eyes were. He was absolutely wasted—another thing that never happened when we were together.

"Tom, you're scaring me. I need you to leave. Go sleep it off and then maybe we can get you some help." I might not love him anymore, but Lindsey didn't need to see her dad like this. I would help find him a rehab to spare her that.

Tom scrunched up his nose in disgust. Before I could see it coming, pain exploded across my face as he slapped the back of his hand into my cheek. My head snapped in the opposite direction. I could taste blood, so I knew he had split my lip.

I reached up to cup my cheek, but before I could, he grabbed hold of my hand and jerked me up toward him. Suddenly, I was on my feet, and he had me pressed right against his body.

"You self-righteous little bitch! You think you're better than me, don't you? I don't need any fucking help. What I need is for my fucking whore of a wife to come home and start being my wife again. I've tried to let you have your little midlife crisis, but it stops now. Do you understand?" He spat.

Tears leaked from my eyes as he squeezed my wrist to the point of pain and shook me. "Tom, you're hurting me. Let go!" I cried. I didn't know how I was going to get out of this situation. I could try screaming, but I doubted anyone would hear me.

He snatched my hair, wrenching a strangled cry from me as he forced me to look at him. His eyes were wild like he wasn't sure what to do or say.

"God, you make me so fucking crazy, Kate." He slammed his lips down on mine and started to grope me. One hand in my hair holding me still, the other hand trying to lift my shirt.

I tried pushing him off me, but he wouldn't budge. Desperately looking for a way out, I could feel my stomach getting ready to reject the food I had eaten as panic flooded my body. All of my focus was zeroed in on how to get out of this situation, so much so that I didn't notice Reid come up behind Tom.

It all happened so fast, my body crumpled to the floor. I looked up long enough to see Reid punch my ex square in the nose, and I cringed at the sickening crunch. Tom howled and staggered back, grabbing his nose as he looked up at his attacker like he was the victim.

Reid seemed to barely contain his rage. He grabbed hold of Tom's jacket and brought him right up to his face. "Who the fuck are you? You think it's okay to force yourself onto a defenseless woman?" He brought his arm back and punched him again. Blood was running freely down Tom's face now. If his nose wasn't broken before, it sure was now.

I stood on wobbly legs to get to Reid. Tom looked like he was about to start crying soon. I just wanted him out of here. I touched Reid's shoulder to stop him. "Reid, this is my ex-husband. He is very drunk and I think he needs help finding the door."

Tom looked between Reid and me. "Are you fucking this guy, Kate?" he shouted.

Reid was having none of it. He reared back and punched him again. The sound of his nose breaking further was enough to make me wince as Tom howled in pain again.

Reid shook him like a rag doll. "The next words out of your mouth better be *I'm sorry*. Or I'm going to make sure you won't be able to touch another woman with that useless husk hanging between your legs ever again!"

Tom immediately sneered at me and spit his blood on the ground "I'm sorry. Now let me go so I can get the fuck away from this useless whore." He spat in my direction.

Rage passed in Reid's eyes again as he punched Tom in the gut. Tom's breath left him with a whoosh, and he went a little pale.

When I thought Reid was going to keep hitting him, he pushed him away so hard Tom landed on his ass. My ex scrambled up, swaying a little. I didn't know if it was from the alcohol or getting his assed kicked.

Tom looked at me and Reid one more time as he got on the elevator. He pointed at me and said, "This isn't over, Kate."

I had to hold Reid back before he grabbed Tom again and beat him to a bloody pulp.

The elevator started to go down and Reid turned, grabbing my face between his big hands. The damage he saw made his face go red with anger all over again.

"If I ever see him again, I'll fucking kill him," he said in a calm voice that left chills on my skin. I cupped my hands over his, leaning against the rough warmth of them, but I winced a little when I put pressure on my throbbing cheek.

He leaned forward and kissed my forehead. "Let's get you cleaned up."

I nodded and led him to my apartment. He shut and locked the front door, double-checking the lock. "I'll be calling the landlord in the morning and telling him what happened tonight. We need a doorman to keep people out that don't live here," he said gruffly.

Grabbing my hand in his, he led me to my bathroom. After flipping on the light, he turned to me. He gathered me up, running his hand soothingly down my back, before he picked me up and placed me on the countertop. He looked through the drawers until he came up with what he needed. He placed the peroxide, cotton swabs, and gauze on the counter next to me. Wedging himself between my open thighs, he went to work.

I flinched at the sting as he cleaned my lip with practiced hands. He was quiet while he worked, but I could feel his tension getting higher with each passing moment. It was obvious that looking at what Tom had done to my face upset him.

I needed to take his mind off of wanting to track down my ex and beat him all over again. "How long have you been an EMT?" I asked.

He blew out a shaky breath and looked into my eyes. "About five years now. I floated around after high school and kind of landed into it. I'd gotten into a motorcycle accident, and the EMTs were amazing. I signed up for classes the next week." He smiled at the memory.

Gently, he grabbed my chin and turned my face so he could look at my cheek. I felt his breath fan across my face as he said, "It doesn't look like he broke anything, but I think you will probably get a bruise. I'll go get you some ice. Stay put."

I did as I was asked and sat still. I heard him in the kitchen getting what he needed, and he was back within seconds. He handed me two night-time pain relievers with a glass of water and told me to drink.

I swallowed the pills with a big gulp of water and I blanched when he put the ice to my cheek. He stood between my legs and held it still. Holding my ice pack with one hand, he gripped my upper thigh with the other. He seemed to be searching my eyes for something as I looked at him.

Taking the ice pack from him, I grabbed his other hand and inspected his knuckles. He had a couple of splits that needed attention.

He looked down at me and shrugged. "Don't worry about it, I've had a lot worse." He gave me a small smile.

I put my ice down and grabbed a clean cotton swab. After pouring some of the peroxide solution on it, I set to cleaning his cuts.

This whole situation seemed really intimate. After I was all done cleaning the blood away, I wrapped his knuckles with some gauze that he had set out earlier. Finished, I looked up to see him staring down at me with some indiscernible emotion in his amber eyes. God, what I wouldn't give to know what he was thinking. I blushed as I looked away.

Reid grabbed my chin gently and moved me to look at him. "I want to kiss you so bad right now, but I don't want to hurt you."

I felt butterflies flutter in my lower belly. My breathing came out in little puffs as I said, "You would never hurt me."

He lowered his hand to my neck. The motion should have scared me, given what I had just gone through, but I leaned into it. I believed what I said—he would never bring any harm to me.

When Reid lowered his mouth to mine, it was the gentlest kiss he had ever given me. Though he was gentle with my lips, he did dominate in other ways. He tightened his hand at my throat, just enough to let me know he was there. Stepping closer between my legs so we were flush together, he pushed me until my back was against the mirror.

I moaned as he dipped his tongue in enough to make me want more. Before I wanted him to, he pulled away. "It's late and you have been through an ordeal. Let me get you to bed."

I nodded, and he picked me back up and carried me to my bedroom. I didn't think I would ever get used to being carried around like my weight didn't bother them.

Reid set me on my feet beside my bed so he could pull back my blankets. He turned to leave, and I grabbed his arm. "Would it be too much to ask if you would stay the night with me?" I didn't think I would be getting much sleep tonight.

He looked at me like I was crazy. "You think I am going to leave you alone after what just happened? If you kicked me out I would still sleep in front of your door, bunny." He gave me a small peck and then left the room.

I heard him in the living room, picking up my takeout boxes and turning out the lights. I turned to my bed and lay down with my ice pack on my cheek.

I heard rather than saw him come in. My back was to my door where he turned the light off. Then I heard the rustle of clothing being taken off and felt a slither of excitement run through my veins.

As he climbed into the bed, all I could see was his

silhouette against the street lights filtering in through my bedroom window. He covered himself up to his waist, leaving his torso out of the blankets. I could hear the smile in his voice when he said, "Don't get any ideas. You've been through enough tonight and you need to rest."

I huffed, and he chuckled. I scooched closer to him, hoping he would take the hint and hold me.

It turned out he was really good at taking hints. He brought his arm around me and pulled me close. He arranged me to where I had my head on his chest and my arm across what I knew was a sexy abdomen. I hadn't seen him with his shirt off since the day at the beach, but I remembered how he had looked.

He was mouth-watering, with the same sexy *V* Heath had, but Reid's waist was more tapered. He wasn't what I would call thin as he was nothing but muscle, but he was certainly lean and tall compared to Heath's bulk. He also had a full-sleeve tattoo running from his wrist up to cover his left pec. The ink was a series of swirls, dots, and sharp lines that begged to be traced. I'd never considered myself a tattoo girl until I met these two.

I nuzzled closer and put my leg over his waist, surprised to only feel skin touching me. He was long and hard pressed against my thigh. I tried not to wiggle, and I looked up at his face expectantly.

He looked down at me and chuckled again. "I sleep naked, and that is from you pushing your luscious body up against me. Just ignore it and go to sleep."

*Fat chance of that happening.* From the feel of his erection against my leg, I would say he and Heath were about the same size in that department. Reid's might have been a little thicker than Heath's, but not much. I moved my leg to get closer, and Reid's chest rumbled.

"If you don't stop moving, I'm going to tie you down and stop letting you touch me, baby," he threatened.

That got me to hold still. I still didn't know how I was supposed to sleep though. With his free hand, Reid rubbed my side. Up and down, up and down. The movement was almost hypnotic. I felt the steady rise and fall of Reid's chest against my cheek as my eyes began to feel heavy. It wasn't too much longer before I felt myself slip into a restful sleep.

## Chapter Eleven

I was having the most delectable dream. I could feel a hot mouth latch onto my nipple as he licked and nibbled softly. I heard myself moaning, and I arched for more. Sensing a hand make its way below my shorts and touching soft skin, I felt the vibration against my breast as he rumbled his approval at my wetness. I didn't want the dream to end, but I could feel myself starting to wake.

As I scrunched my eyes closed, trying to hold on another moment longer, I felt the bed shift. My eyes flew open, and I realized that I wasn't dreaming. I looked down at my body and saw Reid in all his naked glory hovering above me. I smiled and reached up to bring him down for a kiss.

He ran his finger lightly around my pebbled nipple and sighed. "Sorry I woke you, bunny, but when I woke up, these pretty pink nipples were not in this flimsy tank top anymore. They were just begging to be sucked on."

I whimpered when he leaned back down and nipped me again.

"I know you need to get up soon and get ready for work, but I need to taste you first," he said in that husky tone I loved.

That was all the warning I got as Reid sat up and pulled my shorts down. He settled between my legs and kissed me right on my clitoris. My body jerked, and I reached for him.

He looked up at me with those dominating amber eyes. "No touching, bunny. I want you to reach up and grab your headboard. You don't move those hands or I'll stop what I'm doing and spank your bare ass."

I shivered at his command and grabbed the spindles of my headboard.

"That's my good girl." He gave me a wicked grin as he lowered his head again. He held eye contact with me as he ran his tongue from my entrance to my throbbing clit.

Throwing my head back, I gave over to the sensation. He was taking his time, making small circles around where I needed him most. This was absolute torture, and the bastard knew what he was doing. He was licking everything except my clit. "Please, Reid," I whimpered.

He chuckled against my wet center. "I like the way you ask so nicely, bunny, but I'm having fun taking my time. You're my favorite snack."

He took a small pity on me and sucked my clit into his mouth and let it go with a naughty smack of his lips. Then he immediately went back to his small circles. Every so often, he would go lower and fuck me with his tongue. It still wasn't enough.

I decided begging would get me nowhere, so I tried moving my hips to get him where I wanted him. He pulled away and smacked me right on the meaty part of my inner thigh, pulling a small squeal from me. It was painful, but then it turned to warmth, only pushing me higher. He looked up at me with stern eyes "Who's in charge here, Kate?"

I nearly screamed when he put his fingers in me, curling them up. "You, Reid, you!" I was breathing so heavily I thought my lungs would give out.

He still stared at me when he growled. "That's right, I am. This is my pussy, and I will do with it what I want, how I want. You pull that shit again, and I'll stop."

I couldn't form words, so I just nodded vigorously. I didn't have to wait long until he returned to his mission of driving me crazy. I strained to hold on to the headboard while sweat broke out on my brow. "Please, Reid. I can't take anymore." I wasn't above begging at this point.

He finally seemed to take pity on me as he sucked my clit back into his mouth and flicked his tongue. The feel of him licking and his fingers combined was all it took. It was all too much.

He bit down gently, and I lost it. I exploded against his tongue with a scream. I didn't even notice that I had brought my hands down to grab his hair, holding him to me. By the time I realized what I had done, it was too late.

Reid smiled up at me like he'd wanted me to slip up. He grabbed my hips and flipped me onto my stomach. Still holding my hips, he pulled me up until I was on all fours. The change of positions happened so fast that it made me a little dizzy.

"I believe I told you to hold on to that headboard or I would spank this pretty ass, baby."

I felt him come up behind me and thrust his cock between my wet folds. He pulled back and thrust again, the movement rubbing against me. My arms shook as I held myself up. I had just come, but I was already close again.

He ran his hand up my back until he got to my nape. Reaching forward for my throat, he pulled me up until my back was against his front. His other hand came forward and pinched my nipple. I gasped as pain bloomed, but then the warmth went straight to my pussy.

He rasped in my ear. "You're going to stay on your hands and knees while I spank you. It will hurt, but don't worry, you'll like it. If you do well, I'll make you come again. Am I understood, bunny?" It was a miracle that I could say yes, I felt so high right now.

He let go of my throat and pushed me until I was back on all fours again. With his cock still nestled against my clit, I could feel him throbbing against me. I desperately wanted him to start moving. I was so focused on that part of his anatomy I didn't have time to prepare for the smack that landed firmly on my right ass cheek.

I nearly screamed as Reid peppered my ass in quick, hard smacks. He was right, it hurt, but I could feel myself getting wetter with each stroke.

I lost count after a bit, and I started to float. When he was done, I could hear his heavy breathing, causing his cock to move slightly with each breath.

I moaned when I felt my clit throbbing against his hard length. If he slid against me one more time, I would come again. I was shaking with my need to orgasm. Before I could think better, I reached down under me to touch him.

As soon as I did, he groaned and pushed into my hand. As he rubbed against my palm, he slid easily through my wet folds, and I was coming again with his name on my lips. I had no control over myself as my pelvis churned against him.

He gripped my hips, urging me on while telling me to come against his cock. When the orgasm subsided, I was still pushing him against me as he throbbed with his own need. I rocked back and forth, making him fuck me through the slickness of my arousal.

"This was going to be all about you, but I want you so fucking bad." He pulled away slightly before pushing back through my labia. My wetness made it easy for him to slide. I kept my hand flat against him as he thrust against me. With every pull of his heavy cock, he rubbed against my clit, driving me higher again.

I pushed against him harder, forcing more pressure against me. His thrusts hastened and became erratic.

"I'm gonna fucking come, Kate, I want you there with me. Come for me!" he commanded as he smacked my ass one more time. I let myself go, coming so hard I saw stars.

He groaned from behind me as his cock jerked in my hand, and he came all over my pussy. He gave a couple more thrusts, his release adding to my wetness.

We stayed like that for a moment. He just slowly rubbed against me, spreading his cum like he was marking me as his. Before I wanted him to, he pulled away with instructions for me to stay where I was. He came back with a warm washcloth and cleaned me up. After his roughness, I wasn't expecting such softness, but I reveled in it.

After he was satisfied with his work, he pulled me into his arms. We lay back down, and he stroked me all over, telling me how perfect I was, and how he hoped I'd say yes to him and Heath.

Not too long after, the moment was broken by the sound of my alarm clock. Reid got dressed and said his goodbyes with long, sweet kisses. He left with the promise that he would see me later tonight.

After I showered, I got ready for work. I tried and failed to cover my bruised cheek with makeup. Later, I would call my lawyer about serving Tom with a restraining order before the day was over. I didn't recognize the person he was becoming, and I didn't want any part of it.

Gathering my things, I left for work with a smile on my face. Tonight was the night I'd take a chance and grab what I wanted, what I needed, for a change.

\*\*\*\*

"That lowlife, slimy motherfucker!" Jill proved she knew some very colorful curse words, reminding me why I had shut her door when I came in.

She had called me on my desk phone sometime around eleven to see if I wanted to get some lunch with her. I braced myself as I greeted her with our food order. I knew my friend was going to fly off the handle when she saw my bruised cheek and healing lip.

Jill had always been very protective of the people she loved. She was proving that now as she described in vivid detail what she wanted to do to Tom's favorite appendage.

I cut her off when she got to the meat grinder portion of her rant. "Jill, it's okay. I already called my lawyer, and she said she will have him served papers by the end of the day. Once he gets the restraining order, he'll back off." I truly hoped that was what would happen.

The old Tom had dodged confrontation like it was contagious. This new Tom I met last night seemed to thrive on it. I told myself I needed to look into what was going on with him a little more. I wondered what was happening in his life that made him act this way.

When I told him I wanted a divorce, he'd been indifferent. Yes, he'd tried to blame his infidelity on me, but after we signed the papers, he left well enough alone. It didn't make sense that over a month later he was trying to get me back.

Jill wasn't having it. "No! Fuck that. I'm going to have *my* lawyer take you on as a client. We are going to take that piece of shit to the cleaners. He won't have two pennies to rub together when we're done with him."

When Jill was pissed, she got scary. She was absolutely one of those women who, when scorned, would burn the world down.

She picked the receiver up on her phone, ready to dial when I stilled her hand, trying to make her see reason. "Jill, I'm fine. Taking him back to court is asking for more issues. I just want him to leave me alone. I want to move on with my life," I said with a small smile, hoping that would help.

She slammed the phone back down. "Fine! I'll follow your lead. But I swear to God, Kate, if he touches you again, I will kill him myself." She leaned back in her chair with an exasperated huff. "How the hell did you get away from him, anyway?"

I smiled now, remembering this morning. "Reid was coming home and he saw Tom attack me. He beat the shit out of him. I think you'll have to fight Reid for killing rights, by the way. He was absolutely savage."

I paused, smirking as the image of Reid going feral on Tom flashed into my mind. I squirmed under Jill's questioning stare as I came back to reality. "And I'm sure he told Heath by now, too, so you might have to fight him as well."

I got hot just thinking about it. I normally wasn't into the whole *me Tarzan, you Jane* thing, but watching Reid last night had done something for my girl parts. The way both men had defended me from predators made me all sorts of weak in the knees. I would be lying to myself if I said I wasn't falling for them little by little, and that scared the shit out of me. We barely knew each other at this point. I shouldn't already be having these strong feelings for them. I was almost sure they didn't return the feeling. For God's sake, we hadn't even had sex yet.

I must have had it written all over my face because when I looked back at Jill, she had a look that screamed she knew a secret. "So, have you slept with them yet?"

My face immediately flamed, and Jill laughed. "Oh, come on, Kate, like you're any good at hiding your emotions. You have either slept with them or you're getting ready to."

There was no point in trying to keep it from her. "We've done everything but have sex. I was planning on telling them tonight that I want to try this relationship," I admitted.

She clapped her hands together as if she had just won something. "*Yes*! Now, tomorrow when you come to work, you're going to have to spill every dirty detail. Matter of fact, why don't you just video it so I can watch the replay," she said with a saucy smile.

She was so enthusiastic about my sex life that I couldn't help but laugh. I loved Jill, but she was a total pervert and was completely serious about the video. We spent the rest of our lunch eating and chatting about all matters. Everything from some of the manuscripts I had been given to read, to what our weekend plans were. Jill only brought up castrating Tom a couple more times. Overall, it was a good lunch.

By the time I made it back to my desk, Samantha was waiting on me. She needed me to make her reservations at some fancy restaurant for myself, her, and the new author they were bringing in, Emily Schafer. She was the brilliant mind behind the script I had been reading last night.

I was a little bewildered that Samantha wanted me to come with her to the meeting on Friday. When I asked her if she meant it when she wanted me to come too, she just looked at me like I was silly and said, "Of course, I think meeting Emily would be a wonderful opportunity for you." Then she disappeared back into her office.

I had to say I was pretty excited to meet her. I wondered if I would be able to ask her some questions about writing. When I was younger, I wrote for the school newspaper and had always figured when I went to college, I would declare English literature as my major. I recently started working on a manuscript of my own just for fun. I didn't think I would ever get published by any means, but it would be awesome if I could bounce my ideas off Emily to see what she thought.

After making the reservation for Friday at noon, I set back to returning emails and all the other busywork for the day. Before I knew it, it was time to head home. A sense of giddiness came over me as I walked to my car. I couldn't wait to get home and get dolled up to see the boys.

Checking my phone, I saw there was a text from Heath, asking if I wanted to go for a drink and some food before we headed to their place. I replied, saying I would meet them at The Sand Dollar. He sent back a winky face, saying they couldn't wait.

Tucking my phone away, I started the car and headed home, smiling like a loon the whole way.

## Chapter Twelve

Looking at myself in my full-length mirror, I decided I was ready to go. I let my hair hang down my back in loose beach waves, the tips reaching just past my shoulder blades. I kept my makeup to a minimum with some mascara, highlighter, and lip gloss.

Wearing the dress I bought the other day with the nude heels, I had to admit I looked good. The little black dress hugged every curve like it was made for me. The plunging open back definitely brought attention to my ass. The heels only helped in making my legs look long and sleek. I topped off the outfit with some simple gold hoops and a matching bracelet.

For once, when I looked in the mirror, I saw a beautiful woman and not just a middle-aged mom. The woman who stared back at me wasn't bland, she was a woman who had confidence and knew what she wanted. Even if I just looked that way instead of feeling it, I would take that as a win.

Taking a deep breath, I grabbed my clutch and left my apartment to start my trek to the bar, getting more and more nervous with each step that brought me closer to the boys. I sent them a quick text, saying I was on my way now. My phone dinged back almost immediately, saying they would meet me at the front door. Smiling again, I placed my phone back into my clutch.

Rounding the corner that would lead me right to the front entrance, I saw them. They stood side by side, looking absolutely delectable. They were both wearing blue jeans. Heath had on a simple white button-up with the sleeves rolled up. The stark white of his shirt made his hair look inkier than I had ever seen before. When he caught sight of me, I watched as his eyes filled with lust as he took in the sight of me.

Never taking his eyes off of me, he swung his hand, hitting Reid on the back to get his attention.

Turning around, Reid caught me in his gaze. He looked much more casual in his black t-shirt and his well-worn black leather jacket. His hair was slicked back, reminding me of someone who would be in a motorcycle gang. I felt myself flush as I remembered how he had played my body this morning. His eyes held all the promises of what he would do to me once he got his hands on me.

Looking at them standing next to each other, they looked like innocence and corruption. I knew better though, they were both deliciously sinful. They were both raking the length of my body with their hot stares. Their eyes were intense as they looked at me like I was their next meal. Feeling brazen from their heated looks, I let my hips sway a little more than normal as I took my final steps toward them.

Coming to stop in front of them, I looked up and gave them my best 100-watt smile. Heath smiled back down at me before he pulled me in for a breathless kiss, running his tongue across my lower lip. I felt the motion of his tongue mirrored in my core. I was dazed as he pulled away from me.

When I looked up at Reid, his stare was filled with even more desire than before. It was as though he enjoyed watching Heath and me together. He was still looking me up and down, playing his tongue between his teeth. He stopped at my eyes and made a motion with his finger, indicating he wanted me to turn around.

My face heated slightly as I followed his command, turning until I was facing them again. Reid pulled me to him, and I leaned in to kiss him. He surprised me by bringing his mouth to my ear instead.

"You look like my wet dream, bunny. Heath and I now want to skip dinner so we can take you back to our place and eat you instead," he whispered, sucking my earlobe in his mouth, nipping it before letting me go.

I swayed a little when I pulled away. Heath pulled me to his side as we made our way through the doors. I had no idea how we were supposed to get through dinner now.

We followed Reid to a round VIP booth. I couldn't help but look at the other patrons in the bar. Did they know I was with them both intimately? Even though nobody was truly paying attention to us, I couldn't help but blush. I wished I didn't care what others thought of me, but I did.

When we got to the booth, Reid gestured for me to get in first, I slid as gracefully as I could behind the rounded table. Heath followed me in, pushing his thigh right up to mine. He looked down at me again before cupping my chin and running his thumb across my scabbed lip. The look of anger passed over his eyes so fast, I would have missed it had I not been paying attention.

Not wanting our night to turn sour because of Tom, I grab his hand and kiss his fingers. Still feeling slightly sensual, I ran the tip of my tongue against the tip of his finger before kissing it again.

His eyes flared at me before he sighed and asked. "Have I told you yet how stunning you look?"

I smiled shyly. "I believe I missed that."

Reid had flagged down our waitress and ordered us a bottle of wine and was now pressing himself to my other side. Heath put his arm around my shoulders, rubbing small circles with his thumb on my collarbone. Reid's hand snuck under the tablecloth and grabbed my thigh right below the seam on my short dress. I sucked in a nervous breath and tried to calm my nerves. They had barely touched me, and I could feel myself softening for them.

Our waitress was quick to come back, depositing our glasses and chilled wine on the table. Heath ordered for all of us with a smooth voice while Reid used his free hand to pour me a glass. I picked the glass up, brought it to my lips, and drained it in one gulp.

Reid grunted a laugh, filling my glass again. Heath moved his hand down to my other thigh and squeezed. "Slow down, sweetheart. We want you to have your wits about you by the end of the night."

My breath hitched as he moved his hand further up, bringing my dress up with it. I silently thanked God for the tablecloth, otherwise, everyone would be getting quite the show. When I thought he wouldn't stop his uphill climb, his hand stilled. Coming to rest with his pinky against my quickly damping panties.

No sooner than I had calmed my racing heart, Reid's hand started to move as well. He raked his fingers up until they touched the outside of Heath's hand. My thighs were not small by any means. They touched each other, so I thought there was no room for Reid's hand. I was proved wrong when he simply pulled my thigh up and over his, making me spread my legs indecently. He placed his hand adjacent to Heath's, giving me a slight rub over my panties.

I tried to keep my eyes forward and not look down at their hands. If I looked down, I was sure to have a flaming face and everyone in the bar would know what was happening under the table. I was breathing so heavily and was getting wetter with each passing second of having them so close to where I craved them.

It was like they had a psychic link as they both started to play with the edge of my panties at the same time. I had to bite back my moan as they both delved under the fabric. Both of them slid their pinkies easily along the inside of my wet labia. If they didn't stop soon, I was sure to make a scene.

Reid leaned over toward my ear. "Don't make a sound, bunny. You wouldn't want all these people to know we're touching your little pussy," he grumbled with humor in his voice.

I tried to stop the heat from rising as Heath leaned into my other ear. "Should we see if you can come quietly, sweetheart?" he asked before he licked the shell of my ear, making me gasp.

They were both moving in tandem on either side of my clit now. I was already so close I could taste it. I had to hope that with the dim lighting of our booth, nobody would be able to see my face as I lost it. I had no control over myself as I leaned my head back and bit my lip to stop the moan that tried to escape. I felt my legs start to shake as the boys kept up their assault. I gasped as the first wave of my orgasm crashed over me. Heath leaned over before I could make a noise, crashing his lips onto mine, drinking down my soft moans.

When I came down, Heath released my lips and replaced my soaked panties to their proper place. He held his hand where it had been before as he straightened himself.

Reid took his turn as he brought me to his lips for his own domineering kiss as he replaced his hand on my thigh. "We seem to not be able to control ourselves around you, bunny," he murmured against my lips.

He kept me spread open for him but didn't make any more moves to touch above the thigh. I tried to relax as we all came out of our lust bubble. We made small talk while we waited on food. I was a little shocked when I felt myself calming and just enjoying their touch. It felt somewhat normal.

Faster than I thought it should have taken, our food was delivered. I figured the boys would move their hands to eat but they didn't, preferring to eat one-handed.

The steak Heath had ordered melted on my tongue. The glorious mixture of spices lit up my taste buds. This was not food you would be able to get from just any old bar. The wine that was served with the food only added to the flavors. I ate my food with gusto, enjoying every last bite.

I think the boys had a thing for me and food. Now and again I would make a sound of pure pleasure from the tastes exploding along my tongue. And every time, I felt a hand clasp my thigh a little tighter. I was amazed when I managed to get through the whole meal without choking once.

Once we were done eating, the boys wasted no time getting me out of the booth and on the way to the door. Heath slid his hand into mine while Reid wound his arm around the small of my back.

I glanced around to see if anyone was watching us. To my surprise, we only got a few curious glances but the majority of the crowd minding their own business.

We walked back to our complex in comfortable silence. It felt good to just have their hands on me the whole way. Making it to their apartment without another elevator incident shocked me.

Once inside, Heath locked the door while Reid took his jacket off, hanging it up. Heath turned and took my clutch from me, placing it on the table.

Making his way to the couch, Reid gestured for me to join him. I flushed at the memory of us on the couch. He must have been thinking about it too because he smiled and pulled me in for a kiss. Before I could stop myself, I pushed my hands into his hair, begging wordlessly for him to deepen the kiss. He surprised me by pulling me on top of him so I was straddling his hips.

I could feel the cool air kissing the bottom of my ass as my dress slipped up. I had worn one of those skimpy thongs that Jill made me buy.

I was startled from our make-out session when Heath ran his hand along the curve of my ass as he sat next to us. Pulling away from Reid, I looked at him licking his lips as he stared at me with lust-filled eyes. "Before his night goes any further, we need to talk."

I swallowed past the lump in my throat and nodded. I started to slide off Reid's lap, but he stopped me by pushing down on my hips. I could feel his erection pressing against my center.

"He said we needed to talk, not that you needed to move. I'm enjoying my view far too much to have you move." He then rubbed his thumb against me over my panties, making me bite back a moan.

Heath grabbed my attention by leaning toward me, sliding his hand down my ass so he could rub my entrance over the thin material from behind. If they kept it up, I didn't know how we were going to have this conversation.

Heath cleared his throat before he began. "As you already know, Reid and I want you to be ours. But with recent events, we have come to the decision that we want you around a lot more than a normal girlfriend would be around."

Reid was still rubbing me from the front, driving me mad, when he said, "We find that we like to be with you more than we have ever liked being with anyone else. There is something about you that we can't stop thinking about. It's maddening."

I let his words sweep over me as a warm feeling filled my chest. Heath saved me from having to say anything back as he forced me to look at him. "And your ex showing up here didn't sit well with us. We want you to stay with us half the time, and we can stay with you the other half."

His words cut through the haze and had me pulling back. I pushed against Reid's chest and stood up. Both men looked up at me from their seats on the couch.

"What do you mean you want me to stay with you? Like, move in with you?" I felt a cold slice of panic stab me in the chest. I wasn't ready for that. I had just started to gain my independence back and I didn't want to give it up already.

Heath leaned back on the couch and regarded me seriously. "We aren't saying you need to move in with us, sweetheart. We just want to be able to keep you close so we can make sure your fucking ex doesn't make another appearance. We could just stay the night at your place sometimes and you could stay here sometimes. Nothing permanent yet."

I swallowed hard as I looked between them. It was Reid's turn to speak now. "After what I saw him doing to you last night, it would just make us feel better to know you're not in harm's way. Once we see that he isn't going to try anything else, it can go back to normal if that's what you want."

I stood there and considered their words. Was it really such a bad thing to have these two look out for me? I would be lying to myself if I said sleeping with them nightly wasn't intriguing. I had already fallen asleep in both of their arms separately and woke up feeling safe and loved.

I took a deep breath. "What happens if I decide I don't want this anymore? I just got my freedom back. I don't know how I feel about giving it up so soon." As I said the words, both of them frowned my way.

Heath was the one who spoke. "We don't want to make you feel like we're taking your freedom away from you. Reid and I just want to make sure you are safe, sweetheart. We wouldn't like it if that's what you decided. As Reid said, we find it hard to think about anything other than you. But if that's what you truly wanted, we would let you go."

I mulled over his words for a moment and came to a decision. "All right, we can try it your way," I said with a shaky voice.

They looked at each other and then back at me. Heath broke the silence first. "So, you are saying yes to us? Yes to being with us both?"

I nodded and I finally spoke the words they were looking for. "Yes, I want to be with you both."

## Chapter Thirteen

They both smiled like they were the cats that got the cream. Reid put his hands behind his head like he was getting comfortable. "If the answer is yes, then we need to know if you are on the pill. We want to take you without any barriers. We are both clean and we trust that you are too. If you would like to see the papers, I can get them."

I tried to breathe as the reality of the situation sank in. "I have an IUD and I got tested after I found out Tom cheated. I'm clean. I trust you too."

Reid nodded. "Good, now we are going to need you to lose the dress," he ordered in a sultry tone that had me hot.

I could hear my heart beating in my ears at this point. I was so nervous I could hardly stand it. They had both seen me naked, but this seemed far more intimate with both of them staring me down. With shaky hands, I reached for the top straps of my dress. Slowly, I slid one down and then the other, exposing my breasts. The dress gathered at my hips and I pushed it further down, shimmying until it pooled around my feet. I stood back to my full height in my skimpy thong, which was beyond drenched at this point, and my heels.

Both men just stared at me and said nothing. I could feel their eyes eating up every inch of exposed skin.

When they stayed silent, I bent down to take my heels off, and Reid stopped me with his rough command. "Did I say you could take those heels off? I think they will look really good around my neck later. Leave them on, but lose those panties. And don't you dare throw them to the ground. You bring them here like a good girl."

I shivered at his words. Reaching down, I slowly dragged my thong down my thighs. After collecting it from around my ankles, I walked back to the men staring at me from the couch. I held the soaked panties out for Reid to take. He took them, and like the pervert he was, brought them to his nose for a deep inhale. I shouldn't find the move sexy, I should find it gross. So why did I feel my pussy clench when he did it?

His eyes flared as he looked back up at me and spoke to Heath. "From the feel of these, I would say she is already warmed up. Would you feel between her legs for me and see if she is ready for us?"

Before I could even look Heath's way, he had me pulled into his lap. My back was pressed against his thighs, forcing me to put my legs on Reid's. I sucked in a breath as Heath spread me wide open with his hand and shoved two fingers deep into my channel.

"Oh!" I exclaimed, and he curled his fingers, slowly dragging himself out and then diving back in.

I could hear Reid chuckle as he said, "Fuck, you don't even have to tell me she is wet, I can hear it." Sure enough, the room was filled with my harsh breathing and the erotic sounds coming from my sex.

I reached up and started to unbutton Heath's shirt. I needed to feel his warm skin against my hands. Somewhere in the back of my mind, I could feel Reid standing up, but I wasn't paying attention to him. I was so lost in lust, I couldn't see straight.

Heath used his other hand to fondle my breast, and I arched into the movement. My hips started to churn of their own volition as I felt the orgasm barrel down on me. Right when I was about to tumble off the edge, he stopped moving his fingers that were fucking me. I groaned my frustration as I grabbed his hand to make him start rubbing again.

I whimpered when Heath removed his hands completely. But before I could do anything about it, he flipped me so I was on the ground on my knees. That was when I looked up to find Reid standing in front of me in all his glory. He had stripped down, completely naked.

Holding his hard cock in his tight fist, he pumped himself as he spoke. "Heath told me all about how your mouth felt the other night, and I'm a little jealous. I need you to suck me and get me ready to fuck you, bunny."

I smiled up at him. I could clearly see that he was beyond ready to go, but I played along. Taking his cock in my hand, I brought my mouth to him, licking the pre-cum that was beaded at the tip.

I gave him a few more small licks until he grabbed my hair and forced me to look at him. "Stop teasing me and suck me," he said behind clenched teeth. He didn't release my hair from his fist, he just simply guided my mouth further onto his cock, forcing me to take more of him.

I looked up at him as I dragged his head into my mouth and sucked hard, extracting a rough growl from him. The sound went straight to my core. I settled in and got to work. I was moving fast and taking him deeper with each pull. I was on a mission to make him come. I got to taste Heath already, I wanted to taste Reid now. I reached up to play with his balls, and he jerked with another deep moan. I could tell he was close, so I tried getting him in deeper.

"Fuck yes, baby, you suck me so good."

I felt his balls start to tighten, and I almost had him to the soft spot in the back of my throat when he pulled me off of him. Licking my swollen lips, I looked up at him. "You didn't let me finish," I said with a pout.

He was breathing so heavily while he looked

down at me. "There will be time for me to come in your mouth later, bunny, tonight I am going to come in your pussy." He pulled me up to my feet and spun me around. Heath had also joined us in removing his clothes and was waiting for me to face him.

He pulled me in for a deep kiss and he picked me up. I wrapped my legs around his hips and wiggled when I felt his cock poking at my entrance. I tried to slide down onto the length when I felt a sharp slap land on my ass cheek.

I yelped and looked behind me to where Reid was standing. "You wait until we give it to you," he said sternly. Turning back around, I gave Heath my best pout, earning me a chuckle.

He leaned back down and took my mouth again. Drugging me with kisses, I didn't even realize we were walking until Reid flipped the light on in a bedroom. Looking around, I wondered whose room this was.

My curiosity didn't last long as I watched Reid climb onto the bed and leaned against the plush headboard. He almost looked small on the massive bed. Almost. If I was worried about sleeping arrangements, I wasn't now. This bed would fit all of us comfortably.

Heath let me slide down his body until I was on my feet. He turned me around until I was facing Reid. He snaked his hand around the front of my body and rubbed his fingers down against my engorged clit. I was afraid my legs would give out, so I leaned back against him.

He used his other hand to pluck at my sensitive nipples. Leaning down, he whispered in my ear. "I want you to look at Reid while he strokes his cock for you, sweetheart. You are going to stand here and come apart in my arms and look at him while you do it."

He pressed firmly on my clit and started to rub. Dragging his fingers back and forth from my entrance to my clit, spreading my arousal. I looked at Reid and watched as he touched himself. His abs flexed with each stroke. I couldn't believe how turned on I could get just watching these two pleasure themselves.

Heath rasped against my ear again. "Do you see what you're doing to him? If he isn't careful, he's going to come in his hand from watching you. You are so fucking beautiful and we love watching you lose control. Come for us, Kate."

He moved his fingers back and forth more quickly now, and it wasn't but a couple of breaths until I was screaming his name while staring at Reid. If Heath hadn't had such a tight grip on me, I would have fallen to the floor. Bringing his hand up to my throat, he urged me to turn my head so he could take my mouth. He whispered against me. "I want you to climb up on that bed and ride Reid's cock."

He let me go, and I climbed up on the bed and straddled Reid's hips. Now that it was finally happening, I tried to calm my shaking hands. Reid must have seen how nervous I was because he grabbed my hands and brought them to his mouth, kissing my fingertips. Before he dropped them, he nipped my middle finger, dragging a yelp from me.

He grinned up at me. "You're in control this time, bunny. You control how deep I go and how fast this happens."

His words made me relax. He was the most dominant person I knew. If he was giving up control, then he was serious about this. I pushed myself up and lined his hard length with my entrance. I slowly started to sink down onto him. My breath came in sharp puffs.

Reid looked down at where we were connected and ground his teeth. "Fuck, you're gripping me like a vise, baby. I already know I'm not going to last long."

I moaned as I sank further, inch by inch, and I could feel him stretching me. I felt more elated than I had been in years.

I felt the bed dip behind me as Heath pressed his body to my back. He ran his hand down my spine before he grabbed my ass. Reid held my thighs, moving his hand restlessly like he wanted to take control. The feeling of four different hands on my body was euphoria at its finest.

I moaned long and hard, and I finally took Reid to the root. We were both panting as I sat, getting used to his massive size. Heath reached one hand around, placing it between where Reid and I were joined. "You did so well, sweetheart. Now I am going to rub you while you fuck Reid. I want to watch you go wild."

I did as I was told and lifted until Reid almost slipped out and pushed back down. Reid pushed his head back with a long groan. I found a rhythm I liked and rode him while Heath stroked my throbbing clit. I could feel the pressure building.

Heath pushed his hand further down, rubbing his fingers right where Reid's cock was pumping in and out of me, gathering my wetness. Reid must have liked the extra sensation as well as he bucked up into me and hissed between his teeth.

I couldn't lie, the thought of these two extremely hot men touching each other, even briefly, turned me on to no end.

When I thought he would rub my clit again, he surprised me by bringing his wet fingers to my asshole. I stilled, making Reid groan in frustration. Not one to stop the fun, he gave my thigh a sharp slap. I whimpered as the pain turned to heat and sank in.

"Did we say you could stop? You let Heath touch you and keep fucking me." Reaching up, he tweaked my nipple to drive his point home. I started to move again, still feeling Heath's fingers.

Leaning forward, he licked the shell of my ear and said, "I can guess that you have never taken a man here?" He pushed slightly against the tight hole. I shook my head. "Well, sweetheart, we are going to start preparing you to take both of us. I will fuck this tight asshole while Reid fucks your cunt and then we will switch. You will be so full of cock you won't know what to do. Now I need you to lean forward a little and relax. I won't hurt you, I just want you to feel how good it can be."

Doing as he asked, I leaned forward, the movement making Reid's cock rub my G-spot. Reid thrust up into me now, taking some control back. I could feel Heath's finger rub around my hole, trying to gain ground. I took a deep breath and blew it out, pushing back into Heath.

"Oh fuck, baby, that's it," he rasped. Bringing his other hand back around my body, he started rubbing my clit again.

Reid kept up his slow thrusting while he grabbed my throat and pulled me to his mouth for a rough kiss. I didn't ever think I would like to be manhandled, but I found myself loving every minute of it. Heath pushed in as I pushed back, getting the tip of his finger in. It had no problem sliding in from the arousal he had rubbed around my puckered entrance.

The feeling was taboo and strange, but it didn't hurt. Heath started rubbing me slightly faster as he pushed his finger further in. He reached his second knuckle when Reid groaned again. "I can feel you, Heath, she is so fucking tight. She is going to squeeze us to death." Reid grabbed my breast and started to pinch my nipple.

It was all too much, I was so full as Reid fucked my pussy and Heath started to finger-fuck my ass. I was going to go off like a bottle rocket. Reid picked up the pace and pulled me down flush to his chest, opening me up further to Heath.

Reid's voice was strained when he said, "Oh, fuck, I'm gonna come, she feels too good. Kate, I need you to come with me. I need to feel your pussy convulse around my cock."

Heath was full-finger deep in my ass, and the feeling was amazing. He was hitting nerves I didn't even know I had. I felt myself start to tighten, my muscles contracting on their own. I had no control over it as I ground down on Reid and exploded around him. I could feel Reid pulse inside of me as he spilled his seed with a long groan.

I was barely finished with my orgasm when Heath picked me up, flipping me so my back was against Reid's front. Reid recovered quickly as he grabbed my arms and brought them up to the back of his neck. Holding me down so I couldn't move.

Heath came down between my legs and latched his mouth on my clit. I screamed as another orgasm washed over me. Heath proved he didn't care that Reid had just filled me up with his come as he ate my pussy like it was his last meal. He gave me a couple of long licks before coming up my body and filling me back up with his big cock, Reid's release making it easy for him to slide in.

I gasped my pleasure as he pulled my legs up and fucked me hard. I was so over-sensitized that when Reid reached down and played with my clit, I came immediately. This time seeing stars.

I could feel Reid hardening again already against my ass as Heath slammed into me over and over again.

"Fuck, you were right. She is so fucking tight, she's suffocating me."

He didn't let up his assault as he put my legs back down in favor of pulling one of my nipples into his hot mouth. He used his other hand to tweak and pinch the other one. I could feel another orgasm rising beneath their hands. Heath just fucked faster until his thrusts started to become erratic. Reid pinched my clit, and I came one last time with a scream. Heath pulsed inside of me as he rubbed out the rest of his orgasm. "*Fuck!*" He roared above me.

He fell on top of me, trapping me between them. I let one of my hands find Reid's hair and the other one reached down into Heath's. We all three lay there for a few moments, just catching our breaths. Heath was still inside of me when I felt him start to harden again.

He pushed himself up and let Reid roll me over to lie on top of me. He leaned down to take my mouth again. "We aren't even close to being done with you yet," he muttered as he slid inside of me again.

It was a long time before I got to take those heels off.

## Chapter Fourteen

The next morning, I found myself wickedly trapped between two insatiable men. I had been up a better half of the night being shared between them, loving every second of it. I was smiling like a crazy person at the memory. I hadn't even stretched yet but I could feel a delicious ache inside of me.

I couldn't express the emotion that expanded in my chest at the sight of them wrapped around me. I was lying on my side. Reid was pressed up to my back, leaving no space at all. I could feel his groin pressed against my bottom. He had his leg pushed between mine and his arm was lying over my side.

Heath was pressed against my front. He had wrapped his arm around my hip, just below Reid's arm. His legs were also tangled with mine and Reid's.

I was beautifully cocooned between them. The last thing I wanted to do was wake them and break the moment, but by the light filtering through the blinds, I would say it was almost time for me to get up for the day. I wished I could lie there all day, but I had a job I had to get to.

Trying to raise my head to look at a clock, I felt Reid stir behind me. He slid his hand further up my side until he was cupping my breast. I knew he was awake when he pressed his hard length across my ass.

Grinning, I pushed back against him, earning a small groan from him. "Do you want to play this morning, bunny?" he whispered in my ear, his voice thick with sleep. I couldn't have stopped myself if I wanted to as I nodded.

"I am going to fuck you just like this, but I want you to be quiet and not wake Heath. He is rather grumpy in the mornings. I'm going to make us both come so you can walk around with a reminder of who fucked you all day. Does that sound good to you?" he responded in a hushed tone.

Not giving me a chance to say anything else, he slid into me with a harsh breath against my ear. "God, how are you always so ready for me, Kate? I could fuck you a thousand times and still want you again."

I tried to stifle my moan as he tweaked my nipple. He was fucking me so softly I could hardly stand it. I pushed back against him, trying to get him to move faster. I was rewarded with a hard nip to my ear. "Do I need to remind you who is in charge again, bunny?"

Reaching under me, Reid grabbed my hip and brought his other hand up to grasp my throat. Effectively holding me still while he tortured me. I gave a frustrated groan as he chuckled against me. He didn't stop his slow thrusts as he said, "Oh, now look at what you've done. You have woken up the grouch."

I looked up and sure enough, Heath was staring at me with lust in those emerald eyes. Without saying a word, Heath slid down my body. He stopped at the apex of my thighs and spread them, ensuring he had a perfect view of what Reid was doing to me.

Before I could ask what he was doing, his mouth was on me. I screamed as he sucked my throbbing clit into his mouth, flicking his tongue viciously. He was dangerously close to Reid's cock, and that thought alone spurred me on.

The combination of Reid's slow fucking and Heath's rapid licking, had me coming apart at the seams. Heath didn't stop after my first orgasm stopped, he merely lapped me softer as Reid picked up his speed. "Look down at what he is doing to you, bunny. Watch him as he licks that delicious cunt while I'm fucking you," Reid commanded in my ear.

Looking down, I saw Heath staring at me as he rubbed his thumb against me. I couldn't breathe from all the sensations they were dragging out of me. Staring at Heath as he pushed down on my clit, I wailed as I came again.

"No more!" I panted "I can't take it anymore," I begged. Reid just continued his hard pounding. I could hear how wet I was as he slid in and out of me.

"You will take what we give you." Reid growled, moved his hand down to my sex, and spread my labia wide open. Allowing Heath full, unhindered access to my sensitive clit.

I watched as Heath smiled and then sucked my nub back into his mouth. My hips undulated themselves and started fucking Reid back and pressing up into Heath's hot mouth. I couldn't take much more, my body shaking. Reid moaned hard against my ear and throbbed inside of me as he came in hot jets, hurtling me to fall off the edge with him.

"God, I could watch you come all day, baby." Heath winked up at me. I gave him a lazy smile. Now that was a good way to wake up.

Climbing back up the bed and settling back in front of me, Heath kissed me. "Good morning, sweetheart," he said against my lips.

I couldn't help the laugh that escaped as I said, "Good morning."

Grinning at me, he got off the bed and motioned for me to come to him. Reid reluctantly let me go with a parting smack on my ass that made me yelp.

Heath led me to the shower, where he washed every inch of me. He spent a little extra time on my pussy as he cleaned it with care. When he was done, he grabbed the soap for himself. I took it from him and lathered my hands up, preferring to wash him by hand as well, marveling at the silky feeling of him under my fingers. He was still hard by the time I made it to his cock. I couldn't stop myself as I stroked him, wanting to see him come apart for me. He had me backed up to the shower wall with his hands braced on either side of my head as he sucked in his breath between clenched teeth.

Before he could stop me, I sank to my knees in front of him, pulling him past my lips under the hot spray of water. He looked down at what I was doing to him with hooded eyes. His head bowed, leaning heavily against the wall. I felt a surge of feminine power as I watched him come unhinged. It was a feeling I'd never felt before. Like I was becoming a different person. Pure unadulterated liberation.

I loved every second of it.

The noises he made emboldened my movements. Encouraging me more and more with each pull from his cock. Watching him lose control because of what I was doing to him made my self-esteem skyrocket at that moment. He came in the back of my throat with a long feral groan, and I drank him down greedily before the water ran cold.

Like the last time I had showered with Heath, he insisted on drying me off as well. I didn't have anything to wear besides my dress from last night, and I still didn't know what Reid had done with my panties. I guessed that I wouldn't be seeing them again. Heath just grabbed the robe off the back of the door and wrapped me in it with a sweet kiss on my nose. God, I didn't know how I was ever going to recover if I lost this man.

When we exited the bathroom, I could smell bacon and coffee wafting from the kitchen. Hand in hand, Heath and I made our way, following the delicious smells. I came to a halt in the hallway when I saw Reid standing at the stove in nothing but sweats. My mouth started watering, and it had nothing to do with the food.

Setting me down at the table, Heath turned to get us some coffee. I watched both men from my seat as they worked in tandem with one another. Heath came back, placing my cup in front of me as Reid set down my plate filled with bacon, eggs, and toast. I waited for them to seat themselves on either side of me before I dug in.

Moaning around my fork at the first bite, I savored the flavor washing across my tongue. Closing my eyes, I chewed and swallowed before filling my fork again, eating with excitement. I was halfway through my meal when I realized the boys were staring at me.

Face flaming, I put my fork down and grabbed my napkin, wiping my mouth. "Sorry," I apologized. Tom used to hate it when I made a show of enjoying my food. He would say it made me sound like a fat person. "Sometimes food makes me a little happy and I'm starving," I said, a little embarrassed.

Reid laughed, bringing his coffee to his lips for a sip as Heath grabbed my hand and spoke. "Don't ever apologize for enjoying something, sweetheart. We were staring because the sounds you were making were turning us on. I have to say, I am quite jealous of your bacon right now."

There was heat in his eyes when he released my hand, picking his fork up to take a bite of his eggs. I gave a small smile as I resumed my meal.

Reid put his cup down and looked at me. "So Heath and I need to get your spare key before you leave for work this morning. Since we have agreed to split time between here and your place, we're going to get you an appropriate bed for all of us to sleep in. We'll get it set up while you are gone."

I placed my fork down again and looked between

them. "I don't have the money on me for a new bed right now. I'll have to go to the bank to get it from my savings. We'll need to leave soon so I can get it to you before I go to work," I said as I looked up at the clock to see if we had enough time.

Reid shook his head. "I asked for your key, not money, Kate. This was our idea, so of course, we are going to buy the bed. We also have a couple of other stores we have to go to as well today. We need to get our little bunny some accessories," he said with a wink.

I was sure he wasn't talking about a new Coach bag. I blushed again but picked my fork back up. We ate the rest of our meal, and I listened to them talk about what they had planned for the day. Heath had to close the bar down tonight so Reid would be alone with me for most of the night.

The whole time I sat with them, I couldn't help thinking that this whole thing felt really natural. Being with both of them last night had felt that way too. I had expected awkwardness but had experienced none so far. I was so afraid going into this that one would get jealous of the other and then they would blame me. But these two had shared me and neither minded when it was their turn to just sit back and watch. Both of them had handled me with such care it could make a girl fall in love fast. Even when I was married to Tom, he had never once treated me as lovingly as these two had.

When we finished with breakfast, I helped clean up and wash dishes. When the dishes were all done, Heath grabbed me, crowding me against the sink. He grabbed the side of my face and leaned down for a kiss. "I'm gonna miss you today, sweetheart. I can't wait to crawl into bed next to you tonight."

I sighed as I leaned into his hug, kissing him goodbye one more time. I turned and made my way to the door, Reid, hot on my heels. We walked to my door, and I unlocked it.

As I turned to tell him goodbye, he pushed me against the door. Leaning down for a kiss, he stopped. "When you come home tonight, I need you to lock your door, and don't answer it for anyone. I won't be home for a couple of hours after you and I don't trust your ex to not try something again. Can you do that for me?" He pinned me with his stare.

Swallowing hard, I nodded. "Yes, but I served him with a restraining order yesterday, so I'm sure I won't have any more problems with him." He held his hand out, silently asking for my key. I handed it to him, and then he closed the gap, kissing me breathless.

His kisses always had me wanting more as I thrust my hands into his soft hair, pulling him closer to me. He slid his hand into the top of my robe and caressed my naked breast. I moaned as his finger raked over my puckered nipple.

He chuckled as he pulled away from me. "Unless you have time to be fucked in this hallway, you need to get inside. I will see you tonight, bunny." He kissed my forehead and ushered me inside, not leaving until I closed the door behind me.

I stood against the door for the longest time, just breathing. Giggling, I thought about pinching myself because none of this felt real. I had just had the most amazing sex of my life last night with two of the hottest guys I had ever seen.

Shaking my head, I pushed off the door and headed to my room. As I got ready for work, I let my mind wander back to some of the wicked things they had done to me last night. I blushed at the memory. I would be lying to myself if I thought that what we did was just sex. It felt like so much more last night. I had never in my life felt so cared for and loved as I did when we were all intimate together.

If I hadn't been falling for them before, I certainly was now. I didn't know if they felt the same way I did, but I hoped so.

## Chapter Fifteen

"Kate, can you come in here for a moment please?" Samantha called from her office as I was in the middle of responding to some emails. After saving what I had typed, I grabbed my tablet and made my way to her office. She was sitting behind her desk, writing some notes on a paper pad while looking at her computer. Taking a seat in one of the plush pink chairs in front of her desk, I asked what I could do for her.

She looked up and removed her glasses, smiling at me. She was always so professional looking with her black bob haircut, making her look sleek and well-manicured. Her round glasses fit her personality perfectly, as well as her heart-shaped face. I might be a little biased, but I thought she was the smartest person in the office. I had only been working for her for a little over a week, but she had taken me under her wing, and I had already learned a lot about the publishing business.

"Have you had a chance to read over those manuscripts I gave you?" she asked.

I flushed slightly. "I am halfway through the first one. I was going to read more last night but I found myself... indisposed." I looked down at my hands, a little afraid I was about to get scolded. When I looked up again, she was just nodding.

"Okay, no big deal. I want you to go home for the rest of the day and try to get them finished if you can. In fact, go ahead and take tomorrow too. Just take your tablet home with you and you can work from there if I need anything. We have that lunch meeting with Emily on Friday, and I want you to be well-versed in her work. I want your full professional opinion by Friday morning"

I sat there, shocked for a minute. Samantha must

have seen the look cross my face because she laughed and asked me if I was okay.

"Uh, yeah. I just didn't figure my opinion would matter that much," I admitted.

She regarded me seriously for a moment before responding. "Why wouldn't I want your opinion, Kate? I think you show tremendous promise in the literary field, if I'm being honest. When I give you things to work on, you are always professional and prompt when getting them back to me. I think you have a keen eye for the written word, you just need the confidence to go for things you want."

I shook my head as she continued. "I know it was none of my business, but I read a little of what you have been writing. You accidentally left your computer open the other day when you went to lunch and the document was right there. I couldn't help myself. You don't have much written yet, but what you do have is amazing, Kate."

She was looking at me with all seriousness. "And, as much as I would hate to lose the best assistant I have ever had, I want you to pursue what you have further. Anyone that can write like that without an education to back it will always have a valuable opinion in my book."

I felt myself flush again. I had started to just play around with writing for the last couple of days. I really didn't think it would go anywhere, to be honest. I was just trying to get my thoughts down on paper, and it was starting to take form before my eyes. I never would have thought that one of the lead publishers at this firm would think it was worth anything though.

She nodded at me and went back to her computer. I stood up and told her I would have both scripts read by the end of the day tomorrow and to call me if she needed anything.

I was on autopilot as I shut down my computer and grabbed my things to head home. I was still reeling from what Samantha had said when I made it to my car.

Could I really do this? I loved writing, but I never thought I would be good enough to get published. I smiled to myself as I started my car and headed toward home. I had taken the leap with starting of a new relationship, and so far, it was going great. Why not do this for me as well? Even if it didn't work out, I still had my job to fall back on.

Feeling excited about what my future could hold, I felt the need to tell someone I cared about. It was almost lunchtime, so I thought about seeing if Lindsey wanted to grab something to eat with me. I quickly ruled that out as an option when I thought she would probably be in class. Jill was still at work so I knew that wouldn't do either.

Smiling again as the idea struck, I drove past my apartment as I made my way to The Sand Dollar. The fact that Heath came to mind when I thought of the people I cared about wasn't lost on me.

Parking my car, I glanced in the building to see if he was inside. I hopped out of my car and started to walk to the doors. Stopping right as I put my hand on the handle, I had the irrational feeling of being watched. I looked all around to see if I saw anyone I knew. A few people were walking about, but I didn't recognize anyone.

Shaking the feeling off, I walked inside. The bar was empty except for a few employees milling around, getting ready to open. The waitress from last night spotted me and made her way over. "Is there something I can help you with? We aren't open for another thirty minutes, but I can see if we can seat you early."

I shook my head. "Oh, no that's okay, I was just

looking for—"

"Kate!"

Turning toward the bar, I spotted who I came here to see. Heath put down the clean glasses he had been carrying and made his way to me. I breathed out a nervous breath at the sight of him. This man had put me in a hundred different positions last night, bringing me intense amounts of pleasure, and the sight of him still made me nervous.

"Hey, Amanda I got this. Will you finish putting the glasses up for me please?" He talked to the waitress without taking his eyes off me. "Hey, sweetheart, is everything okay?" he asked me, concern written along his brow.

I nodded. "Yeah, I got sent home for the rest of today and tomorrow so I can finish up those manuscripts for a meeting on Friday. I also had something kind of exciting happen so I figured maybe we could get some lunch and talk about it. I wanted to share the news with someone I care about, and you came to mind." Was I rambling? I felt like I was rambling.

Heath just stared at me with a grin playing on his lips.

I let out a nervous laugh. "But I can see that you're busy and this was just silly of me. I should have known better than to interrupt you at work. I'll just go home and I can talk to you—"

Heath cut off my next words when he brought his lips to mine, effectively shutting me up. When he pulled away from me, I swayed a little. He grabbed my hands and brought them to his mouth, giving my fingers little kisses.

"You aren't interrupting anything, sweetheart. I was just about to take a break and get something to eat before we open. Have you eaten yet?" At the shake of my head, he led me to the bar. Pulling out the stool for me, he kissed my neck and told me he would be right back.

He headed toward the kitchen, opening the door, and asked whoever was working for two house burgers and fries. He was back to me before I could even miss him. He sat on the stool beside me, turning to face me. We faced each other with our legs tangled together. He grabbed my hands and threaded his fingers between mine. "Now, tell me all about your exciting news."

So, I smiled and told him everything that Samantha had told me. Even relaying the fact that I used to write back in high school and I was so excited to get back into it. I told him that I had a really good feeling about this, and I wanted to go for it. He listened intently and gave me his input when it was needed.

Our food had come, and we began to eat as we were still talking. We sat and talked for what felt like hours, even though it had only been maybe thirty minutes. I shared with him that it had been a dream of mine when I was younger to write a novel but just never had the opportunity.

He told me that this bar had always been his dream, and it was Reid who pushed him to take the leap. He said that if he hadn't had someone in his corner cheering for him, he probably would have never bought this place and now have a successful business, so he was going to do the same for me. I believed that he and Reid would always help me flourish and make me a better version of myself.

When our food was long gone and customers started filing in for lunch, Heath stood and cleared away our plates. Then he came back and pulled me into his arms. "If you need someone in your corner to push you to follow your dreams, just know that Reid and I will never hold you back. We will do everything we can to help you achieve your goals."

I pushed up on my tiptoes, wrapping my arms around his shoulders, and kissed him. I normally let him and Reid take the lead when it came to this stuff, but I couldn't resist. His words of encouragement touched me. I had never had anyone besides Jill push me to do things for myself, and it felt good to have two more people rooting for me.

I pushed my breasts into him as his hand traveled lower to grab my bottom. Pulling me into his growing erection. He broke away from me and murmured against my lips. "If you don't stop soon, I am going to take you to my office and bend you over my desk."

I gave him a mischievous grin as I licked his bottom lip, earning me a growl.

He walked me to my car, keeping his hand firmly in mine. He stopped and turned to me, brushing my hair back he leaned down for another small kiss. "I wish I could come home with you, sweetheart, but I have to stay and take care of things tonight. I will be counting the hours until I can crawl into bed next to you."

"I can't wait," I murmured softly.

He opened my door for me and waited until I started the vehicle before going back inside. Waving goodbye, I pulled away from the curb and headed home.

**\*\*\*\***

Placing the finished manuscript on my coffee table, I sat back on my couch with a smile. I absolutely loved Emily's book. It was funny at times, had just the right amount of drama, and the spice scenes had me blushing at some points.

Leaning back, I put my hands above my head and stretched. I grimaced at the time. It was already past six in the evening. I had come straight home from Heath's bar, and after changing into my sweats and tank top, I had settled on the couch and started reading. That was after I saw the massive bed dominating my bedroom with a note in the center.

It was from Reid, of course, saying he couldn't wait to see me spread out on the bed for him to devour later.

I decided I had read enough for the day and I would start on the other script tomorrow morning. My stomach decided it was time to remind me that I hadn't eaten since noon when it rumbled loudly. After getting up from the couch, I headed toward the fridge to see what I could make. Deciding on shrimp fried rice, I grabbed everything I needed and deposited the ingredients beside the stove.

As I got my pans out and started the rice, I thought it was too quiet in here for my liking. I had restless energy about me I needed to release. One of the main reasons I had decided to rent this apartment was because of the surround sound speakers that were hardwired throughout the walls. They ran off Bluetooth, so I got my phone out and pulled up my favorite station on my music app.

Turning my volume up almost full blast, I danced around the kitchen as I cooked my meal. Some of my favorite memories were of Lindsey and me dancing together in the kitchen. If I closed my eyes hard enough, I could still see her sweet little face looking up at me as we swayed to our music.

I was swaying my hips and bouncing up and down, rocking my hips like the artist was saying he liked, while I added my eggs into the pan and scrambled them. If I had any windows in my kitchen, I was sure any neighbors would be getting a free show. I didn't have a bra under my tank top so my breasts were in full swing with the music.

The song changed and I was about to pop lock and drop it when hands came around my waist. I screamed and swung my spatula over my head to strike my attacker and was rewarded with a startled huff as the hands disappeared from my hips.

I turned around poised to strike again when I came face to face with Reid. He was holding his forehead "Remind me to never sneak up on you again," he said with a chuckle.

I grabbed my phone and turned the volume down. Putting my weapon down, I went to him and held his face. "Oh my God, I am so sorry. I didn't think anyone would be sneaking up on me like that. Are you okay?" I asked.

He stuck his bottom lip out in an adorable pout. "I don't know, I might bruise." He moved his hand to show me his forehead.

I inspected the red spot, pulling his head toward me to get a better look. "I think you'll survive, do you want me to kiss it to make it feel better?" I asked with a grin.

Still sticking that lip out, he nodded. Laughing now, I pulled him toward me and kissed his red forehead. I started to pull away but he caught my hips, dragging me into a kiss. He licked my bottom lip, asking silently for me to open for him. I obliged and our tongues danced. He pulled away first. "Hey, bunny, I missed you today."

Wrapping my arms around his shoulders I leaned in. "Me too, I got some exciting news at work today." I turned around and finished the fried rice while I told him about my day. He leaned against the counter, listening intently to me.

After doling up our food into two bowls, I handed him his with a kiss. "That is exciting, Kate. Meeting

Emily sounds like an awesome opportunity for you," he said encouragingly. "Thank you for cooking." He gestured to his food. "It smells amazing."

We took our food to the living room and cuddled up on the couch. I asked how his day was, and he told me all about it, saying it wasn't too busy with only three page-outs. I wasn't an EMT, but I decided that having a slow day was probably a good thing.

We finished our food and Reid took our empty bowls to the kitchen. I heard him doing the dishes soon after. I tried to help him, but he shooed me back to the living room, saying I cooked so he would clean. That was unexpected as I did all the housework when I was married. I had to say, I loved being taken care of for once.

Reid joined me back on the couch, wearing sweats he had pulled from the duffle bag I saw he had brought with him. We cuddled up under one of my huge soft blankets and flipped the TV on. Deciding on a movie to watch, we relaxed back and enjoyed each other's company. Reid was sitting with his feet propped up in front of him on the coffee table, and I curled up to his side.

It wasn't too long and we forgot about the movie, preferring to enjoy each other instead. I couldn't help wondering how long this new can't-keep-your-hands-to-yourself phase would last. I hoped it never stopped because I never felt sexier than I did while one of them was kissing me.

Reid had me on my back with himself wedged between my legs. We had been making out like a couple of teenagers for half the movie. Before I knew it, the credits were rolling and Reid was turning off the TV. After picking me up from the couch, he carried me to my bedroom.

I giggled as he threw me on the bed and climbed back on top of me. Running his hands up my stomach, he grabbed both my breasts and brought them to his face. "I love these tits. They are so soft and fit just right in my hands."

"You don't think they are too saggy?" I asked, that old insecurity rearing her ugly head.

Reid looked at me like I kicked his dog, and I couldn't help the laugh that escaped. "Don't talk about my friends that way, they're perfect. Just like you." He finished by pulling my tank top down and kissing my tightly pebbled nipples. I leaned back with a short moan, letting him have his way with me.

When he looked back up at me, I was ready for more. "I want to show you some of the goodies I bought for you today, bunny. I need to go get my duffle bag. When I come back, I want you completely naked and sprawled out on this bed," he ordered before he climbed off of me and left the room.

I scrambled to do his bidding. After removing my sweats and panties, I threw my top off and lay back down on the bed to wait. It wasn't long before Reid came back into the room.

"Oh, now see, you are a good girl." His words sent an odd sense of pride through my system. He set his duffle down on the floor and started to dig in it. I couldn't see what he was grabbing but he must have been satisfied because he stood back up in no time. He set his items down before he brought his shirt up and over his head. If I was curious to see what he got out of his bag before, I wasn't now. All I could think about now was getting my hands on him.

I must have had my thoughts on full blast because he smiled and shook his head. "Not yet, bunny. First, I want to play. I need you to get on your hands and knees, ass toward me."

I rushed to get into the position he told me to. I felt the bed dip as he came up behind me. He pushed his hand against my back to make me lower my chest to the bed. The position forced me to thrust my ass high up in the air.

"We are going to try something new tonight, bunny. Heath and I agreed that I would start getting you ready to take both of us." He reached his hand underneath me and started rubbing around the wetness he found there. Moaning into the mattress, I pushed my ass back into his hand to get more pressure. He brought his drenched fingers up to my ass and rubbed them around my puckered hole.

"I'm going to stretch this little hole tonight, then I am going to fuck that little cunt of yours until neither of us can take anymore."

I sucked in a deep breath as he started to push his fingertip into me. My wetness made it easy for him to slip in. Using his other hand, he touched my pussy again, making me roll my hips in time with him. "That's it, baby, you help me get these fingers in your ass. I will have you addicted before you know it," he promised.

I moaned his name as he pushed his finger in all the way, pulling out slowly just to push in once more. His finger dragged across nerves with each pull.

I was getting closer to release with every rub of my clit and push of his finger. Soon he pulled out and dripped something cold right on my asshole. The sensation sent a shiver up my spine. He rubbed the liquid around and around, making me beg for him to put his finger back in. "Please, Reid, use your fingers again, I'm so close."

He groaned as he pushed not one but two fingers back into me. Two fingers were slightly less comfortable than one. I could feel him stretching me with each thrust. "Fuck, you are going to strangle my cock when I get inside of you. Unfortunately, that's not going to happen tonight. You are nowhere near ready for something my size."

My moans were getting louder now. Reid was fucking me with his fingers a lot faster than before and pushing harder on my clit. "Oh, Reid! I'm going to come!" I screamed.

"Come for me, Kate, come around my fingers," Reid demanded.

At his command, I came hard, pressing back against him, desperate to get the most out of this orgasm. He didn't let up. He rubbed faster and fucked his fingers harder until he rolled me into another orgasm before the first one had even finished. I could hear Reid behind me groaning too. "Oh, Kate you're soaking my hand, you are so fucking hot."

He finally slowed his fingers, allowing me to come down. He removed his fingers, and I whimpered at the loss. "Don't worry, baby, I have something else for you," he said as he pressed something hard and cold back to my empty backside. "I want you to relax and press yourself back until this is fully seated in that beautiful ass."

I did as he asked, breathing deeply, and I pushed back. I knew enough that what I was pressing against was more than likely a butt plug. I whimpered as I pressed until I was to the widest part, pausing. "It's okay, bunny, you can do this. Try to take it in little passes." His words of encouragement spurred me on. I pushed back and forth, back and forth. Until, finally, the whole thing was in.

"You did so well, baby. I am so proud of you," he said lovingly. His sweet words made my chest expand.

"Now I am going to fuck you, bunny. You did such a good job of turning me on that I know I'm not going to last that long, but don't worry, I will make sure to take care of you first." He finished with a tap on the butt plug, sending the vibration up and extracting a moan from me.

The bed dipped again as he stood up and removed his sweats. "I'm going to flip you over so I can see the rest of this gorgeous body. Don't you lose my plug. If you do, I'll spank that ass red and we'll start over, am I understood." It wasn't a question, but I nodded anyway.

He got back on the bed and flipped me over. I clenched and held on to the plug for dear life. He was on top of me in a second, looking down at me, his hard length, right where I wanted it. "That's my good girl, now I'm going to eat my fill of your cunt. You hold on to that plug and don't come until I tell you to."

He was down my body with my clit in his mouth before I knew what was happening. I screamed as he sucked hard and pushed his fingers into my pussy. I didn't know how I was supposed to hold off the orgasm that was quickly approaching. He wasn't playing fair as he finger-fucked me so fast I was seeing stars. He opened his mouth and flicked his tongue against my swollen clit so I could see what he was doing, the sight nearly undoing me.

"Do you want to come, baby? You look like you are really trying to hold it back." He grinned up at me as he curled his fingers inside of me, rubbing my G-spot. The bastard knew what he was doing.

"Yes! Yes, Reid, I need to come!" I screamed down at him. He chuckled as he leaned back down and gave me a long lick. He then pulled my clitoris back into his mouth and continued his torture. I was holding my breath and shaking by the time he pulled his fingers away and crawled back up my body, settling between my legs again.

"You come with me inside of you, bunny," was all he said before he thrust deep inside of me. I sucked in a huge breath as I tried to adjust to the sudden stretch.

"Fuck, you're even tighter now with the plug. Are you okay? Because I need to fuck you, hard," he said behind clenched teeth.

Nodding with all the desperation coursing through my body, I said, "Please!"

That was all the permission he needed. Reid fucked me hard, taking my breath away. I was impossibly stretched, but it felt so good. He sat up on his knees, bringing my legs up with him. This position made him go even deeper. He reached down and pinched my clit, and I exploded around him. It was a shock even to me when I managed to keep the plug in.

He gave me a deep groan and he continued his assault. "Ah, fuck! It's too much!" He growled right before he pressed his thumb down on my clit and sat back, rubbing that magical spot inside of me in long deep passes. I erupted again, unable to stop my muscles from seizing. He slammed into me and rubbed his climax out with a long moan before collapsing on top of me.

We both lay like that, trying to catch our breath for a long while. He never removed himself from me, but I could feel him softening. He finally raised his head enough to look at me and kiss me sweetly. Our tongues slid together. Pulling away, he looked into my eyes. "You are so goddamn perfect for me, Kate," he said as he kissed me again.

After rolling off me, he left the room and came back with a warm washcloth and cleaned me up. He then carefully removed my plug and cleaned it in the bathroom. I curled up under the blanket and started to drift. When he came back, he crawled into bed and pulled me to his front. I fell asleep to him kissing my shoulder and his soft praises.

## Chapter Sixteen

The next day was more of the same. Sometime during the night, Heath had snuck into bed with Reid and me. I awoke that morning sandwiched in between my two guys. They both woke with me and made love to me. Reid held me down while Heath showed me exactly how much he missed me the night before. They both took turns making me come with their mouths, fingers, and cocks until Reid begrudgingly had to go to work. He had left me in Heath's arms with the promise he would see me that night. His kiss held all sorts of promise.

Heath didn't have to be at the bar until right before opening today, so he lazed around with me all morning. We got up and showered together, an act that I was becoming very accustomed to. The feeling of our wet bodies sliding together under the hot spray was quickly becoming something I craved. He had slipped the plug back into me in the shower with instructions that I was not to take it out until he left for work. He wanted me ready to take both of them by next week, and the only way to do that was with practice. He rewarded me for taking the plug so nicely with his wicked mouth.

After we dried and dressed, Heath led me to the living room where he sat me down and handed me the manuscript I needed to read today. It took me a couple of positions to find the perfect one to accommodate the plug, but once I found the right one, I relaxed into the feeling. He then made breakfast for us both and we ate and enjoyed each other's company.

I sat with my feet in his lap, reading, while he worked on his laptop and made calls to his vendors. It was so comfortable to just be around him, I hadn't even noticed the hours that slipped past us. Before I knew it, he was kissing me goodbye with the promise that he would see me in time for dinner tonight.

The rest of the day slid by in a haze as I immersed myself in Emily's book. The woman truly knew how to paint a picture. I finished the script shortly after four in the afternoon. After making some notes about both books, I decided it was time to see what I could make the boys for supper. After inspecting my fridge, I came to the conclusion that I needed to go to the store.

Grabbing my keys and purse, I headed out, going through my mental list of things I needed on the drive there. I had decided to make them my famous, by my daughter's accounts, chicken alfredo.

Once I found a good parking spot, I climbed out of the car and headed inside. I had almost made it to the doors when I felt the hairs on the back of my neck stand up. I got the same strange feeling I got the day before like someone was watching me.

Turning to survey the parking lot, I didn't see anyone I knew. I even bent down to see if I could see inside some of the parked cars. Still not seeing anyone, I rushed inside to get around other people. I tried to tell myself that I was being ridiculous, but I just couldn't shake the feeling.

I wondered briefly if maybe Tom was behind this. I hadn't heard anything from him since I filed the restraining order against him, but that didn't mean he had forgotten about me. I decided I would do a little digging when I got home. It was time I figured out what was going on with him.

I went about my business of getting everything I needed for alfredo, as well as picking up some essentials. When I got all checked out and headed to my car, I didn't have the same feeling I did earlier.

I called my lawyer on the way back home to make sure she had served Tom his papers. She confirmed that they were indeed served. Thanking her, I put my phone away and drove the rest of the way home.

I briefly thought about telling the boys about what I had felt yesterday and today but decided against it. They would probably just worry and that helped no one. Besides, I was probably imagining things.

Once I made it home and unloaded my food, I sat on the couch with my laptop, starting my search. After typing Tom's full name into my search browser, multiple links popped up. The top one was his dealership website. Clicking on it, I didn't see anything out of the ordinary. There were the usual car listings and videos with his cheesy smile on his face.

I clicked on one of the videos and watched the infomercial highlighting his new inventory. He looked like what you would think a sleazy car salesman would look like. Even going so far as to hire bikini models to hold up his "sold" signs. He went on about his thirty-point inspection and how his cars were the best deal around. I rolled my eyes when he mentioned his top-notch customer service. I had met his "first-class" employees and seen his one-of-a-kind cars. I wasn't impressed.

Tom had always prided himself on finding junk cars, slapping a Band-Aid on them, and then selling them for a marked-up price. His employees were just as bad as he was too.

I remember when his dad owned the dealership. It was a better place to shop for a reliable car when Big Tom owned it. Unfortunately, when he passed, so did his way of doing business.

I felt my eyes widen at the end of the video when it changed into a wide pan of the entire car lot with Tom and Vivian standing side by side in the middle of it all. The last time I had seen Vivian she was bent over Tom's desk, ass naked. Looking at her now, it looked like she had some work done. Her breasts were considerably bigger than they were a few months ago and her face looked like it was stuck in a permanent smile. I cringed. Botox was a scary thing.

I wondered if Tom had bankrolled those enhancements. I knew what he paid his employees, and it certainly wasn't enough to cover plastic surgery. I would bet that left a bitter taste in his mouth after she left him for a different man. Karma sure was a bitch, although she had a wicked sense of humor.

Backing out of the website, I scrolled a little longer until I saw a news article that piqued my interest. The picture was of Tom, but it was actually a mugshot. I felt my jaw drop as I scrolled and read the article.

*Local business owner charged on multiple counts of fraud, to be seen in court this month. Owner of Tom's Used Auto, Thomas Hart, involved in falsifying car titles sold at business, may be facing years in federal prison for crimes committed. Court date is set for Monday, April 17th. More on court proceedings to follow.*

"Holy shit," I mumbled behind my hand. I couldn't believe what I was reading. I had always known Tom stretched the truth when selling his vehicles, but I never would have guessed he was doing anything illegal. He must have posted bail, but he was obviously going against the whole suggestion about not leaving the state.

When Tom came to my door the other night, he was so drunk he could hardly stand. This would surely explain his need to drink. If Vivian truly did leave him for another man, then he would really have nothing else to lose. The whole thing made me wonder if he felt I owed him something. His life seemed to be falling apart, and it had started when I left him. A shiver ran up my spine at the thought of him taking his unfortunate luck out on me.

Hitting the back button, I searched for more on the case. Before I could get too far, the lock on my door jiggled. My breath caught in my throat before I slammed the computer shut and jumped off the couch.

Had Tom come to finish what he started the other night? Staring at the door, I wondered if I should call the police or try to find something to defend myself with. Just as I was thinking of making a run for my bedroom, where I could barricade myself in and call the cops, the door opened. I bit back my scream as Reid walked through the door.

I released my breath in a rush and practically ran into his arms. His breath left him in a huff with the force I hit him with.

"Well, that's one way to welcome me home." He pulled away long enough to look at me. "Are you okay, Kate? You look a little pale, are you going to be sick?" he asked, concern written all over his face.

I looked up at him and opened my mouth to tell him what I had discovered but stopped myself with a shake of my head. I had barely even started to date these men and I was already going to bombard them with my problems? I didn't want to scare them off so soon. It was bad enough Reid already had to defend me from my ex, he didn't need to hear any more of my drama.

Reid was staring at me now, searching my face for an answer. "What is it, bunny?"

I looked at his chest and then back up to his face, trying to give what I hoped looked like a brilliant smile. "I just— I wasn't expecting you back so soon and you scared me. I was going to have supper waiting when you guys got home, and I must have lost track of time."

He was still looking at me skeptically like he didn't quite believe me. I pushed up to kiss him, trying to get him to leave it alone. I felt him holding himself back for a beat like he was still going to push the issue. I swiped my tongue along his lip, silently begging for him to drop it.

A thrill jolted through my body as he pulled me closer and sank into the kiss. I nibbled on his lower lip as he grabbed hold of my ass and rubbed his erection against me. Conversation avoided successfully.

"God, I missed you today. Do you know how hard it is to go to work smelling like you and be able to concentrate?" he asked as he pulled away from me.

Before I could answer, he picked me up and walked further into the apartment, depositing me on the kitchen island to more fully devour my lips.

By the time he let me go, I was so needy, and I whimpered a little at the loss. He laughed as he looked down at me. "I need to shower before we do any of those dirty things playing around in your mind, bunny. And I heard you mention something about food?"

I laughed as I hopped off the counter. "How does my famous chicken alfredo sound?"

He leaned down for another quick peck. "That sounds like heaven." Then he turned me around to face the stove and smacked my ass as he walked away. "Make my food, woman." He chuckled as he walked toward my bathroom.

"Caveman!" I called after him playfully. And just like that, I forgot all about Tom as I focused on making my men their meal. Whatever his problems were, they were just that, his problems. If he hadn't ruined our marriage, then maybe I would have been able to help him, but he burned that bridge years ago.

I busied myself preparing our meal and put it out

of my mind. I was just about to drain the pasta and add my sauce mixture when Reid emerged from the bathroom, looking like my wet dream. He only wore a towel slung low around his muscular waist. He was drying his hair with a smaller towel. I watched as the motion rippled across his damp abdomen. The flowing tattoo across his pec was almost hypnotizing to watch as he flexed from the motion of his arm. His hair was mused when he lowered his towel. It lay messily over his forehead, partially blocking his eyes. I had to catch my drool before it dribbled down my chin.

He grinned when he looked up at me. "Do you need any help with that?"

I looked down at my hands and realized I was still holding the pot above the sink, poised to dump my noodles in the strainer. Clearing my throat, I found my voice. "You are very distracting. Go get dressed."

Turning back to what I was doing, I managed to drain the noodles and added the sauce and chicken into the pot.

I felt Reid come up behind me before he spoke. "Are you trying to tell me what to do, bunny?" he asked before he bit my earlobe. "You let me know how that works out for you." He grabbed my waist and turned me around to face him. I couldn't help the giggle that escaped as his lips crashed down on mine.

The kiss was domineering, to say the least. He shoved his tongue in and demanded mine to move with his. I moaned into his mouth as he caught my hand and led it to his erection. "Do you see what you do to me, bunny? I go all day with a soft cock, and the moment I see you, I'm painfully hard. Stroke me," he commanded with a long groan as I gripped him under his towel.

I squeezed hard and pumped him from tip to base as I leaned in to kiss and lick his chest. He clearly liked what I was doing as he pushed into my hand. Before I was ready, he jerked away from me, tucking himself back into his towel.

"Don't you worry, you'll get up close and personal with that part of me later. I don't want to be the one responsible for you burning food," he said before he turned and headed back down the hallway to my bedroom.

Smiling to myself, I turned back around and continued cooking. Five minutes later, I was pulling the garlic bread out of the oven when Heath came through the front door. I set the bread down and walked to him. He enveloped me in his arms and kissed me from my lips, down to my neck, and back up again. "Hello, sweetheart. It smells amazing in here."

After detangling myself from him, I headed back to the stove and started to serve our food. Within minutes, we were all seated at my table enjoying our meal and discussing our day. I omitted everything I had discovered about Tom. Instead, I talked about Emily's books and all I had to do to get ready for tomorrow.

The boys and I laughed as they shared stories about things that happened at work. The feeling of sharing our day with one another felt so domestic, it made my heart squeeze a little.

After supper, the boys ushered me to the living room as they insisted on cleaning the kitchen up. Before long, we were all seated on the couch, watching some mindless TV show. I was seated in the middle, of course, and we all shared the same blanket.

I wasn't sure who started it, but somehow, we all ended up tangled on the floor, the show long forgotten. I didn't see how it was fair that I was the one who was completely naked and they were still halfway clothed, but they assured me it was. I had lost count of how many orgasms they had given me by the time they flipped me to my knees.

I watched with lust-filled eyes as they both stripped out of their clothes and proudly stood in front of me. I licked my lips as they both stood there with their hard lengths pointing at me.

Heath was the first one to step up, offering me his cock like a particularly juicy lollipop. I grabbed him with one hand and sucked his head into my mouth, swirling my tongue. "I don't think I will ever get used to your mouth, baby," he said with a long deep groan.

I smiled around his cock at the praise. Reid stepped forward a moment later and pulled my face toward him. I continued to stroke Heath as I gave Reid the same treatment. Switching back and forth between the two, alternating sucking and stroking. I gave them little moans now and then, letting them feel the sensation.

They were both breathing heavily when they pulled away. Reid sat down on the couch and motioned for me to come closer. I settled between his legs and started licking him from base to head again. I felt Heath come up behind me and grab my ass, lifting it so he could have access to my pussy.

Heath pushed into me with a forceful thrust of his hips that had me cursing. Reid pushed forward, pressing his length into my waiting mouth. A deep moan escaped me as Heath kept up his punishing thrusts.

"Do you like the feel of Heath's cock in your little cunt while you suck my cock, bunny?" Reid asked.

I just sucked harder, letting that be my answer. I was rewarded when he groaned and grabbed my hair, wrapping his fist around the length.

The sounds of Heath's groans and the slap of our skin spurred me on. Making me push my mouth further onto Reid. I bobbed my head up and down quickly, determined to take all of him. With each pass, he found the soft spot in the back of my throat, and I could tell it was driving him crazy. When I was finally at his end, his balls resting against my chin, I swallowed around him.

"Fuck!" He growled before he took control, fucking my mouth as I hollowed my cheeks and focused on my breathing.

They fucked me in tandem. When one pulled away, the other pushed forward. I could feel all of it coming to a climax when Heath's thrusts became erratic and Reid's breath became strained as he stared down at me. Heath reached around my hips and pinched my clit, sending me spiraling down with a moan that traveled up Reid's cock.

That was all it took. They both pressed forward and came hard. Reid's mouth was slightly ajar as he groaned and held himself at the back of my throat, spilling his seed. I swallowed, not wanting to lose a single drop. I could feel Heath throbbing as he shot hot streams of his release inside of me.

Pulling me back while staying inside of me, Heath brought me to his chest while Reid came forward to take my mouth. Heath was kissing my neck as he spoke to Reid. "Take our sweet girl to bed. After that performance, I think she deserved a couple more orgasms. Tie her down if you have to. I would like to see how many times we can make her come before she begs us to stop." I could feel his grin against my neck.

I hissed between clenched teeth as he nipped me, and Reid started touching my slick folds again. "I thought Reid was the bossy one?" I asked breathlessly.

Heath chuckled, his chest jostling me. "Oh, sweetheart, you have no idea."

## Chapter Seventeen

"Are you about ready to go, Kate?" Samantha asked from her office door. I nodded as I jotted down a few more notes. I wanted to be fully prepared for my first meeting with Emily. I had this nervous energy about me all morning. I'd woken up anxious to get my day started.

The boys had opted to stay in bed this morning without me. Heath didn't have to be in today, but Reid had the late shift. They'd tried to keep me in bed by pinning me down and taking turns kissing me. Both of their hands traveled south to do wicked things to my body. It took all of my willpower to push away from them and take my happy ass to the shower with a saucy smile on my face.

On a normal day, I would've loved to have stayed in bed with them and just spent the day finding bliss in one another's bodies. Not today though. Today was the day I advanced, not only in my career but in my life. To most people, this lunch meeting wasn't a big deal, but for me, it was an opportunity to seize something for myself.

Samantha had told me I could ask Emily any questions I wanted to, and I intended to use that to my advantage. I wanted to know what made her want to start writing. If it wasn't too much, I wanted to ask her thoughts on some plots I had bouncing around in my head. I didn't know any authors personally, so I definitely didn't want to squander this opportunity.

Twenty minutes later, we were pulling in front of the Italian restaurant I had made our reservations at. I got out of the car with the promise to get our table and start setting up while Samantha went to find a parking spot.

The hostess showed me to our table, and I ordered three glasses of water and some bread to start.

When Samantha joined me a few minutes later, the table was set and I had laid out the notes we wanted to cover for this meeting.

I could feel my phone vibrating in my purse, but I ignored it. I didn't want to be unprofessional by texting when Emily got here. We had gotten to the restaurant ten minutes before we agreed to meet, but I didn't want to take the chance.

It wasn't too much longer, and we saw the hostess bringing someone to our table. We both stood as Emily approached with a warm smile on her face. She looked to be just a little younger than me, I would say no older than thirty-two. She had a head full of blonde curls and a lot of orange in her hazel eyes. The light sprinkling of freckles that ran across her nose told me she was a minimal makeup gal like myself. She wore a pair of jeans with strappy wedge heels and a white blouse with flowers on the scoop collar and flowy sleeves.

Samantha reached forward and extended her manicured hand out to greet her. "I'm so glad we could find time to meet up, Emily. Kate and I have read both of your manuscripts. I think I speak for us both when I say they're amazing."

Emily flushed as she shook my boss's hand.

She looked at me as I held my hand out next for her to shake. "It's such a pleasure meeting you. I have to say, I feel like I know you already just from reading your work," I said with a bright smile.

Emily released my hand, and we all took our seats. "Well, you certainly know how to make a girl feel special." She spoke with a nervous laugh.

Samantha chuckled. "Well, we know when to give credit when credit is due."

The waiter came shortly after. We all ordered our food, and Samantha ordered a bottle of wine for the table. We made small talk while we got to know Emily. She was a very interesting person. It struck me as odd how many similarities we shared. She was also recently divorced and moved for a fresh start.

"I started writing when I was in my twenties. I wasn't happy in my marriage, and I used it as an escape from reality. I never would have thought that I would be good enough to get published." She was very animated when she spoke.

"I always wanted kids and my husband never did. I was really unhappy for a long time. When I finally got the guts to ask for a divorce, that's when I decided it was time for me to try. I had already written five manuscripts while I was still married. The two that I submitted to you were what I thought were my best ones," she said with a hopeful smile.

She was looking at me now. "So, what about you? You have the look of someone with a story to tell."

I flushed and took a sip of my water. Was it written all over my face? I told her about my failed marriage and everything in between. When I finished, I expected the same pity in her eyes that everyone else seemed to get.

To my surprise, she was smiling. "Well, it might not have felt like it, but what you went through was probably a blessing. Not everyone gets a second chance to build a life that they truly want."

I hadn't thought of it that way. Emily was either wiser than her years or a true optimist. She looked at me over her wine glass now. "So, what are you doing with this second chance you have been given, Kate? What new adventure gets you excited to get up in the morning?"

I smiled and thought of the men I left in my bed that morning. Those two were helping me break out of my shell more than they would ever know.

The sad reality was I hadn't been happy when I first moved here. I was heartbroken and beaten down. There was a reason I had lived next to them for a month before I had even known I had neighbors. I had been so consumed by my self-pity, I hadn't even left my apartment. I hadn't wanted to explore the new city I was calling home until after they'd entered my life.

Jill had begged me for weeks to come out with her to celebrate my divorce. I'd blown her off until she showed up that night and all but dragged me to that bar. That was the night I met Heath and my world changed for the better.

To the outside world, it might look like the only thing those men did for me was give me amazing sex. But for me, it was so much more than that. They were showing me how to expect more from myself. I was learning to love myself for who I was. I wasn't even as self-conscious as I used to be.

They expressed quite frequently how beautiful and perfect I was, and I found myself believing them more and more with each passing day. I didn't even start writing again until I had met them.

"I have a few reasons I get up in the morning," I said with a secret smile, "but one of my main ones is the prospect of new opportunities." We talked for the next twenty minutes. Even when our food came, we continued our conversation.

We talked about everything from family to books we liked to read. I had told her about recently taking to writing again and she said she would love to read what I had so far. I was thrilled, of course.

"Kate here shows tremendous promise as an author. I have read some of what she has, and I have to say I can't wait to read more," Samantha chimed in with a wink. I couldn't keep the smile from my face. "But, as much as I'd love to sit here and talk about Kate's up-and-coming book debut, we're here for you, Emily. We needed to go over some notes with you about your manuscripts and some editorial proposals as well as cover art."

We spent the next hour going over everything for Emily's books. She loved some of the suggestions I had made and the ideas that Samantha had for the cover.

When it was time for us to head back to the office, Emily slipped me her card. She told me to text her with any questions I had or to just get out and have some drinks together. I hugged her goodbye with the promise that I would see her again soon.

I hadn't made a new friend since elementary school, and that was Jill. I made a mental note to tell her all about our meeting and make some plans to go out for a girls' night with Emily.

It was just after two o'clock when we got back to the office. Samantha had gone over everything she needed me to do on the car ride back. Once I was at my desk, I settled in and got to work.

A couple of hours later, I popped my head into her office. "Hey Samantha, I'm all done. Is there anything else you have for me?" I asked.

She looked up at me over the rim of her glasses and smiled. "I'm pretty sure we're at the point in our relationship where you can call me Sam, Kate."

She chuckled as I blushed. "No, that was all I had for you to do. You only have about an hour left of the day. If you want, go ahead and work some more on that book of yours. You really need to set a word count goal for each day to stay on top of it." She winked at me and went back to her work.

I walked back to my desk with a smile on my

face. Opening my document, I got to work. An hour later, I was saving what I had written and emailing it to myself. I would work on it some more this weekend.

Sam came out of her office, shutting and locking the door behind her. "You did great work today. Take the weekend and relax. We'll hit the ground running on Monday." She smiled at me as she made her way to the front door.

I sat back in my chair with a sigh. I had a stupid grin on my face. Today had gone exactly like I hoped it would and I was ecstatic about it.

Remembering it was just going to be Reid and me this evening, I figured I should ask him what he wanted to do for supper tonight. I was feeling like sushi.

Pulling my phone from my bag and unlocking it, I realized that I never checked it earlier today when it buzzed me. There were three messages from a number I didn't know. Bile rose in my throat as the images loaded.

Two images. One of me. I was smiling, sitting in the restaurant window with Sam. It had been taken outside looking in. Tears clouded my vision as I looked at the second image. It was of my car in the parking lot. My tires were slashed and in big bold red spray paint, the word *WHORE* was written down the side. The last was a text message that read, **I'll be seeing you soon.**

Throwing my phone down onto my desk as if it burned me, I stood in a rush. I ran to the nearest window to see the parking lot.

Sure enough, my car was sitting there looking exactly like the picture. I looked around the office and realized I was the only one left here for the day. I sprinted to the front door and locked it. Running back to my desk I reached for my phone and dialed 911 with shaky fingers.

After the operator said they would send a unit my

way and told me to stay locked inside the building, I called one of the two people in this world that made me feel safe. He picked up on the first ring.

"Hey, sweetheart, I was just thinking about you. Are you on your way home?" Heath asked with a sensual voice. I couldn't hold the sob back as I tried to speak.

"C-can you come g-get me?" was all I managed.

Heath wasted no time as I heard him jump up from whatever he was doing and grab his keys. "Are you at work? What happened? I'm on my way. Stay on the phone with me and don't you fucking move."

All I could manage was a strangled whimper in return. The whole time I was on the phone with him, he was talking me down from my panic. He was afraid I would pass out before he could get there because I was on the verge of hyperventilating.

He must have hauled ass to get to me because in less time than it should have taken, I saw him whip into the parking lot. He'd gotten to me faster than the cops had. I watched as he jumped out of the vehicle and started to run to the doors, only to stumble when he saw my car. I watched his face go from worry to rage in two seconds flat.

He was banging on the door as I ran to let him in. As soon as he was through the doors, he locked them again and pulled me to him. I wrapped my arms around his waist, buried my face in his chest, and sobbed.

He rubbed my back methodically and tried to soothe me with soft words. I finally calmed down enough to pull away and look at him. He grabbed my face with both of his hands and regarded me seriously. "What happened, Kate?"

I handed him my phone so he could look at the texts I'd received. I watched his jaw clench and heard his breathing pick up. He was gripping my phone so hard that his knuckles were white. When he looked back down at me, he looked ready to murder someone. "Do you know who did this?" he asked between clenched teeth.

I had a pretty good guess, but I just shook my head no. He looked at me like he didn't quite believe me, but he said nothing as he pulled me to him again.

Just being in his arms seemed to calm my nerves a bit. I felt myself start to breathe normally again, and my mind was starting to clear. Even though I was still in shock over the whole situation, having Heath here was a comfort.

I watched as he pulled his phone out and called Reid before I could tell him not to bother him at work. I stopped myself when he gave me a look that said not to even try his patience as he told Reid it was an emergency and he needed to get here as soon as he could. He shoved his phone back into his pocket before he gathered me back into his embrace.

Fifteen minutes later a black car pulled into the parking lot with Jill hot on their heels. Dispatch must have called her when they figured out it was her building.

She paused to look at my car before she turned. Red-faced, she unlocked and slammed through the front entrance. "I'm going to kill that son-of-a-bitch. I swear to God, Kate! This has gone too fucking far," she yelled.

I tried to go to her, but Heath wasn't letting me go that easy. "Jill, calm down before you get yourself arrested." I tried to talk the beast back.

She looked at me like I was the crazy person in the room. "Calm down? You want me to calm down after seeing what that piece of shit did to your car?" she screamed.

I flinched back and Heath tightened his hold on me, pulling me closer to his side. "You don't know it was him that did it." That sounded weak to my own ears.

Jill's eyes widened even further. I was saved from more of her yelling as two detectives walked in.

The one who spoke first looked to be in his mid-thirties. He looked to be of Latin descent with his jet-black, shoulder-length hair, chocolate-brown eyes, and olive-toned skin. His voice was smooth as silk. "Whose car has the customized paint job out there?" he asked as he pointed toward the lot.

I opened my mouth to speak, but Jill got in his space before I could. "Is this some kind of joke to you? Do you think it's funny that my friend is being terrorized by her ex? Detective...?"

I felt Heath's hands flex at the mention of Tom, but he said nothing. I was surprised when the detective didn't even flinch at Jill's venomous tone. She may be small, but when she was good and pissed off, she was a force to be reckoned with.

He pushed his hand toward her as a way of greeting. "Detective Damon Santos."

Jill looked at that outstretched hand like it was a snake. He smirked at her and let his hand fall back to his side before shoving it in his pocket "Does it look like I'm laughing, Miss...?"

Jill squinted her eyes at the detective before looking down at his badge. "It's Brookes, as in Brookes Publishing. This is my building, Detective Santos," she said, scowling at him now.

He grinned at her. "Well, Miss Brookes, since this is *your* building, you should be able to tell me what happened in *your* parking lot."

I needed to defuse this situation before it got even more heated and Jill got into trouble. She opened her mouth to say something I was sure would have been inappropriate when I spoke up. "It's my car that was vandalized."

Heath gripped my side and said, "She also got some very threatening text messages."

That got Jill's attention. "What do you mean? Let me see your phone," she demanded.

She didn't give me time to hand it over as she snatched it from me and walked away with it. Detective Santos followed after her.

The other detective stepped forward. He was a hard-looking man. He had dark circles under his cold eyes. "My name is Detective Pete Green. I need to get your statement, if you would explain to me what led up to these events this evening." He regarded me seriously.

I started to explain what had happened when the front doors slammed open again. I turned just in time to see Reid looking around wildly until his eyes locked on me. I felt a pang of guilt run through me as I took in his work attire.

He made a beeline straight for me, and I opened my arms for him to gather me into a tight embrace. I looked up at him as he asked if I was okay. I nodded with fresh tears in my eyes, emotion clogging my throat. He caressed both sides of my face as he kissed me lightly before we broke apart, only to have him and Heath firmly bring me to their sides.

Detective Green was openly staring at me with a slight look of disgust in his eyes. I tried not to shrink back under his hard gaze.

"As I was saying, I need your statement," he said in a chipped tone, darting his gaze between the three of us. Either he didn't care for public displays of affection or he didn't approve of our lifestyle choice, I couldn't be sure either way.

I gave him what he wanted, telling him about the pictures and the threatening text.

"You didn't see anyone suspicious-looking

today?" he asked in a mundane voice. Like he had already decided this wasn't worth his time. When I shook my head no, he asked if I could think of anyone who would want to hurt me.

I stammered before Reid spoke up for me. "We already know it was her ex-husband. That son of a bitch showed up at her apartment the other night and tried to beat the shit out of her." Reid was red-faced when he finished. You would have to be blind to not see how angry he was. I had the indescribable need to soothe him as I rubbed my hand down his arm.

Detective Santos rejoined us at that moment and was watching the situation with careful eyes. Detective Green smirked at Reid. It was obvious that they knew each other and didn't like one another. "How do you know it was her ex-husband? It looks like she entertains multiple men. Could it be one of the others?" he insinuated before he tsked at me like I was a wayward child. "I don't know what you women expect to happen when you trollop around with multiple men, leading them on." He sneered.

My mouth dropped open as I gasped and my face burned at the accusation. I felt Reid let me go and move toward the detective. Before he could get more than a step, Heath got in his face and pushed him back. "You need to calm down," he said harshly.

Reid pointed at the detective. "He just implied that Kate is a whore and deserved what happened to her! That fucker is going to get what he deserves in a minute," he seethed.

"I heard him, but all you're going to do is get your ass thrown in jail. Just because he is a close-minded *prick*"—he paused to glare at the detective before turning back to Reid—"doesn't mean you get to beat the shit out of him."

Jill came up beside me and held my hand, trying to comfort me. Detective Santos was pushing his partner toward the door, telling him to go take pictures of my car. Trying to get him to remove himself from the situation.

Reid finally calmed and Heath backed down. "I'm sorry about Pete. He's having some hard times at home right now and is under a lot of stress. I'm not trying to make excuses for his behavior though. He will no longer be involved in this case," Detective Santos said with a sad smile.

"I don't give a shit if he's having a hard time at home or not. The next time he implies that my girlfriend deserved any of this, I won't hold Reid back, I'll join in, *Detective*," Heath threatened.

Damon nodded. "I think we have everything we need. I will be visiting your ex-husband personally to see if he has an alibi for today. According to Miss Brookes, the cameras in the parking lot would have recorded what happened. I will review those when I get back to the station. I'll call you if I have any news at all." He gave us all one last look, lingering on Jill before he turned and was out the door.

Jill turned me around to face her and gave me a tight hug. "You're not staying in that apartment where he can get to you. We'll go and get you a bag, but you are staying with me this weekend," she said with resolve.

Reid stepped up and grabbed her attention. "That won't be necessary. She'll be staying with us until they catch that fucker."

Jill turned and went toe-to-toe with Reid. I cringed at the thought of both of their strong personalities clashing. "What's stopping Tom from just taking his ass across the hall to your door? If he can get to her apartment, he can get to yours," Jill said.

Heath took their arguing as an opportunity to scoop me up and take me to the office lounge. He sat down on the couch with me in his lap and ran his hand down my back in soothing strokes.

I could barely hear them going at it from here. Heath turned me to look at him. "It's gonna be okay, sweetheart. We will figure out what's going on, but in the meantime, Reid and I will take care of you," he promised.

His sweet words were my undoing. I laid my head on his shoulder, burying my face in his neck, and started to cry. I hadn't realized how much I was holding in. I hadn't even really reacted when Tom hit me the other night. But I was letting it all out now. Heath kept rubbing my back and rocked me gently.

By the time my eyes ran dry, Reid joined us. He sat down next to Heath and leaned in to kiss me sweetly.

Jill came and squatted in front of us. "You're going to stay with Reid and Heath for a while, okay? Reid told me that they are going to work out a schedule so at least one of them will always be with you at all times. If you need anything at all you call me, understand?"

I nodded as she leaned forward and smoothed my hair down.

I felt like such a burden at that moment. The fact that they felt obligated to take care of me made me feel guilty. Reid, Heath, and I had only been dating for such a short amount of time, and they shouldn't have to deal with this. I didn't know if they knew what they signed up for when they took me on.

We all left sometime later. I rode in Heath's vehicle, pushed right up against him. My car was being towed to a local body shop, where it would be assessed for damages and turned in to insurance.

When we got home, they tried to get me to eat something, but the idea of food was repulsive. I just wanted to be done with this day and sleep.

They ushered me into their bathroom where we all got into the shower. They both took their time washing and holding me. There was nothing sexual about it, and everything they did was a comfort.

After I was dried off, Reid carried me to bed where he laid me down in the middle, and they both climbed in, surrounding me. I lay there for the longest time, thinking about the implications of this night. I wondered how much they would put up with before they decided enough was enough.

They signed up for a partnership, not someone else to take care of. I made a promise to myself as I lay there and listened to their breathing even out as sleep took them.

I promised that I would end things with them if I couldn't get this Tom drama under control. They deserved to have someone who didn't have so much baggage to carry around. It would hurt like hell, but I would do it to save them.

## Chapter Eighteen

The next morning, I got a phone call from Detective Santos before I had even gotten out of bed. Reid and Heath sat up with me and listened intently to the conversation. Damon said he had viewed the security footage of the vandalism on my car but that led nowhere. Someone had cut the power to the camera right before the event.

My heart dropped as the thought of me being able to put this all behind me vanished. He also informed me that since Tom was still a resident of Georgia, he had to pass it off to the local sheriff in my old hometown.

I tried to stop the mortification from creeping up to my face. I came from a very small town, so I knew that once word got out about this, everyone and their dog would be talking about it for months. Damon promised to call as soon as he heard word from Sheriff O'Neal about Tom's whereabouts.

Before we hung up the phone, he strongly urged me to have people around me at all times until they figured out what was going on. I guessed that meant I was staying in all weekend with the boys. Pulling my phone from my ear, I leaned against Heath as he brought his arms around me.

"It'll be okay, Kate, we won't let anything happen to you. Hopefully, Detective Santos will get to the bottom of this quickly," he said quietly against my cheek.

I tried to find comfort in his words, but all I came back with was guilt. Reid sat in front of us as he reached to push my hair behind my ear. He tried to smile to reassure me, but I could see his anger simmering beneath the surface.

I still couldn't fathom what I had done to earn this type of loyalty from these men. We had barely known each other for a couple of weeks, but I knew with every fiber of my being that these two would go to war for me. That alone should have made me feel secure in all aspects of this relationship, but instead, it made me feel like such a burden.

Reid mistook my look of guilt for apprehension as he grabbed my chin, forcing me to look at him. "You don't have anything to worry about, bunny. We'll figure this out, but in the meantime—" He grabbed ahold of my ankles, pulling me away from Heath's arms. I was on my back with him on top of me before I could even yelp.

He looked down at me with a sly grin. "How about we take your mind off of all this and express how happy we are to be able to spend the whole weekend with you"—he looked from me to Heath as he finished with a sinful smile—"un-interrupted."

I couldn't help the nervous giggle that bubbled up my throat as I watched Heath prowl closer to us. I had a ridiculous smile on my face as I glanced back at the man on top of me.

"You're so beautiful," he muttered right before his mouth descended onto mine.

I sighed as we sank into the kiss, coming up for air only to have Heath take his place kissing me as Reid slid down my body. They proceeded to show me just how they could take my mind off my problems.

****

Even after I had begged and pleaded, neither one of them had made love to me. They said they preferred to take care of me this morning, saying today was all about me. So now, two hours and countless orgasms later, I sat on the couch in their living room.

I sat, but really, I lounged awkwardly. I had

discovered it was kind of difficult to sit with a butt plug shoved up my ass. I begrudgingly tried to relay that fact to Reid, but he laughed and told me he could make it even more difficult for me to sit if I liked. I clamped my mouth shut after that and tried to get as comfortable as I could.

They instructed that I was to only wear Heath's t-shirt for the rest of the day. Given the fact that I had no clean clothes over here, I didn't have much of a choice. When I tried to put on yesterday's panties, Reid promptly told me I was no longer allowed to wear panties in his presence. I laughed it off, thinking he was joking, until I saw his dark glare.

The rest of the day was oddly domestic. Reid went to my apartment to grab some things for me to keep here. Unloading the bag into one of the spare dresser drawers, I noticed Reid was completely serious. There wasn't a single pair of panties in my bag. He had grabbed my laptop though, so I could work on my book. I sat and wrote for a good portion of the day, getting lost in the story that unfolded behind my very eyes. When I wrote, I fully immersed myself in the story, finding myself feeling exactly as my characters were feeling. I was only pulled out of my story weaving when Heath brought me back to reality to feed me and tell me I needed a break.

After my break, Reid lounged on one side of me, flipping through channels until he found a show he was interested in. Heath sat with us for a while but eventually had to go into the bar and go over scheduling issues.

He and Reid really were managing their schedules around me. The fact that I was making their lives harder was not lost on me. Reid was very intuitive, I found. He saw when I was feeling guilty and promptly took my mind off of it as he pulled me into his lap.

He turned me until I had my front draped across

his legs with my ass thrust into the air. My breath left me in a rush as he tapped on the plug and asked me if I was ready to have it removed.

With a nod of my head, he pushed his fingers inside of me with a long groan. "I think you like my plug. Your pussy is awfully wet," he said as he removed his fingers in favor of rubbing my clit.

Within minutes, he had me unable to form cognitive thoughts as I wailed my release. After he removed the plug, he moved me to lie on the couch as he lay behind me, cuddling me close.

We lay like that for so long that I eventually dozed off for an afternoon nap. I awoke as Heath took Reid's place behind me.

Reid sauntered into the kitchen, leaving us behind. I turned on my other side and faced Heath, tangling our legs together. We embraced each other, kissing softly, teasing each other for the longest time.

I could feel that he was just as turned on as I was as I reached down to rub him through his jeans. I unbuttoned them and reached inside. He fell heavily into my palm, and I squeezed around him, getting a hiss from him in return.

I pumped him a few times before I rose to straddle his hips. The no-panty rule was working in my favor as I easily slid onto him. I felt powerful as I rode him, watching as his face contorted in pleasure. He was breathing heavily, restraining himself from taking over as I slowly fucked him.

He pushed his thumb against my engorged clitoris as he got close to release, silently begging me to fall over the edge with him. I did just that when he started to pulse inside of me as he spilled his seed with a long groan.

As I leaned down to kiss him, Reid walked into the room with pizza and beer, proclaiming supper was served. He obviously knew what Heath and I were doing. He put the food and beer on the coffee table and pulled a washcloth out of his back pocket.

Before I could take it from him, he reached between us and placed the cloth where Heath and I were still connected. It was an intimate moment as he stared into my eyes. The vision of the thin material being the only thing that separated his hand from Heath's cock turned me on all over again.

He stared into my eyes as I felt Heath pull out and he started to clean me. Reid was giving me a wicked smile before he pushed his mouth to mine, forcing his tongue inside. Biting my lower lip, he proclaimed that I would need to ride him like that later too. I bit back a giggle as I gave him a saucy smile that had his eyes flaring.

We all disengaged and were seated under a huge blanket with pizza within minutes. The sun was going down as we started a movie and leaned against each other. Long after our pizza was gone and halfway through the movie, my phone trilled with an incoming call. Detective Santos sounded very sober when I answered and placed him on speaker.

"I'm sorry I don't have much news, Ms. Hart. We still haven't had any luck in finding your ex-husband. I was informed this afternoon that he does have a warrant for his arrest. He is out on bail, and he missed his court date. Sheriff O'Neal said that by the looks of your old home, nobody has been there for a while. He did get a search warrant and found some very … disturbing things."

I was having a hard time breathing as panic set in my chest. I asked him what they had found. There was a heavy pause before he continued.

"From the looks of it, he has been watching you

for a while. There are candid pictures of you hanging all over the wall in his office. The photos had unsettling slurs written all over them. He also had a detailed list of your whereabouts for the past few weeks."

He paused to let the information sink in before he continued. "When you were married, did he ever have violent tendencies toward you or your daughter?" he asked.

I knew Heath was rubbing his hand up and down my back trying to soothe me, but I felt nothing. I could feel the start of a panic attack approaching rapidly as I tried to choke out my words. "N-no," I managed barely. "He's only ever been violent with me once, and that was just the other day," I admitted.

I heard him sigh into the phone before he spoke. "We think he may be suffering from a mental break following his legal problems and he is using alcohol to cope. We think he may be blaming you for leaving him and causing his life to spin out of control. He isn't in his right frame of mind right now."

My mind was racing as I stood to pace around the living room. Tears burned the back of my eyes as I asked what I should do until he was caught.

"Right now, we suggest staying with people you know. Don't go out alone. I know this isn't the best solution, but it's all we can do until Mr. Hart is caught and brought in for questioning."

After ending the call, I stood there, stunned, staring at my phone. Somewhere in the back of my mind, I could hear Reid and Heath talking to me, but I wasn't listening. I still didn't understand why this was happening. I got away. After putting up with Tom for nineteen years, I got away!

I should be allowed to have a clean break, shouldn't I? It pissed me off that he acted like I was the cause of his problems. He had made me into a compliant little housewife who had no say in her own damn life. But now he wanted to blame me? I had to put my life on hold because of him when we were together, and now I would have to do it again.

I didn't realize I was squeezing my phone with white-knuckled force until Heath tried to grab it from me. I was shaking with rage as I looked up into those emerald eyes. He looked at me with such sympathy that it enraged me further.

I jerked away from him and made for the front door. I wanted to be alone in my own apartment. I needed to know I still had some form of freedom.

I got all of three steps before Reid was hauling me around getting in my face.

"And just where do you think you are going?" he demanded with a scowl. I tried to push against him, but it was like pushing against a wall.

"Dammit, Reid! Let me go, I am going home." I pushed against him again, but he wasn't budging.

He twisted me around and held my hands behind my back, causing me to thrust my breasts out. I knew my anger was misplaced, but it felt good to lash out as I tried to kick behind me.

He easily dodged my kick and pulled me closer to him, biting down on my ear. I bit back my yelp, not wanting to give him the satisfaction.

"I know that you're pissed off right now and you want to take it out on someone. But if you try that again, I will have you over my knee, and I will take my anger out on your ass," he bit out between clenched teeth. A bit of lust broke through the haze of my rage at his promise.

Heath came to my front and ran his thumb along my cheek, gathering a tear I hadn't known I'd shed. "I know you're scared right now, but fighting us is the last thing you need to do. We've already decided you aren't going anywhere, so why don't you calm down and come talk to us? Let us take care of you, sweetheart," Heath said softly.

I could deal with the fact that Reid was just as angry as I was, but for some reason, the way Heath always kept his calm rubbed me wrong at that moment. I knew I was being irrationally angry, but I just needed to take it out on someone. On any normal day, when Heath was so sweet with me, I would melt for him, but not today.

On some level, I knew I was trying to push them away for their own good when I said, "Fuck you! Why don't you and Reid sit and talk it out by yourselves? You two seem to know what's best for me. I didn't ask for you to take care of me and I don't want it. I don't need another man in my life trying to control everything that I do!"

I saw the hurt flash in Heath's eyes before it disappeared, and his lips thinned in a passive expression. At that moment, I didn't care if I hurt them both.

"All I have ever wanted for myself is the freedom to make my own decisions. After a *long* shitty marriage, I finally got it. I was finally free…" My voice broke as I held back more tears. "But now, Tom has taken it away, again! And you two are just helping him at this point. Let me go, I don't want this anymore. I don't belong to you." I tried to jerk away from Reid again, but he held on tight.

When I looked back up, I saw a darkness pass over Heath's eyes that had me backing into Reid. I felt Reid chuckle behind me.

"Oh, now you've done it," he said against my ear.

## Chapter Nineteen

I tried to swallow past the lump in my throat as Heath stared daggers at me. "You don't belong to us?" he asked with an edge to his voice.

His smile was humorless as he cupped my out-thrust breast through my shirt. He pinched down on my nipple, hard, extracting a small scream from me at the pain that followed. Soon the pain turned into that sweet heat that I'd learned to crave.

When I refocused on Heath, he looked mighty angry now. "I understand what you're saying, Kate. The last thing we want is for you to feel trapped in another relationship where you have no freedom. But the fact remains that it's not safe for you to be without us right now."

He turned around, and I almost whimpered, I wanted him to stay here and fight me. I opened my mouth to yell at him but stopped as he turned and sat on the couch. Lounging back and spreading his legs, making a show of readjusting himself. I licked my lips as I got an eyeful of his bulge.

My body couldn't decide if it wanted to fight or fuck. There was definitely something wrong with me.

"Reid, bring her here for me. Strip her and lay her across my lap. I think it's time she learns just who exactly she belongs to," Heath said with that dangerous edge to his voice.

Reid released me long enough to strip Heath's shirt off me and throw it behind him. He then hauled me up, and my world was upside down as he slung me over his shoulder.

I squealed as he dropped me back down, draping me over Heath's lap like I had been across his earlier that day. I tried to scramble up but was caught when Heath trapped my legs under one of his, and he smacked my ass hard enough to make me yelp.

"That fucking hurt!" I screamed at him but made no more attempts to get away.

He smacked again, and I bit my lip to squelch the noise coming up my throat.

"Yeah, it got your attention though, didn't it? This is how this is going to go." He paused to smack me on the meaty part of my thigh, holding his hand there letting the heat sink in.

I bit back a moan, not wanting to let him on to how much I enjoyed it. Reid sat down next to him and cradled my upper torso and head in his lap. He grabbed both my wrists and held them above my head with one hand, seizing me for their punishment. My heart squeezed a little when he pushed my hair out of my face and turned my head so I wouldn't get a crick in my neck. Even angry, they cared about my comfort.

Heath brought my attention back to him with another sharp slap to the opposite cheek he struck before. "You obviously need a release, and if you can't sit and talk to me, this is what you are going to get. I'm going to spank this beautiful ass until you let out that anger you're holding on to. Once you have calmed down, we can talk. If you thought I was a nice soft lover, you are about to learn otherwise right now. I might prefer to be gentle with you, but I am not soft." He emphasized his point by grinding his erection against me.

He ran his hand up my spine before digging his fingers into my hair and pulling. My breath hitched, and I arched into him, silently begging for more. "You say stop if it becomes too much, and I'll stop," he said calmly before returning his hand to the curve of my ass.

I felt a chink in my anger at his words as a warm

feeling bloomed in my chest. Even angry at me, he would make sure never to hurt me.

Before I could say anything, Heath's hand arched back, and he peppered my ass with his slaps. At first, it had me bracing, holding my breath at the pain, but before long, I felt myself relaxing and enjoying the heat sinking into me.

I let go of the anger that was riding me and sank into the moment. His firm strikes never hit the same place twice. I was moaning softly by the time he slowed his strikes, rubbing and kneading my ass in between each fall of his palm.

I felt the tears that leaked out of my eyes hit Reid's denim-clad thigh beneath my cheek. Not from pain but from all the pent-up emotions I always kept bottled inside. I never would have imagined that this would be the release I needed, but I was feeling better with each fleshy smack.

When he arched his hand again, I wasn't ready for the slap he delivered right on my pussy. I screamed as he rubbed between my soaked folds.

"Fuck, sweetheart, you are so wet. You like this don't you?" Heath asked as he kept up his achingly slow rubs. He used his other hand to spank me again and I pushed my ass back for more.

"I can smell her arousal from here. It's making me so hard it hurts," Reid admitted from above me.

Heath ceased his punishment, and I nearly groaned with the need for him to keep going. "Now, are you calm enough to talk to us?" he asked softly as he rubbed my sore behind.

I shook my head. "I just need to have some control back in my life. I feel like everything is being taken from me again and I can't do anything to stop it."

Heath stopped rubbing me for a moment before

he spoke. "I understand your frustration, sweetheart. But like I said, it is too dangerous for you to be on your own right now."

I almost felt a flash of anger rise back up inside of me. "But," he continued, "that doesn't mean you can't be in control around Reid and me. Maybe boss us around for a change."

I jerked my head up, trying to look at him from Reid's lap. Was he being serious? The thought of being the dominant one in our relationship hadn't even crossed my mind. But the idea excited me more than I liked to admit. Don't get me wrong, being the submissive was hot, but thinking of bossing the boys around seemed … intriguing.

"What do you want, bunny?" Reid grinned at me as if he knew exactly where my mind had gone.

"I want to be in charge. This time at least." I wiggled so I could feel the press of Heath's hard length against my belly.

"I want to…" I blushed at the thought of telling them exactly what I wanted. I swallowed, trying to bring moisture back to my mouth before I forged on. "I want to suck you while Heath uses his fingers on me." My face flamed hot.

I felt Heath's hand tighten on my ass as if my words excited him. Reid grinned down at me before I felt his cock twitch against me.

"Then, by all means, bunny. Do your worst," he said before he relaxed further back into the couch.

I gasped as Heath pushed his fingers inside of me, curling them to hit that magic button inside of me.

Trying to make myself focus, I pushed my hands against Reid's legs so I could get a good angle. He pulled himself out of his jeans, and I wasted no time pulling him past my lips. Heath upped the speed of his fingers as he watched me suck Reid's cock.

"Fuck yes." Reid hissed as he gathered my hair behind my head to hold in his fist.

I was so incredibly turned on right now that I couldn't have stopped if someone tried to make me. I sucked hard as Heath continued to smack the fleshy parts of my ass and thighs, never stopping his fingers from moving. I was going to come soon, and I wanted Reid right there with me. I pulled him back further until he was almost to the back of my throat. I gagged as he pushed the rest of the way. My eyes were watering as I swallowed around him.

He moaned with each pull of my mouth. I felt my orgasm rising faster and faster as Heath fingered me. The only sounds in the room were his fingers gliding through my wetness, Reid's strangled groans, and my crude sucking noises.

The best part about finding my own control was knowing I could give it over to someone I trusted most. Which was a good thing, as I had no control anymore over my body as Heath pushed in and circled his thumb on my clit before he spanked me one final time. I screamed around Reid's cock as I came.

He let out a harsh sound as he pushed to the back of my throat one last time and came in hot jets. I swallowed down greedily, licking him clean while he jerked with aftershocks.

Before I talked myself out of it, I pushed away from them. Standing there under their hot gazes, I tried to get my wits about me. Trying desperately to think of the next thing I wanted them to do.

Heath looked up at me with wanton eyes. "Now what, sweetheart?" he asked with a devious grin.

I straightened my spine as I looked down at him. In my best authoritative voice, I said one word. "Strip."

I could tell Reid wanted to take back control by the flare of his eyes as I stated my command. I had to bite back my grin as I felt a surge of feminine power when they both stood and slowly stripped their clothing.

I bit my bottom lip as they shed their shirts, tossing them to the floor beside them. Soft golden skin and black ink filled my vision. No matter how many times I had watched them take their clothes off, I was still mesmerized by how their muscles flexed and worked as they moved.

They both watched me with heat in their eyes as they pushed their jeans down those powerful hips. When they stood back to their full height, bare of any clothing, all I could do was stare at those hard cocks bobbing between strong legs.

A naughty thought crossed my mind before I could shut it down. I wondered briefly if they would even go for such a thing. A look of pure panic crossed both of their faces as they looked at my wicked smile as if reading my mind.

Reid was the first one to voice his concern. "Don't even think about it, Kate. We may be a threesome and neither of us minds touching one another while we are fucking you."

Heath finished the thought for him. "But we are not going to touch each other without you in the middle of us. We don't swing that way."

I giggled as I continued to think about it for a moment. Maybe one day I could get my boys to play. But that day wasn't today.

I looked at Heath. "I want you on your knees in front of me," I ordered.

If I had blinked, I would have missed it. One minute he was standing, and the next he was kneeling in front of me, eager to do my bidding.

I swallowed hard as I looked down at him. Now that I was here, I wasn't sure I would be able to tell him what I wanted. Being in charge of anything wasn't something I was used to. I had never been able to demand that my own needs be met. I was always rolling over and never putting myself first.

I mentally shook myself. It was time for all of that to change. I said I needed control over my own life, and dammit, I meant it. I looked down at my Greek God and hardened my resolve as I spoke.

"Lick me," I said almost shyly.

He smiled before he did exactly that. He kept eye contact as he leaned forward, gripping my hips in a firm grasp. Flicking his tongue out from behind those insatiable lips, he licked me in a long swipe, lapping up my arousal with a deep groan. My knees nearly buckled as I gave over to his ministrations. I moaned as he sucked and released me with loud smacks. The erotic noises sent hot zings throughout my body.

My core trembled as I watched what Heath was doing to me. His mouth firmly latched on to my sex before he released me long enough to look up into my eyes. I could see my arousal coating his lips and chin right before he smiled and returned to his mission of driving me crazy.

I thrust my fingers into his dark, silky locks as a shuddered gasp left my mouth. I felt another surge of power coursing through my body. Seeing this man on his knees for me was turning me on more than words could describe.

I looked over at Reid with hooded eyes. He looked desperate to get in on the fun, but he was patiently waiting for my command. "Your turn." I panted. "Come kneel behind me," I ordered around a gasp as Heath speared me with his tongue.

Reid wasted no time, and soon I felt him at my backside. He laid a kiss on my lower back as his hands traced my curves, waiting for his next assignment. I looked down and around my shoulder at him, trying not to blush this time. "Lick me," was all I said. I watched his eyes flare with devious excitement before he leaned in, swiping his tongue along my asshole.

I nearly jumped out of my skin at the sensation. I widened my stance to give them more room. They took advantage and deepened their thrusting tongues. Both of them licking and sucking.

Reid pushed his tongue inside of me as Heath sucked my clit into his hot mouth, and I just about lost all motor skills.

"Touch yourselves," I said around a ragged moan. I was feeling extremely powerful at the moment, and that was driving me just as high as their mouths were.

Both of them groaned against me as they grabbed those big cocks. I watched as they pumped themselves with their tight fists. Faster and faster, they went. Their need to find the finish line, taking hold.

I pulled my leg up and over Heath's shoulder. He didn't miss a beat as he helped me balance by tightening his hold on my hip. Both of them seemed to dive deeper, the position giving them greater access. I swore I could feel their tongues touching every so often as they made mad swipes up and down my intimate areas, never leaving an area untouched by their mouths. The thought made me all the hotter.

"I'm going to come!" I exclaimed. "I need you there with me. Come for me." Both of them groaned as their movements became jerky.

Reid's tongue dove into me with fucking motions as Heath sucked my sensitive bud into his mouth, flicking it wildly. I held on to the tops of their heads as I went on my tiptoes. Unable to hold off any longer, I rode their faces as I screamed my release into their waiting mouths.

Unable to stay upright one second longer, I collapsed into their arms. I felt Reid's cock jerk against my back while he rubbed his orgasm out against me as he groaned, "Oh, God, yes," into my ear. His hot release spewed against my back as Heath leaned forward.

Sliding an arm around me, he pulled me into him as he came in long jets across my stomach. He raked his lips across mine as he grunted, "*Fuck!*" He growled as they both jerked against me with aftershocks.

Before I could think to move, Reid had me up and carried me to the bedroom. My time in control was over, but I was okay with it. They needed control just as much as I did. Besides, I couldn't help but love every second of submitting to them.

They spent the next couple of hours making love to me. Telling me that I was theirs and I wasn't to fight them about that fact any longer. They wanted to take care of me, and I needed to let them.

Heath had been right to help me release my anger the way he did. I apologized for the way I acted, telling them that I didn't mean anything I said about not wanting them. They understood, of course.

Two dominant men submitting to me made me see that the level of their dedication to me went beyond the physical. I knew deep down that they cared for me more than any of us had been able to express. And maybe it was because our relationship was still new. I couldn't fault them for not telling me how they truly felt, I hadn't conveyed such things either. No words of love were spoken, but I felt their love in their unique way that day.

## Chapter Twenty

The next few weeks passed in a comforting routine. I had stayed with the boys for a week with no incidents before I tried to convince them that it would be safe to stay at my place, but they were having none of it. Reid threatened to tie me down to the bed if I so much as thought about running off by myself. I believed him so I promptly dropped the subject.

We fell into a habitual schedule after a while. Heath took me to work every morning, and Reid picked me up every evening. I was given strict instructions to stay at work and not leave the office by myself. Heath even made sure to deliver me meals from his bar and eat with me most days. Making all of the office women extremely jealous in the process, and not of my food. I couldn't blame them, he was hot.

On the days that Heath didn't feed me, I would eat lunch with Jill or Emily at the office. They both came up with new and exciting ways to castrate my ex every day. Jill would only take breaks from talking about Tom long enough to ask if I had heard from a certain detective.

She tried to play it off as a casual curiosity, but I knew better. Jill had the hots for Detective Damon. My mind was playing with the idea of getting those two together after this was all over.

We all took turns making meals in the evenings. I complained only once that they were going to make me fatter than I already was. They'd gotten very angry after I had made the self-deprecating joke and had promptly taken turns punishing me for the insult against myself. They evidently wouldn't stand for anyone insulting me, even if it was me dishing out the insults.

If one of them had to work, then the other one would stay with me. No matter who I ended up in bed with that night, I always ended up wrapped around both of them by morning. I had expected us to get sick of each other after so long, but we had only grown closer over time.

I had started to anticipate their needs and wants as they did mine too. I also assumed that our passion when making love would fizzle out over time as well, but it only seemed to be getting better and exquisitely dirtier as we learned what made each other tick.

I knew now Heath could also be just as dominant in the bedroom as Reid. He just preferred to let Reid do all the bossing. One of his favorite things to do was to tie me to the bed with my head hanging off the edge so he could fuck my mouth while Reid fucked me from above. He would order me to swallow his cock, which I would happily do.

I also learned that Reid got off on watching just as much as he did with participating. There were times when he would just sit back and tell Heath and me what to do and where to touch. It was a major turn-on seeing him pleasure himself to us.

They had also learned things I liked that I hadn't even known I liked. For example, if one was pulling my hair while fucking me from behind and the other held me by the throat and played with me, I was bound to explode quicker.

Also, I now knew I had what was called a praise kink. Who knew there was such a thing? But when one of them told me I was "a good fucking girl," I went wild.

Every day, they prepared me to take both of them. They had upped the plug size that I was instructed to wear for hours at a time, saying I only had one more size left before I could take one of them. I always got rewarded for my submission with mind-blowing orgasms.

After week two, I had gotten a visit from Detective Santos for an update. The police had started to check into Tom's credit card purchases to see if they could track him that way. That road had quickly gone nowhere. It was like the man had fallen off the face of the earth and nobody knew where to find him. I was just thankful that he hadn't gotten bold enough to try anything else.

At the start of week three, the autobody shop called with news that I could pick my car back up anytime I was ready. After talking it over with the boys, I decided it was best to let Lindsey have the car for a while. I knew without a doubt that Tom would never try to hurt her in any way, so leaving the car with her was a safe option.

I never told Lindsey what happened between her father and me. She didn't need me to muddle the image of her dad any more than it already was. What was going on with Tom shouldn't be one of her concerns.

I took these last weeks to work heavily on my book. Every free moment I had, I used to write. Emily helped me by reading chapters as I had finished them and sent back her notes. Our friendship was still in the early stages, but it was definitely blooming into something great.

I had fallen into the story so hard that by the end of the third week I was completely finished. Heath and Reid had taken turns proofreading my work and both of them expressed how much they loved it.

I used pieces of my own life to create this book so it would forever hold a special place in my soul even if it was never published. While holding my breath, I pushed the *send* button. Emailing my manuscript to both Jill and

Sam. I smiled as I placed my laptop on the coffee table with a sigh.

It was Saturday evening, and I had both boys with me this evening. I was usually content to just stay in for the night and snuggle down on the couch with them. Not this time though, I had restless energy running through me as I bounded up from my seat. I spied Heath sitting at the dining table, poring over the papers in front of him.

I sauntered over to him. He looked up at me and leaned back, silently giving his permission. I straddled his lap and made a space for myself between him and the table. Leaning down, I kissed his neck all the way to his ear before nipping it gently, just the way I knew he liked.

His fingers flexed against my bottom as he squeezed, letting me know he was enjoying my explorations. "You keep doing that and I will be having you for supper, sweetheart," he rumbled below me.

I giggled as I sat back up to face him. "I want to go out and celebrate. I just sent my manuscript off and I feel really good about it."

I watched the fun smile waver slightly from his lips. I knew he was fighting an internal battle between his need to keep me safe and his want to see me happy.

I cut in before he could speak again. "You and Reid both will be with me." I tried with a smile. "And we can go to your bar, you know your bouncers will keep an eye out for Tom. I just want to go have a nice meal with you guys, maybe drink a little. I can invite Jill and Em to come along too." I finished with a pout.

Heath still seemed to be thinking about it when I leaned in to whisper in his ear. "I can wear one of those extremely short dresses I bought a few weeks ago and put on a dance for you." I traced my tongue along the shell of his ear before leaning back.

His eyes darkened. He grabbed the back of my

neck and brought me to his lips. After drugging me with his kisses, he looked at me seriously. "All right, we can go."

I clapped my hands together and squealed a little bit.

"But if I see anything at all that makes me think Tom is around, we will be out of there faster than you can blink," he said with a point of his finger. I smiled and bit the tip of his finger, earning me a sharp slap on my ass cheek.

He chuckled as I practically leaped from his lap and sprinted to the bedroom to start getting ready. I texted the girls a time to meet us and continued my search to find the shortest dress I owned.

****

An hour later, we pulled up to the front door of Heath's bar. I suggested we walk because it was just a couple of blocks, but both men looked at me like I was crazy. I decided not to argue with them.

When I exited the bedroom after getting dressed, it took everything I had to not let them keep me home. Reid had taken one look at the tight little red dress paired with black fuck-me shoes I had on and proclaimed I wasn't allowed to leave the house.

I had caught myself admiring the dress in the mirror after putting it on. It was a quarter sleeve with a deep V cut that stretched down just above my navel. It was a plain deep-red color with the length stopping at mid-thigh. The scandalous part was the slit that went dangerously high. I had to promise to give Reid a private dance in it later to get him to agree that I should wear it.

We made our way inside and met Jill and Emily at one of the VIP booths. This was the first time Emily had seen either Reid or Heath. The look in her eyes was pure shock as she scanned their bodies from head to toe.

Jill nudged her with her elbow and mouthed "I told you so."

The next few hours were spent trying to talk over the loud music in between downing our drinks. Jill commented on how happy I looked lately, and I knew it had a lot to do with the two men beside me.

We all ordered food to munch on and the drinks kept coming. Heath had gotten the chance to push right up against me, taking advantage of the situation by playing with the slit in my dress. The motion instantly made my heart rate pick up.

At some point, Emily had determined that the song playing was "her jam" and we needed to dance. I just loved this girl's fun, carefree spirit. We left the boys behind as we made our way to the dancefloor, still keeping in their sights.

I stared at them as I swayed my hips sensually, throwing my hands above my head as the music pumped through my body. Although they weren't touching me, I felt the heat from their gaze. It was doing fantastic things to my girl parts. I turned to show them my backside when I caught eyes with a familiar face.

Detective Santos was making his way to Jill. He wasn't in his suit and tie, so I figured it was his night off. I had to admit he filled out that t-shirt and jeans well. The way his long hair was hanging free around his face would make any red-blooded female drool. I had sex almost nightly with the two hottest men I could ever dream of, and I still found Damon extremely attractive.

I couldn't help the smile that cracked across my lips as I watched shock cross Jill's face. He regarded me with serious eyes for a moment before yelling over the music. "I hope you aren't here by yourself, Ms. Hart."

I couldn't help the giggle that bubbled up as I saw Jill's face go from surprise to something akin to anger.

"She isn't here alone. I'm standing right here with her," she said righteously.

Emily and I glanced at each other like two teens about to get chastised before we dissolved into a fit of giggles.

Damon looked down at Jill with a smirk. "I was hoping she would have a little more protection. You're a little too ... little, to be in charge of protecting anyone," he teased.

I watched Jill's eyes flare as she stepped up to the detective. "I'll show you little." She poked him in his impressive chest.

I started to get between them when I felt hands go around my waist hauling me back. I knew who it was immediately and let him take me to have his wicked way. "That looks like it could go nuclear at any moment, best to stay away before it blows," Reid said right into my ear.

I felt him move his hands down closer to my thighs as he started to sway to the music. Grinding himself into my bottom. I loved the feel of his hands roaming my body. I turned my head so my cheek was resting against his chest as I lifted my arms to thrust my fingers into his blond locks.

I looked over to Emily only to see her back away from me with a little grin and wave. She flowed into the sea of dancing bodies, letting the music take her.

Nobody paid attention to us on the dance floor. They were all too busy immersing themselves in the music. I had my eyes closed as I seductively rolled my hips into Reid's groin. I felt another body come in front of me.

Keeping my eyes closed, I smiled as I felt Heath's hands join Reid's in exploration. "I got tired of watching and decided I needed to touch you too, sweetheart," Heath said against my lips. His tongue started a delicate dance against me as he took his time devouring my mouth. He didn't let up when I felt Reid's fingers find their way into the slit of my dress.

My breath hitched when he touched my naked flesh. He groaned into my ear as he ground his erection into my rear. "You naughty little minx, you don't have any panties on."

I huffed a laugh. "I was told I wasn't allowed any and I always do as I am told."

Reid wasn't talking to me now. "If we don't get her home soon, I am going to go lock us in your office and fuck her on your desk," he threatened.

That didn't sound like a bad idea to me as I pushed back into Reid's cock again. I watched as his eyes flared, and he looked dangerously close to doing just that. Heath took my hand and started tugging me to the door.

I looked back, trying to find Jill. "We can't leave without telling Jill, she'll worry."

Heath stopped and pointed to a very not-worried Jill. She was up against a nearby wall with a six-foot-something Latino pinning her down, devouring her mouth.

My mouth made an *O* shape as I took in the scene before me. Jill had her hands playing in his hair, holding on for dear life. He had his body hard against hers with one hand behind her and the other firmly against her ribs under her breast. Detective Damon proved that he could calm Jill's beast just fine as I got just a hint of tongue before it was thrust into her mouth.

I never knew watching someone kiss could turn me on, but I learned that it was doing just that right now.

"I think she'll be fine. Let's go," Reid said, pushing me toward the door.

The ride back to our apartment seemed to take no time at all as I mauled Heath in the passenger seat while Reid drove. He pulled me onto his lap to straddle him, and his hands pushed my dress up my hips so I was completely exposed to both of them.

He held two fingers up to my mouth for me in a silent command. I brought them in and sucked hard before I swirled my tongue around them. He groaned before he pulled them out and placed them on my puckered asshole.

My breath left me in a rush as he sank them in knuckle deep while his other hand gripped the back of my neck, keeping me in place. I heard Reid groan from the driver's seat as he reached over to pull one of my breasts out of my dress to pinch my nipple, eliciting a deep moan from me. He continued to punish my nipple as Heath slowly dragged his fingers out before sinking them back in, deeper this time.

He brought his mouth to mine. "I am going to fuck this tight hole tonight, sweetheart. What do you think about that?" he whispered against my kiss-swollen lips. I sealed my lips to his in a hungry kiss, letting that be my answer.

I was just about to take him out of his jeans to fuck him right in the truck when Reid slammed into *park* and grabbed me out of the vehicle. He righted my dress before carrying me to the front door.

Before I could blink, we were all fumbling around in the elevator on the ride up. Reid was obviously at the end of his rope as he shoved me to the wall, lifting my legs in the process. "You like teasing us? Making us watch you dance like a vixen?" he asked between kisses.

He pushed my dress up just enough to get his hand between us. I gasped as he shoved his fingers inside of me roughly. "I can tell you like to be a little tease, bunny. You're soaking my fucking hand."

He held me in his stare as he removed his fingers to suck them into his mouth. He rolled his eyes back as he tasted me, making me quiver at the sight.

Before he could put his fingers back into me, Heath took his place. "You remember the first night we met, sweetheart? I wanted to fuck you right here, just like this," he said as he pulled me to him, rubbing himself against my sex. I was basically dripping with arousal, so I was sure we were making a mess of the front of his jeans.

I groaned in frustration as the elevator dinged at our level. Heath chuckled against my lips. "One day soon I am going to do just that, don't you worry," he promised.

They were tugging me out of the elevator and toward their door the next minute. I was so absorbed in my naughty thoughts I didn't notice that Reid had come to a complete stop in front of me. I slammed into his back, causing me to almost fall on my ass. Heath steadied me as I got a look at what they were staring at.

All of my arousal left my body in a rush as I paled and immediately sobered at the sight of my front door. It had been forcefully kicked in, and the intruder didn't seem to care enough to close it on their way out.

Hot tears sprung to my eyes. Before I could think better, I ran for the door, avoiding the outstretched hands trying to stop me.

A sob escaped my mouth as I looked at the scene that was my apartment. Everything was completely trashed. All my dishes were shattered on the floor. My tables were upturned. My pictures on the wall looked like someone had punched the glass out of them. There were deep slashes on my couch, and the TV was busted.

I bet if I went to my bedroom I would find the

bed that Heath and Reid had bought me slashed up as well. I tried to grab the door frame to steady myself but fumbled. Heath was there to catch me as I fell.

I could hear Reid standing behind us as he talked to 911. My tears were openly falling, and I didn't even try to quiet myself. Everything I had saved for was in this apartment.

The last of my independence was attached to this place and these things. Tom had yet again taken something precious from me. I shook off Heath's grasp as I bolted to the bathroom. I was going to be sick. I barely made it to the toilet before I emptied my stomach.

I heard Heath's curse as he came to me. He held my hair away from my face and rubbed my back as I finished heaving. "It's going to be okay, baby. We are going to find that fucker and we'll make sure he pays." Heath promised as he helped me stand.

Standing on wobbly legs, I walked to the sink to rinse my mouth out. That was when I saw the bold writing on the mirror. *FUCKING WHORE!!!* was written in angry red letters, covering the expanse of my mirror.

Another sob escaped my lips as I read the words. Heath tried to lead me out of the bathroom as Reid made his way in. He was off the phone now as he took in Tom's message. I watched his face go from worried to filled with white-hot rage before he lashed out. He punched the mirror, shattering it.

When he faced me, the look of worry crossed his eyes again. His knuckles dripped blood to the floor from where he had split them. Without thinking, I grabbed a clean towel from the cabinet and wrapped it around his hand.

When I was done, he gathered me into his arms before he brushed my hair down my back with his uninjured hand. I knew he was talking to Heath when he spoke. "He better hope the cops catch him before I do. I'm going to fucking kill him," he promised in an eerily calm tone.

The boys both ushered me to their apartment where we waited for the police. When they arrived, they asked their questions while taking pictures of the crime scene. I answered them on autopilot. I could hear how dull my own voice sounded as I spoke, but I couldn't find the will to care.

I almost laughed at the thought of my apartment being an active crime scene. When did my life become so ridiculous? I could see the boys looking at me with concern in their eyes.

I looked away from their gazes which only served to feed into my guilt. Once again, I felt that they would get tired of me soon with all of the baggage that I toted around with me. Maybe it would be better for everyone involved if they just ended it with me now. Now was the time to end their headache.

I started to walk far enough away from them so they couldn't touch me. If they were touching me, I wouldn't be able to do what needed to be done.

Before I could speak one word, Heath hushed me. "Whatever you're about to say should be kept to yourself. We have all had a long night and nothing needs to be discussed tonight. Let's just all go to bed, and we can talk in the morning."

*And that is final*, was what he didn't say. I let them lead me to the bedroom and undress me. We all lay under the blanket, and I let them hold me. I could let myself feel one more night of their comfort but that was it. I had promised myself I would end things with them if I couldn't put a stop to this Tom drama. Tonight just proved what needed to happen.

## Chapter Twenty-One

I woke the next morning the same way I'd fallen asleep. Wrapped in a cocoon of limbs and still wracked with guilt. I looked around the room, gathering that it was still rather early. There was just the faintest light coming in through the window. I could barely see their faces.

I lay there and watched them sleep for the longest time, contemplating what needed to be done. Blinking away my tears that threatened to fall as my chest constricted with unhashed emotion.

I couldn't do this to them anymore. They deserved to be with someone who was whole. Someone who didn't need so much work. I just wished I would have had the guts to do this weeks ago before my heart got involved.

It was no longer a question of if I was falling for them. I fell a long time ago and I just hadn't admitted it to myself. I loved them so much that sometimes it was hard to breathe. And that was why I needed to end things with them. They needed someone they could build a life with. Not someone who had a crazy stalker ex they had to protect against.

I tried to shimmy my way to the end of the bed. I was a coward and didn't want to face them just yet. If I did, I knew I would have burst into tears while trying to explain why I was no good for them.

I needed to find my phone and call Jill. She would come to get me, and I could stay with her while the cops dealt with Tom. Even if my apartment wasn't completely trashed, I wouldn't be able to stay there anymore. I couldn't deal with being so close to Reid and Heath. Being that close and not being with them would hurt too much.

I should have known trying to get out from between them wouldn't work. I made it probably a foot down the bed when I felt strong hands haul me back up. Coming face-to-face with amber eyes and a sleepy grin. "Where do you think you're going, bunny?" Reid asked. His voice was thick with sleep.

I was trying to come up with an excuse when I felt two more hands grab me and pull me back to a hard body. "Mmmm, you feel so good and soft this morning, sweetheart," Heath murmured against my neck, kissing his way up to my ear. Reid took his advantage and nuzzled closer, effectively sandwiching me in between them.

I could feel both of them hardening and lengthening against me as their hands roamed. Heath let his hand wander further down until he was tracing my belly button. Sliding further down with every pass. I could feel myself getting wet, preparing for them.

Reid rubbed his cock against my mound as he grabbed my cheeks with one big hand, forcing me to look at him. "I asked you a question, bunny," was all he said as he stared at me with a hooded gaze.

Heath's fingers were just about to touch my throbbing nub when I opened my mouth to speak. "I-I was going to get my phone and call Jill," I said, hoping that would be answer enough.

I felt my adrenaline spike as Reid continued to stare at me before he tweaked my nipple, hard. My yelp turned into a moan as the hurt turned to heat and Heath's middle finger pushed down on the bundle of nerves at my core.

"Why would you need to call Jill this early? Whatever the reason, it could have waited until later." Reid squinted his eyes at me in suspension.

My mind was so fuzzy right now with what Heath's fingers were doing to me as he pushed his erection against my ass. It was so hard to concentrate on what I needed to do.

"I was going t-to have her come get me so I c-could stay with her for a while," I finally managed o say. All at once, they both stopped moving.

I closed my mouth and tried to push up. Heath only tightened his grip and Reid glared at me. "Now why would you do that? We said we are going to take care of you while everything gets straightened out. Do you not think we're capable of keeping you safe, Kate?"

He looked pissed as I tried to explain. "N-no I know you can keep me safe. It's just that... I feel like..." How could I say this without making them feel bad?

Heath leaned down and spoke right against my ear, sending shivers down my spine. "It's just what? Do you not trust us?" he accused.

"It's not that at all!" I nearly yelled. "I just think you guys deserve to be with someone who doesn't have so much damn baggage to carry around. You guys don't need me in your life, making shit more complicated. It's not fair to you. Maybe we should just cut ties before this gets any more serious."

Heath laughed humorlessly and rolled onto his back, taking me with him so my back was pressed firmly to his front. He hooked his feet around my ankles, spreading my legs wide in a familiar position. Reid came to lie on top of me, making a space for himself between our legs.

He looked down at me with dark eyes. More aggravated now that I had explained myself. "What gives you the right to tell us what we need before even talking to us? How is it that you think deciding to leave us is fair?" He growled.

Heath's hands were back to roaming now as he grabbed my breasts, pinching and rolling as he went. Bringing me to the point where pain turned to pleasure. I bit back a moan as Reid slammed his mouth down on mine, forcing his tongue inside, demanding mine move with his.

When he pulled back, he spread my legs further apart and slapped me lightly on my clit before shoving his fingers inside, pulling a short scream from me. "You want to know what I need, Kate? I need you, every fucking day. You're all I can think about. I know Heath thinks the same way I do. We're so goddamn crazy about you. You belong to us, and you're not going anywhere. Do you hear me? I don't give a shit about your baggage. It's all ours now, so you may as well accept it."

He didn't even give me a chance to respond as he lined up his big cock and slammed into my wet depths. His thrust was so powerful that if Heath hadn't been holding me, I would have slid up the bed.

I cried out as he kept up his grueling pace as Heath pushed his fingers between Reid and me, rubbing my clit. He grabbed my throat with his other hand, holding me still for Reid to use as he saw fit.

I couldn't escape now even if I wanted to as Reid kept up his ruthless pounding between my legs. Digging my nails into Heath's sides, not stopping the scream that ripped from my throat, I held on for dear life.

Reid threw my legs over his shoulders and leaned back. The position made his cock rub against my G-spot. He obviously had some residual anger riding him from last night, I realized, as he slammed in and out over and over again.

"You like the way he fucks that little cunt, sweetheart? He wants to feel you come around his cock." Heath hissed against my ear as he pinched my clit, rolling it between his fingers.

My muscles convulsed as I shattered under their ministrations. A fresh cascade of arousal flooded my pussy as I clamped down on Reid like a vise.

He kept his pace with a deep groan. "You think you can just walk away from this, bunny?" Reid panted.

Before I wanted him to, he pulled out with a slap on my outer thigh. The sight of his cock wet from my release made me hotter.

"We're going to mark you as ours today. Roll over and ride Heath's cock, now," he commanded with a little more bite to his tone. I scrambled up and straddled Heath's hips. Before I could line him up and seat myself on top of him, Heath pulled me in and kissed me senseless.

"Reid's right, Kate, we're crazy about you. I don't think we could let you go at this point, even if it was the best thing for you." He stared into my eyes, letting me see all of his emotions. I felt tears pricking the back of my eyes before I looked away from his searing gaze.

Rising, I guided him into me and then sat completely onto his hard length. His abdomen clenched as he grabbed my hips and held me to him. I was so full it was hard to breathe. I rose up and let myself sink back down. Starting my rise again, I felt hands holding my hips down, halting my accent.

"Not so fast, I need you to take Heath as far in as you can and lean against his chest," Reid said from behind me. Before I could do anything, he slid his hand around my front and placed something cold against my clitoris. Turning my head to face him, he took my mouth again as Heath fondled my breasts.

With a click, the toy Reid had placed against my clit started to vibrate. I moaned and started to grind against Heath's cock and Reid's toy. With a slight push on my back from Reid, I did as he asked, lying against Heath's chest, the position holding the vibe in place and making my ass very vulnerable. I wouldn't be lasting long with the vibrations coming from the toy.

Heath started to move his hips, slowly spearing me from the bottom. I brought my hands to his silky black locks and pulled, getting a deep groan from him in return. He wasn't moving fast enough for me, so I started to move on top of him to get the friction I wanted. The movement earned me a sharp slap on my ass, pulling a yelp from me.

"You hold still and let Heath do all the work down there, while I do the work up here." Reid started to push something cold into my ass.

I panted wildly at the feeling of Heath's slow torture, the vibe at my clit, and the plug getting further in my ass. I couldn't help myself as I pushed back toward Reid, earning me another loud smack. I didn't yelp that time. No, the heat from his hand on my ass spurred me on, dragging a long moan from my mouth. I wanted more.

It was Heath's turn to groan from underneath me. "Fuck, she is soaked and she clenches down on me with each slap on her ass."

This time the smack came from Heath as he pushed deeper into me. "Yes!" I managed to say in between labored pants.

They found a steady rhythm that was driving me crazy. Heath was still fucking me slowly, each upward thrust bringing the vibe harder onto my clit. Every time he would pull away, Reid would push the plug deeper into me. It was bigger than the others I was used to, so it took me longer to adjust.

In between all of this, they would alternate their

slaps on my ass. Driving me higher and higher. I could see stars behind my eyes as I pulled at Heath's hair, demanding silently they give me what I needed.

It was all too much when they both pushed in at the same time and I came hard. I couldn't stop my hips as they ground down onto Heath, riding out my orgasm. When I was shaking and about to collapse, Heath pulled me up his body. "Turn around and face Reid. Suck his cock while you ride my face," he ordered.

I turned to do his bidding, and he didn't wait for me to sit. He grabbed my hips and pulled them down to his waiting mouth. I screamed as he ate my pussy like I was his favorite meal.

Reid wasted no time. He was up on his knees, between Heath's spread legs, stroking himself. I was already close to coming again when he pulled my head forward and pushed himself between my lips.

I was moaning so loudly around his cock, I knew he could feel it vibrating up his length as he fucked my mouth. I grabbed Heath's cock and started to stroke it just like I knew he liked it, hard and fast. He pulled me down hard with a groan I felt in my womb as he thrust his tongue inside of me. I nearly screamed as I came against his mouth. He didn't let up, pulling me further down as I stroked harder and sucked longer. Rolling me into another orgasm.

Reid reached the back of my throat and held himself there for a moment with a long groan as I swallowed around him. "That's my good girl, swallow that fucking cock." He growled as he fucked my throat in short, fast passes. My pride swelled as I swallowed again, trying to hold him there.

He pulled away suddenly, taking me with him and kissing me on the way down. "We're both going to take you now, Kate. You are going to ride on top of me while Heath fucks that tight ass of yours." He growled against my swollen lips.

I was sliding down his length as Heath came up behind me, slowly removing the plug. It had done its job and was no longer needed.

I become nervous at the prospect of taking them both. Reid pulled me down to his chest and kissed me tenderly this time, rubbing his hands down my back, cupping my rear. "Relax, we'll go nice and slow until you are used to the feeling." He soothed me.

Holding me steady, he started to spear into me as Heath pushed himself against my puckered hole. He had taken the time to lube himself up to make this the most pleasant experience he could. I tried to relax and push back against him, letting him in a little further. I groaned deep in my chest as his head breached my entrance. "Fuck, she is going to squeeze the life out of me," Heath rasped with a broken voice.

I raised just enough to put my hands on either side of Reid's head. He took that opportunity to grab my breasts. Pulling one tight nipple into his mouth and pinching the other, lighting me up.

Heath was gaining ground with each little thrust, and I was panting loudly now. I knew Heath was only halfway in at this point. I felt the sweat running down my spine as my body strained to take both of them. "I don't know if I can take much more!" I exclaimed between clenched teeth.

Reid reached over and grabbed the vibe, setting it back against my clit. "Yes, you can, Kate. You were built to take us. Now, relax and let him in." He growled before he grabbed the fleshy part of my hips, squeezing me. I didn't know how he made such a harsh command sound so loving.

They found a good rhythm as they both fucked in

short strokes. The vibe did its job of getting me ready for release again. Finally, I could feel Heath completely seat himself inside of me.

They both held still, letting me adjust. I tried to calm my breathing and get used to the feeling of being so full. Heath was rubbing his hands up and down my back and into my hair. Lightly tugging it before he moved on. Reid's hands were clenching and releasing restlessly on my thighs now. I could see the sweat gathering along his brow from the restraint he held on himself.

"We are going to start moving now, bunny. You just hold on to me and we will take care of you," Reid gritted out between clenched teeth.

I could hear Heath panting behind me as one hand settled in my hair and the other on my hip. He pulled out, and I felt every nerve I didn't even know existed, light up. "Fuck, this isn't going to last long. I can feel Reid's cock dragging along mine inside of you." Heath hissed as he started to push back in as Reid pulled out. They were slow at first, trying to find a steady pace.

I felt myself finally relax fully and let them move me the way they needed to. It wasn't long before I was screaming my pleasure between them. They were moving fast and hard as Reid ramped up the vibe, adding one more step to the mix that had me tumbling over the edge again with a strangled moan. I could feel how wet I had gotten—it was coating the inside of my thighs and making it easier for Reid to glide in and out.

The sound of wet skin slapping together drove me higher and higher. Reid grabbed the vibe and threw it off the bed, preferring to use his fingers this time. He thumbed my nub, grabbed my throat, and looked into my eyes.

"You like being filled up don't you, bunny? Know this, we have officially branded you as ours. This is our pussy. This is our ass. We will do what we see fit with it. You are not allowed to leave us. Now, fucking come again like the good girl I know you are. Now, Kate!" he commanded with a growl.

I erupted, screaming their names, grabbing on to anything I could get my hands on as I clamped down.

"Oh fuck! I'm gonna come!" Heath roared as he gripped my hair harder, tugging me back against his chest.

"I'm right there with you!" Reid groaned as his abs flexed under my fingers. He squeezed my throat and held me tight as he came with a long, strained grunt.

Heath's strokes became erratic as he slammed fully into my ass, flooding me with his release. It was all too much, and I chased them into oblivion as I came one last time.

We all fell down on top of one another in a heap. I was boneless as they arranged me between them. I was facing Heath as Reid kissed my shoulder and rubbed my side. Heath dragged my leg up and over his hip, bringing us closer together. We lay there as the sun finally came up, just touching each other.

They took their time as they rubbed my body all over and told me how well I did. They told me how much they appreciate me and how much they don't want to be without me. It was right there on the tip of my tongue to tell them how I truly felt about them, but I kept my mouth shut. Was it too soon for proclamations of love? I closed my eyes and just relaxed back into them. Completely spent and satisfied, I dozed off between them.

## Chapter Twenty-Two

After the next few days, it felt like everything had settled between the three of us. I thought our relationship was fine before, but now somehow it felt more solid. They hadn't spoken the words when they made love to me, but they had shown me with their bodies how much they loved me every day. I knew that the amount of time they had put into taking care of me should have been enough to make me realize they were committed wholeheartedly. But it wasn't until we were all connected that I truly felt it.

After my life-altering sexual experience, Damon called to make sure I was doing okay. I was still pretty shaken up, but Heath and Reid had helped settle me with their affections. Damon told me that he had spoken to his captain, and it was decided that they would keep a cruiser outside my office building while I was at work. When I was home, the boys would take it from there. There still hadn't been any sightings of Tom.

I'd started to feel like this was just going to be my new normal from now on. The thought was unsettling, to say the least. I called Jill and let her know what had happened. I was shocked when she didn't lose her shit. She was surprisingly calm as she talked to me, and her voice held sympathy in place of her normal anger at the situation.

My apartment had been released back to me on Monday after the police got everything they needed. I'd called Sam to explain what was happening, and she had told me to take as much time as I needed to sort things out. I truly was lucky to have such an understanding boss.

My landlord, Rick, had called me and expressed

his deepest sympathies for what had happened. I thought it was his way of trying to avoid a lawsuit for not ensuring the complex was completely locked down to those who didn't live here.

Reid had not been happy when I accepted his apology. He had taken the phone out of my hand and promptly given Rick a very vulgar tongue-lashing. By the end of the call, he'd made it known that he could lease my apartment out again, as I would not be returning. Reid even told him that when their lease was up they would not be signing a new one as well.

When he looked back at me there was no remorse in his eyes. Reid and I had gone toe to toe after that. I may let him dominate me completely in the bedroom, but I would be damned if I let him rule my life outside of that.

"Why would you do that?" I'd screamed. "I still need a place to live after all this is over!" I could feel the familiar burn of unshed tears as they brimmed my eyes.

"If you think for one minute that I'd let you stay in a place where you're not safe, then you have a lot to learn, bunny," Reid had replied dryly.

His absolute calmness with me had driven me up the wall. I needed to fight at that moment.

I laughed but there was no humor in the sound. "Okay, Reid, would you like to enlighten me then? Just what the hell am I supposed to do? Where am I going to live? You can't just make that decision without speaking to me first."

"If the choice of your safety is involved, then no, I don't need to discuss it with you. You obviously don't see yourself as valuable enough to fight for. Otherwise, you wouldn't have let Rick's indiscretion go so easily. I will *not* allow you to be mistreated by anyone!" He growled my way.

The argument had only escalated to the point where Reid had finally had enough. He'd hauled me over his shoulder and marched my ass to the bedroom where I was promptly tied up and received a literal and erotic tongue lashing. He informed me that we would all be looking for a new place together as he slid deep inside of me.

My chest still ached at his words that swelled with his unspoken emotions.

"I can't go back to living without you, bunny," he'd whispered to me with his forehead against mine.

I may have acted like I wanted my own place, but I would be lying to myself if I thought I could be away from them. They had snuck their way into my life, digging their claws in deep, and I loved it.

We spent the day cleaning up what remained of my belongings after that. Heath had shown up shortly after we started and helped haul my ruined furniture to the dumpster.

It was a very emotional day for me. This apartment was my first step to independence, and I hated that Tom had ruined that for me. By the time we were done cleaning up, I only had a few boxes of belongings that hadn't been ruined. We moved my things into what was now the boys' spare bedroom.

I tried to go back to work the next day, much to Heath and Reid's displeasure. To my surprise, it wasn't Reid and me who butted heads like usual. Instead, it was Heath and me who had gotten into it.

"I think you need another day to process what's happened," Heath had calmly said.

"And just what am I supposed to do? Sit and dwell on how my life has been flipped upside down?" I argued. I couldn't just do nothing.

"I didn't say that!" he yelled as he ran his hand

through his hair in a frustrated motion before pinching the bridge of his nose. It was almost like he was trying to stop himself from losing his temper with me. "But it would be nice for not only you but for all of us to be able to just take a day and fucking breath for once." He'd almost seemed to be pleading with me. "All I can do when you're away from me is fret and worry that something's going to happen to you," he admitted in a hushed tone.

If I hadn't needed to cling to my anger at that moment, I would have heard what he was trying to say to me.

"And then what? If you haven't noticed, they still haven't caught Tom. I could give you another day to just cope with this shitshow, but we're just going to have to deal with it again the day after that. None of this is going to go away until they catch him, and in the meantime, I need to work! I *need* to have my independence back!" I'd all but screamed.

"I'm trying to make sure you have what you need but it's impossible to do when you aren't safe to be without us," he'd gritted behind clenched teeth.

I opened my mouth to say something I'd surely regret when Reid pulled me aside as Heath left the room to cool down.

Reid tried to calm me like one would a feral cat with his soothing touch. He explained, "This is just as hard on Heath and me as it was on you." He almost seemed to growl at me. "Heath sees himself as one of your protectors and he can't safeguard you when you're not with us. You're bound and determined to get your freedom back and I get it, I really do. But think about where that puts us. We get to sit back and hope that nothing happens to you while you're away from us. Do you understand how that feels? To be completely and utterly vulnerable to the whims of a psychopath that has a vendetta against the woman we—"

I sucked in a harsh breath and my heart squeezed as he paused, looking away from me for a moment. He clenched his jaw before continuing "We care about you too much to have anything happen to you." He smiled softly at me before caressing my cheek lovingly.

Feeling lower than dirt, I dejectedly looked down the hallway where Heath had disappeared. I'd been so busy wrapped up in my own emotions, I hadn't even stopped to think about how this might be affecting their feelings. For two men who needed to be in control, to have none in this situation would be a hard pill to swallow.

I grabbed Reid's hand and led him to the bedroom to find Heath sitting on the bed with his head in his hands. The sight of him in obvious distress nearly had me undone.

I forced my way onto his lap. When he looked up at me, I could see all the unspoken words and emotions rolling around in those emerald eyes.

Grabbing Reid's hand, I pulled him until he caressed my back with his front.

"I'm sorry," I whispered as I grazed my lips against Heath's. "I understand where you're coming from and I'm sorry," I said again as emotion clogged my throat. "I'll give it one more day before I go back to work, but I can't give that part of myself up permanently. I need to be able to have some independence in my life otherwise I'll start to feel trapped all over again."

Heath's eyes sparkled with relief. The joy I saw in both of them was more than enough reason for me to stay home that day. It wasn't long after and we were all tangled together finding our bliss.

We spent the rest of the day in bed enjoying each

other. Only leaving our room to use the restroom and grab food. We made love multiple times with intervals of napping, touching, laughing, and talking in hushed tones.

Going back to reality came all too early the next day. Heath had driven me to work like usual. He waved at the police cruiser in the parking lot on his way past. After parking, he walked me to my desk. Before he left, he pulled me to him and gave me one of those fight-for-your-life kisses. The type of kisses that made me a little dumb when I finally came up for air.

He made me promise that I would call him if I needed anything today. "Are you sure you don't need me to bring you lunch?" Heath asked, obviously looking for an excuse to come back and see me.

A warm smile came over my lips at his attempt. I shook my head and told him I would eat with Jill today. I wanted to find out if she had gotten into a certain cop's pants yet.

He gave me a playful grin before kissing me one last time. When he pulled away, he had a look in his eyes like he wanted to say more but he refrained. He left with the promise to see me later tonight.

I didn't realize Sam was standing in her doorway as I watched Heath leave. I nearly jumped out of my skin when she greeted me with a cheery, "Good morning!" She raised her eyebrows and her head tilted toward me. She had certainly seen Heath's and my intimate goodbye.

Clutching my chest, I nodded at her and returned the sentiment. She grinned at me. "I have to say I'm quite jealous of you, Kate, you have one fine piece of man there. And the way he looks at you." She fanned herself for emphasis.

I couldn't keep the smile from my lips as I felt my cheeks flush. I didn't fill her in that my other man was just as hot as this one. I cleared my throat before I spoke.

"Thank you for giving me time off. It really helped a lot," I admitted.

She waved me off like it was nothing. "Well, if you're ready to get this day started, grab your tablet and come on in when you're ready," she said with a smile as she turned, walking back into her office. I shook my head to clear the remainder of the lust trapped there. Grabbing my tablet I followed her, ready to take on the day.

## Chapter Twenty-Three

"Oh, I love you so much!" Jill exclaimed as I walked into her office carrying takeout bags from our favorite Mexican place. She was holding her arms out in a give-me motion as I laughed and handed her the food. "You have no idea how much I've been craving their queso. I am so glad they deliver." She squealed as she opened her box.

I giggled and couldn't help myself. "You wouldn't happen to be craving this food because of a certain Latino's attention, would you?" I said with a wiggle of my brows.

I think out of all the years I have known Jill Brookes, I had never seen her blush. Not even when she got her period in history class and bled through her pants. When one of the boys in class started laughing at her, she simply turned around, punched him in the nose, and said, "Now we are both bleeding, you dickhead?" No way would she blush and get embarrassed by something so silly.

That changed today, as she flushed bright red before she choked on her bite of quesadilla.

I sucked in a startled breath as I stood up and patted her back as she coughed and sputtered. She put her fork down as she cleared her throat, giving me a self-deprecating smile. "I don't know what you're talking about."

I raised an eyebrow at her. "You do realize that I was there the night you guys were basically fucking against the wall in the bar, right?" I laughed as she reddened even further.

"You saw that, did you?" she asked with an embarrassed smile.

It was so fun to tease her. I had never seen Jill as flustered as she was right then. "So, are you going to give me all of the dirty details or not?" I asked with a secret smile.

Jill looked down at her food while she ate a few bites. When I thought she wasn't going to tell me anything, she finally broke.

"That man is so annoying! He doesn't back down to me like most people do and I don't know how to take it. He's so goddamn stubborn. I was in the middle of ripping him a new one, and then he just kissed me. Can you believe the nerve?"

She was talking so fast I didn't even think she stopped to breathe. "I tried to push him away but then he just manhandled me until he had me pushed against the wall. He just picked me up like I weighed nothing. I was stuck between a rock and a hard place, and he was the hard place. Nobody has ever had the balls to treat me like that." She huffed as she took an angry bite of her chips and queso.

She chewed fiercely before she released a pent-up breath as she looked at me again. "I have never been so turned on in my life, Kate," she admitted as she threw her head back against her chair with a sigh.

I gave her an encouraging smile as I chuckled. "I know the feeling well."

She shook her head. "I mean it. The way he pushed his hard body against me and just demanded that I kiss him back did things to me. Things that had me wanting to drop to my knees and beg him to touch me. I wanted to give over to him and let him take control, Kate." Her face reddened again at the confession. I was taken aback slightly.

Jill may look like someone who doesn't have a care in the world, but I knew she had some dark shit in her past. She didn't like to talk about it, but I was there to help her pick up the pieces all those years ago. She had ruled her life with an iron fist since that day, never allowing herself to be out of control again. I loved her to death, but Jill was a tough bitch. If she was willing to give up her control, I knew it was serious.

I regarded her seriously for a moment. I knew she wouldn't want to talk about him, but I had to ask her anyway. "Do you need to talk about it? He didn't bring up memories of Jason, did he?"

She flinched at the mention of his name.

"If you want him to leave you alone, I'll have Reid talk to him."

She swallowed hard and shook her head. "No, this felt different. I know I haven't known Detective Santos for that long, but I'm almost certain he wouldn't hurt me. Not physically, anyway. I would bet he would know how to please a woman with what he has packin' though. I felt something long and hard as he pushed me against the wall. I don't think it was his standard issue I felt against my belly." She was trying to steer the conversation back away from the darkness of her past now.

It was obvious she didn't want to go down that road again, diverting me with humor. "You know, you might have better luck getting laid if you call him Damon and not Detective Santos," I said, earning me a snort from Jill.

"Yeah, he told me to call him Damon, but I like the way his eyes flare when I refuse to call him by his first name," she said before we both dissolved into a fit of giggles.

"Wait, back up," I managed around my laughs, "you mean to tell me that you didn't find out what type of hardware he is working with? I figured you took him to your fuckpad after the bar," referring to her hotel room she kept reserved specifically for her one-night-stands.

"No, he got called out shortly after you left the bar. I think he ended up at your apartment to look around," she said around a big bite of food.

Now it was my turn to flush. "I'm so sorry. I didn't want to ruin your night too." I could feel my eyes start to burn slightly. The reality of what Tom was doing to not only my life but others' too, sat like a lump in my gut.

Jill shook her copper-haired head and scowled at me. "Don't. Don't you dare apologize for what that fucker is doing to you. None of this is your fault. If I would have known that he was going to treat you like this, I would have helped your dad drag you out of there kicking and screaming years ago."

Thinking of my dad always left a pang of hurt in my chest. I still missed him every day. "I wished I would have listened to him all those years ago," I said with a sad smile. We sat there in silence for a while, both consumed by our own thoughts.

I couldn't help but wish that my dad was still around. He passed away right after Lindsey turned thirteen. I was almost sure he would know what to do in this situation. My dad had treated me like his princess and I knew that he'd expected Tom to do the same.

Though Tom never treated me the way he should have, he was never hateful. He was unpassionate more than anything else. Like I didn't really matter to him. Which still begged the question as to why he was acting this passionately now. I knew his business was gone and he was in trouble with the law, but that still didn't answer why he was seeking me out now. Like I owed him something.

Shaking off the thought, I looked back up at Jill

with a small smile. "Anyway, enough dwelling in the past. When are you going to see Damon again?" I asked expectantly.

Jill smiled back at me. "I don't know if that is such a good idea. You know me, I like to flirt and have fun and not be tied down. And that man has 'serious' written all over him." She tried to give me a bright smile, but I could tell it was fake.

I nodded and dropped it. I could tell she was done with the subject. At the end of the day, I just wanted to see my friend happy, but I couldn't help thinking that maybe her future was staring her in the face and she would just be too damn stubborn to notice it.

We finished our lunch over small talk. On my way back to my desk, I glanced out the window and saw the police cruiser still sitting in the spot they had occupied that morning. Giving them a small wave, I got back to work.

The rest of the day seemed to fly as I worked on some of the projects Sam had given me. She had taken my simple job of answering phones and upped the ante lately by giving me more manuscripts to proofread. I felt pride surge through me with each new assignment she gave me.

Shortly before three o'clock, my cell phone rang and I looked down to see a familiar face. I felt all my girl parts clench as his deep voice rumbled over the speaker pressed to my ear. "Hey, bunny, how's your day going?"

I smiled as I leaned back in my chair. "Hey, it's going well. I hadn't expected to hear from you so soon. Are you missing me already?" I asked in a teasing voice. His answering chuckle sent goosebumps down my arms.

"I'm always missing you. I especially miss the way you moan in my ear when I am fucking that tight little pu—"

I sucked in a breath as I pulled the phone away from my ear and looked around my desk for anyone that could be listening.

I knew it was ridiculous to think anyone else would be able to hear my conversation. When I didn't say anything, Reid laughed again. "Did I render you speechless, bunny?" he asked.

I clenched my thighs together to stop the ache I felt rapidly building. Putting the phone back to my ear, I replied, "No." I could almost see his smile through my phone.

"I called to let you know that I'll be a little late to pick you up tonight."

I frowned at his words, feeling disappointment that surprised me.

"I have to stay a little later than normal tonight, but I'll make it up to you when we get home." I could hear the promise in his voice. "Is there any way Jill could sit with you until I get there? I know the cops will be watching the building, but I would feel better if someone stayed with you inside too. It should only be about thirty minutes later than normal."

I could tell he felt like he was letting me down, so I tried to reassure him. "Yeah, that's totally fine. I have some work I need to catch up on anyway." I tried to sound more upbeat than I felt. The silence stretched like he was trying to believe my words. "Really, it's okay, do what you need to do and then we can go home."

He sighed. "I'm sorry, bunny, I really will make it up to you. We can get takeout and watch some silly rom-com if you want. Maybe fool around on the couch during," he offered, bringing a smile to my face.

"That sounds wonderful, babe. I'll see you in a couple of hours."

We hung up the phone and I got back to work. I

didn't know when it happened, but I had gotten so used to our little schedule. Having it thrown off had me feeling off-kilter. I shook my head to clear my thoughts.

I was being ridiculous. It was only thirty minutes, and I could wait that long. Those boys had ramped up my expectations so much over the last month that I had a hard time dealing with not getting what I wanted when I wanted it, apparently.

About an hour later, people were starting to shut down their computers for the day when my cell rang again. I smiled, thinking it was Reid, but I was a little startled when I read *Detective Santos* across the screen instead.

"I call with good news, Ms. Hart. We finally got a hit on your ex-husband. His credit card was charged to a motel about twelve miles away from your apartment."

I felt a sigh of relief pass through me at the news. "Oh, thank God. What happens now?" I asked in a hopeful voice. I could feel my shoulders release some of the tension that had gathered there.

"Now, we go nail him. I already called the motel and spoke to the front desk clerk, and he confirmed that he checked Tom in himself, and he hasn't left the room since. I wanted you to know just in case you got worried when the cruiser we have outside of your building left. They're the closest ones to the motel, so they are going to head over and make sure he doesn't go anywhere before I can get there."

I looked out the nearest window, and sure enough, the squad car was backing out of the parking spot and turning its lights on. I smiled as I felt myself relax for the first time in days.

"Thank you so much, Damon. Let me know if you need anything else from me. I'm so glad this will finally be over."

Looking back from the window, I saw Jill walking my way with her purse in hand. I waved at her to come over.

"The pleasure is all mine. I look forward to putting this asshole behind bars."

We hung up, and I looked back up at Jill. "They found him!" I practically screamed. I winced as I looked around the office seeing that almost everyone was filing out now. The workday was over, but I couldn't leave yet. Even though they had caught Tom, Reid would still be furious if I left without him with me, just in case.

"Are you sure?" Jill looked at me with a smile that I was sure matched mine. "Where the hell is he?"

With all the enthusiasm I felt, I relayed the conversation I had just had with Damon. only pausing to say goodnight to Sam as she left. Soon we were the only ones left in the office.

"It's about damn time they catch his ass. I am so hooking you up with my lawyer now. We will make sure that man never sees the outside of a prison cell ever again," she said with a wicked smirk.

I just smiled back at her. There was no point in arguing with her, she would win. Truth was, I would let her pursue anything she wanted to at that moment. I was just happy to finally get my life back. I couldn't wait until Reid picked me up so I could tell him all about it. He and Heath would probably do a happy dance when I told them the news.

I started to put some of my files back away and clean up my desk. Reid would be here soon, and I wanted to be ready to go when he arrived.

Jill was rummaging through her purse when she put it down on my desk with a curse. "I must have forgotten my phone on my desk. I'm going to go to the bathroom and then go get it. I need to get my lawyer on the phone and start planning your lawsuit."

I rolled my eyes as she walked toward her office. Turning back around with the ridiculous smile still plastered on my face, I continued putting my files away. No more than thirty seconds had passed and I heard the click of Jill's heels coming back toward me.

"Did you realize your phone was in your pocket?" I said with a small chuckle.

I expected to hear Jill say something about losing her mind, but what I heard instead had my blood running cold. "No, sugar, I realized you were hiding something from me." A deep voice slurred, followed by the clicking noise of a gun being primed.

## Chapter Twenty-Four

There weren't a lot of things in this world that truly scared me. Sure, I had a healthy fear of some things, but being earth-shattering terrified? There weren't many instances.

One was when I was waiting on that pregnancy test at the tender age of sixteen. Five terrifying minutes before I realized my life was about to change forever.

Or when I found Jill lying in that bathtub, pale and almost lifeless all those years ago. There had been so much blood that day that I was sure that I had lost my best friend forever.

I had felt the cold slither of fear snake down my spine when my dad had gotten into the car accident that took him from this world. Getting that phone call from the hospital had been one of the scariest phone calls of my life. I would never forget the rush to get to the hospital to say my goodbyes before it was too late.

None of those past events compared to the fear that gripped my throat at the sight of my ex-husband pressing a loaded pistol to my best friend's temple while he sneered at me.

Tom looked terrible standing in front of me. His clothes were filthy like he hadn't changed out of them for days. I could smell his body odor from where he stood across from me. His eyes were bloodshot, making him look strung out. His nose and under his eyes were still black and blue from when Reid had broken his nose.

Jill looked at me with wild eyes. "Kate, get the fuck out of here." Her begging plea turned into a whimper when Tom pushed the pistol harder into the side of her head. I shook my head. She should know better than that. I wasn't about to leave her behind.

My phone rang, startling me. My heart felt like it would thunder out of my chest. I saw Detective Santos's name flashing across the screen. My hands shook as I tried to reach for it.

Tom kept his death grip on Jill, bruising her arm, as he pointed the gun my way. "Not so fast, sugar. Take your phone and throw it on the floor, shatter it. You won't need it where we're going."

I did as he asked but not before swiping my thumb across the screen, answering the call. Hoping I wouldn't break it completely, I threw it to the floor. If it still worked, then Damon might be able to hear what was happening.

Looking back up at Tom, I raised my hands in front of me. "Whatever you want, Tom. I'm sure we can work something out. You don't need to keep Jill here," I said in hopes that he would let her go.

He let out a humorless laugh as he brought the gun back to Jill's head. "Now why would I do that, Kate? She just ensures that you do as I tell you until I get what I want."

Jill gritted her teeth in pain as Tom tightened his grip. "How did you even get in here?"

I could tell by the way she cringed that his breath must have been rancid when he turned his face toward her to speak.

"I've been lingering in your bathroom since those cops left on the fake trail I led them on." He looked back at me now. "I have been trying to get you alone for days now, my wife. I figured that the cops were probably trying to track my credit card purchases. So, I bided my time. I watched you from afar. Never getting close enough to tip off those guys you have been fucking. You really have whored yourself, sugar. You've turned into such a slut since we separated, haven't you?" He scrunched up his nose like he was disgusted.

I didn't dignify him with an answer. Maybe his words would have hurt me before I met Reid and Heath, but not now. I didn't give a shit what people thought of me anymore, especially not him.

"I learned your schedule. I even watched your men. I figured the best time to make my move would be before the blond one came to pick you up in the evenings. So I figured out a way to stall him. His coworker found his tires slashed today, making him call in late, causing blondie to be late picking you up."

He tapped the gun to his temple before returning it to Jill's temple. I could plainly see that he had gone completely insane.

"I made a visit to a local motel. It wasn't hard to book a room and pay off the clerk to lie for me. If you give someone enough money, it's easy to get them to say whatever you want them to. That worked to lure your detail away and now here I am."

I couldn't stop the tears from leaking down my cheeks as he finished his story. "I don't understand what you want from me, Tom. I thought you were done with me, so I left. Just tell me what you want." I sobbed, my mind racing, trying to find a way out of this situation.

He practically growled at me. "I want my life back, you stupid bitch!"

I flinched as if he struck me.

"After you left, everything started to fall apart. I lost my business and that cunt left me right after I paid to have her tits done. I took a second loan out against the dealership for that surgery and then she just took off!" He was visibly shaking with rage, and I feared that his finger would pull that trigger by accident, taking my best friend away from me permanently.

I tried to step forward, getting closer. I needed to

get that gun away from him. "Tom, you can't think that any of what has happened is my fault." I tried to make him see reason.

He laughed again and twirled the barrel of his gun in Jill's hair. Tears were leaking from her eyes now.

"You know, I was okay when you left. I even started throwing your shit out immediately after you moved out. Vivian and I had a blast burning your shit and fucking in our bed. And then I started going through some of your important papers. Do you know what I found, Kate?"

I felt my eyes widen, and I started to shake with realization. I just figured out what he had wanted from me this whole time. How could I have been so oblivious?

He smiled cruelly at me. "Were you ever going to tell me that daddy left you $500,000 when he died?" He spat in my direction. "You got that money when we were still married. The way I see it, at least half that money is mine. I find it funny that he made sure to put it in an account that I couldn't even access. That old fucker never did like me, the feeling was mutual of course. And it only took one call to our old attorney to figure out that you never updated your will, sugar."

All the puzzle pieces fit together now. "So you're doing all of this for money? How are you planning on using the money when you're stuck in federal prison on charges of fraud, not to mention murder?" I took another step forward.

Before I could make it far, he stopped me by pointing the gun in my direction again. "That's for me to know and for you to, well, you won't be finding out because you'll be dead."

He leveled the gun at me, and I sucked my breath in, bracing myself for what was to come next.

Before he could pull the trigger, Jill jumped into

action. She pulled her arm forward and brought her fist down right on my ex's manhood.

The sudden attack on his favorite body part caused him to lose his grip on her. She pushed him as he doubled over in pain. She ran in my direction, screaming at me to run. She slammed into me, pushing me toward the door. It seemed so far away at that moment. I ran as fast as my legs would take me.

My hand was almost on the handle as my world exploded in gunfire. I couldn't comprehend what was happening as two shots were fired and then everything got quiet.

Jill's hand clenched in mine before it went lax. Looking back at her, I met her eyes as they widened before looking down at her chest. The front of her crisp white shirt blossomed with dark red. She swayed a bit, releasing a strangled breath before she lurched forward.

I caught her on the way down, both of us landing on the hardwood floor with a thud. I tried to push my shaking hands down onto her chest to stop the bleeding. "Oh, God!" I shuddered. There was so much blood.

In the back of my mind, I could hear somebody screaming, I didn't realize it was me until Tom came to stand in front of me. "Jill! It's okay, everything's going to be all right. Stay with me. You're okay, you're okay!"

My hands wouldn't stop trembling as I looked for something to stop the bleeding. I used my fingers to hold the wound, but the blood just kept pouring out.

She choked as she looked back up at me with terrified eyes. "Run," was all she managed as her eyes fluttered shut.

I tried to shake her, but it did me no good. "Jill!" I screamed, my tears blurring my vision.

Tom grabbed a fist full of my hair and hauled me up to my feet. I cried out as pain flared across my scalp.

He dragged me away from the door. Away from my friend who was surely dying.

I felt an unholy amount of anger surge as I tried to fight back. I was not going to go down without a fight this time. I had been a bystander in my own life for too long and I was finally ready to fight for myself.

I kicked out and struck him right in the knee. He stumbled a bit but kept his grip. "This will be much easier on both of us if you just hold the fuck still!" he yelled at me as he brought the gun down, slamming the barrel across my face.

Pain exploded across my cheek that had my vision dimming at the edges. I could already feel my eye starting to swell shut. I tried to remain standing, but I was finding the action hard.

"You shot Jill, you son of a bitch! How could you?" I screamed. "You aren't going to win. They'll hunt you down!" I let all the venom I felt running through my body out with my words.

I reached up and tried to claw his eyes out. A small victory when he let me go to hold his face. I tried running back to my desk to call 911, but he recovered too quickly and tackled me. The force of the fall caused my head to bounce off the floor.

Everything faded out for a moment. When I came to, the pounding in my head was nearly enough to make me pass out. I could taste blood in my mouth. I tried to roll over so I could crawl to my desk when Tom rolled me back over, coming down on top of me. I tried to fight him off but failed miserably. He easily picked up my torso and shook me violently, slamming my head into the ground once more.

Sharp pain bloomed across my skull again. Blackness threatened as I fought to stay conscious. He held my hands above my head with one of his as he brought the gun to under my chin, forcing me to look up at his bloody face. I may have felt a sense of accomplishment for causing his gaping wound if it hadn't been for my impending death.

"You stupid fucking bitch!" he spat at me. "If you would have not fought me this could have all been over by now! I was just going to have you transfer me the money. It wasn't supposed to be like this! I just wanted to scare you. But now you took away my choice. That bitch is dead! And now I have to kill you so you don't run to the cops. I'm not going to go down for this. I'm gonna kill you and then run."

I tried to buck him off as he moved the gun to my stomach. I guessed a quick painless death was too much to ask for.

For the third time that day, the gun went off, burying a bullet deep in my gut. I screamed in agony as pain ripped through my body. He let go of my hands as he sat up on top of me.

I grabbed the barrel of the gun still shoved to my belly and looked up at my attacker. The father of my child. The person I had shared a life with. I looked up at the man I once thought I loved with wide eyes. There was nothing of that man left in the eyes that stared back down at me.

My vision blurred again as I heard a loud yell of rage and Tom's weight was lifted off me. I turned my head to see Reid tackle him to the ground next to me.

The gun was flung across the room. I tried to crawl toward it but didn't make it far before my arms gave out on me. I was helpless as I lay and watched as one of my loves fought my would-be murderer.

I knew I was losing too much blood as my limbs started to go cold. My vision kept fading in and out as I watched Reid climb on top of Tom, pelting his face with savage blows. Tom's face was a bloody mess by the time Reid wrapped his hand around his throat, trying to squeeze the life out of him.

I could hear sirens now. I felt a little relief at the thought of someone helping Jill. I had the sinking feeling that I wasn't going to get to tell my boys how I felt about them. I loved them so much, and they would never even know. More tears brushed my skin as they escaped.

My vision blurred. It was like I was losing time with each blink, and it sounded like people were yelling at me through a tunnel.

Blink. Reid was about to kill Tom.

Blink. An officer was hauling Reid off of Tom.

Blink. Reid was above me begging me to open my eyes.

Blink. He was pushing on my stomach to stop the bleeding, yelling at me to stay awake.

Blink. Reid was being pulled away from me, screaming with tears in his eyes.

Blink. A strange man was pushing on my stomach saying something about my heart rate.

Blink. Tom was in handcuffs, staring at me with hatred in his eyes.

Blink. Now Heath was here, but a group of uniformed men was holding him back.

Blink. Heath was screaming at the men, trying to force his way through.

Blink. More sirens.

Blink. Darkness.

## Chapter Twenty-Five

What a lot of people didn't realize was that dying was the easiest thing they would ever do. After letting go, it was peaceful. Everything that led up to death was what hurt the most.

All the failures. As a mother, a wife, a friend. Failures were a part of life but that didn't make them any less painful.

All the heartache. Losing loved ones or being betrayed by the person who was supposed to love you the most in this world. Heartache cuts you soul-deep and would always leave a scar behind after it was over.

All the fighting. Forcing yourself to fight for your own happiness was also excruciating. It was much easier to just give up.

All of those things were agonizing.

Not to mention being shot, that shit hurt like a bitch.

But dying? It was like falling into the best sleep you've ever had. Coming back from the dead was also painful. This was a lesson I had to learn the hard way.

I heard the steady beep of the heart monitor before coming back to the land of the living. Trying to open my eyes was proving to be one of the hardest things I had ever done.

Everything came roaring back like a bad dream all at once. The blood seeping out of my best friend. The look of pure loathing from Tom as he shot me. The tears in Reid's eyes as he begged me to hang on just a little longer. The sound of agony coming from Heath as he tried to get to me. Maybe it was better to keep my eyes closed. I could pretend everything was still okay.

Just when I thought about doing just that, I felt a

soft hand grip mine and give me a gentle squeeze.

A soft wobbly voice cut through the fog in my brain. "Mom, it's me, Lindsey. I need you to open your eyes for me. I need you to come back to me." She hiccupped around her broken plea.

My baby was here. I tried to open my eyes, but I couldn't. Everything was just so heavy. I should be in pain, shouldn't I? I had been beaten and shot. Why couldn't I feel anything?

"Please," Lindsey begged with a soft voice. I felt as she put her head against my hand, the wetness from her tears spreading on my fingers. I could feel the darkness starting to take me again. I tried to move my fingers, but nothing was working. I tried to fight it as reality faded away and I was taken back into oblivion.

****

Voices roused me from my warm, dark place. I failed as I tried to open my eyes again. I didn't know how much time had passed but Lindsey wasn't holding my hand anymore.

"This can't be normal. It has been four days and she hasn't so much as twitched." I heard Heath's hushed tone as he spoke to someone I couldn't see.

I tried, really tried to move my hand. If I focused hard, I could almost feel my fingers. "It's normal after having this type of trauma to the brain for the body to stay in a sedative state for this long, Mr. Gillup. Her body is trying to heal," came a soft masculine voice I didn't recognize.

I could hear the frustration in his exhale at what the doctor was saying. I was still trying to open my eyes. I wanted to see my boys so badly at that moment. I could feel the heaviness creeping back in already. I needed to tell them I was okay. That I was still here with them.

I felt something pokey brush against my hand

before I felt his soft lips kiss my fingers. Reid held my hand against his mouth while he whispered to me. "You have to fight this, bunny. Do you hear me?" His voice was smaller and more broken than I had ever heard before. "I am a selfish bastard and I need you to pull through this. We need you, Kate." His voice faded out as I slipped back into unconsciousness.

****

A demanding voice pulled me from myself. "You listen here, you stubborn bitch." Jill growled in a harsh whisper.

I felt a surge of pure joy fill my chest. She was alive. "You don't get to leave me. Do you hear me? We did not go through all of that just for you to leave me. You think I enjoyed getting shot? I didn't, that shit hurt. You are not going to leave me alone. I can't handle this life without you. I absolutely refuse to let you go. You open your eyes right now, Kathrine Hart." Jill's angry voice filled my ears.

I could feel my eyes start to flutter as I tried to open them. "I did not sneak all the way in here, past that bitchy nurse, for you to lay there unconscious. Open your eyes and look at me, dammit!"

If I didn't listen to her, she was sure to start shouting. I tried speaking, but my mouth was so damn dry. I was finally able to get my eyes open and I saw a watery version of my best friend sitting next to me. She had tears in her eyes as she stared at me.

"Oh, thank God!" She sobbed. Her trembling hands grasped mine fiercely.

I swallowed past the lump in my throat as I rasped out, "You're so bossy." I tried to smile but stopped when my cheek flared in pain and my head hurt so bad it made me want to close my eyes again.

Jill laughed at me through her tears. "Well, it

worked, didn't it?"

I tried to laugh with her but my guts felt like they were about to shred apart. I hissed at the pain.

"Don't. Don't try to laugh. Tom got off a good shot and I don't want you to fuck up anything that the surgeons fixed," Jill reprimanded.

I looked back up at her. "I was so damn scared, Jill."

She was openly sobbing now. "I know, babe, I know. We are just lucky your man showed up when he did." She nodded to my left.

Turning my head ever so gently, I soaked in the scene in front of me. Both of my boys were asleep sitting on the couch next to my bed. They looked so tired it made my heart ache. It also looked like neither of them had groomed in a long week. Their hair was as rumpled as their clothes were.

Jill leaned forward and whispered. "They refused to leave you. The nurses tried to tell them they couldn't stay because they weren't family." She chuckled. "You should have seen how they reacted. I'm surprised their yelling didn't bring you out of your coma. Lindsey even tried to get them to go home just to shower, but they wouldn't budge. She ended up going and getting them a few hygienic things and clothes from their apartment for them to use here."

I could feel my chest swelling with the love I had for these two. When I met Heath that first night, I never would have guessed that I would be finding the loves of my life shortly after. They had no idea how much they had changed my life.

I felt the crushing weight of guilt fall on me at the thought of them never knowing how I truly felt about them. I almost left this world without telling them how special they were to me. I looked back at Jill and squeezed her hand. "I almost didn't get to tell them, Jill," I confessed. "I let all this time pass by and I didn't even tell them." I couldn't stop the sob that ripped from my throat.

"Didn't tell us what?" Heath asked as he woke from his sleep, Reid following right after. They both rushed to my side, kneeling beside me.

Reid smoothed my hair and looked at me with watery eyes. "Oh, God, Kate, I thought you were gone." He gasped. "I thought that I was too late. If I had been there when I was supposed to be none of this would have happened. I am so, so sorry, baby."

He shook with the force of his cries as he put his forehead on my shoulder. His broken voice made my heart stutter. I weakly lifted my hand and pushed my fingers into his golden locks.

His body shuddered as he soaked in my touch. "None of this is your fault, Reid. You can't blame yourself."

I looked up into Heath's eyes and could tell he was barely keeping it together. He wrung his hands, wiping them down his jeans. He needed to touch me. To reassure himself that I was okay.

I pulled my hand out of Jill's and reached for him. He latched on to me, bringing my hand to his lips. Kissing me oh so gently. "Tell us what, Kate?" he repeated with a quiet voice.

I looked at both of them with tear-soaked vision. "That I love you," I admitted. "When I look at you both it hurts to breathe. I can't go one day without wanting you. All I can think about is the two of you." I paused to inhale a shaky breath. "I thought when I was young that I had actually loved Tom, but I see now that this is what love feels like. And I know you both feel the same way. Because I've learned to love myself because of the way you love me."

Heath stared at me as his tears escaped down his face. "You're right, sweetheart, we do love you. And you scared the shit out of us. All I want to do is kiss you right now. But I don't want to hurt you," he said with a raspy voice.

"Kiss me, please."

Heath took his turn first, and his kiss was soft as he brushed his lips against mine. It was over before I wanted it to be and then Reid took his turn.

His kiss was a little firmer, but not as firm as I wanted it to be. When he pulled away from me, he let out a quiet shaky laugh. "You are way too fragile for any of that right now, bunny."

I was looking up at my men with hope in my eyes. I was mainly hoping that I healed quickly so I could show them just how much I loved them.

Jill cleared her throat, breaking the moment. "Well, as touching as that was, I believe I need to get back to my room before *Nurse Ratched* makes her rounds," she said with a quirky smile. "I'll check on you tomorrow, babe. Get some rest, but not too much rest. I expect you to wake up when the sun comes up tomorrow."

She was sneaking out the door before I could come up with something smartass to say in return. After she left, Heath moved to her vacated seat, rubbing my arm in soothing motions. Reid settled on the other side of me, doing the same to my leg. I felt my eyes getting heavy as I watched them.

"It's okay, bunny, we will be here when you wake up. Sleep," Reid said as he tucked my hair behind my ear. I didn't have much of a choice as I slipped off again with a smile on my face.

## Chapter Twenty-Six

"You are a very lucky woman, Ms. Hart," my silver fox of a doctor relayed to me. His name was Dr. Ian Young, and he was scrumptious. He had the most beautiful piercing blue eyes. Coupled with his slicked-back dark brown hair and a thick speckling of silver at his temples, it made him a genuine hottie.

His silver goatee that covered his strong chin made him look very distinguished. I couldn't see past his lab coat, but I could definitely tell that he worked out. I would bet money on the fact that he had washboard abs under those scrubs.

I briefly wondered if he was also Jill's doctor. I had to bite back my giggle at the thought of her hitting on our physician.

Reid must have been able to read my thoughts because he leaned down to whisper in my ear all of the vulgar things he was going to do to me if I didn't stop looking at my doctor like I wanted to eat him up.

I smiled up at him with what I hoped was my most innocent face. He just rolled his eyes at me, but I caught the hint of a grin before he looked away.

I had apparently been unconscious for a full week and a half. It had been another long week since that first day I'd woken up to my bossy best friend yelling at me. The boys had stayed with me the entire time. I finally did convince them to go home in shifts to at least shower. But when I tried to get them to go home to sleep, all hell had broken loose.

The argument quickly ended when Reid started tallying up all of the spanks he was going to give my ass when I was better. I enjoyed a good spanking as much as the next girl, but even I knew when to stop while I was ahead.

Detective Santos had stopped by after I'd woken up to give me an update on Tom. Evidently, Reid had done such a number on him that he had to be admitted to a separate hospital for a couple of days after the arrest.

Reid and Heath had both grumbled about the fact that he had even survived the altercation at all. They were both hungry for blood after what he had done to me, but at the end of the day, they were just happy that I was alive.

After his doctor had approved his transfer, he had been promptly carted off to jail to await his trial. From the sounds of it, he wouldn't be seeing the outside of a prison cell for quite some time. Jill had sent her attorney to speak with me, and she had led me to believe that she could get him put away for life. Two attempted murders would do that to a guy.

Jill was released to go home before I was. She had been shot at twice but only hit once. The bullet had gone through her left shoulder blade and out the front, right above her breast.

When she had shown me the X-rays of her chest, I had cried at how close it had come to taking her away from me permanently. I was still thanking God for Tom's bad aim. Jill would need some physical therapy, but other than, that she was going to be just fine.

When Damon had stopped by to give me the news of Tom, I saw him duck into her room as he was leaving. When I had asked her what he'd wanted, she had diverted the conversation to something else. I hoped that she would give him a chance, but I knew how stubborn she could be.

Lindsey had been to see me every day in between her classes. The first few days after I had awoken, had been the hardest. I felt so guilty when I looked at her. I was the reason her dad was behind bars, and it crushed me that she wouldn't get to have a relationship with him anymore.

She got very angry with me for even thinking that any of this was my fault. "Tom made his choice, and he chose wrong, Mom. There is no way in this world that I would ever blame you for what he did," she admitted with tears brimming those familiar gray eyes. "I refuse to feel bad for the man who dug his own grave. He may have been my dad at one time, but now he is just the fucker who tried to kill my mom."

It was my turn to cry as I looked at my baby girl. "I still can't help but feel bad that you won't get to have a relationship with him anymore. I loved my dad so much and would still be a daddy's girl if he were here. I didn't want you to miss out on the experience of a father-daughter bond," I said.

Lindsey smiled a watery smile. "Yeah, well, Grandpa was always a better dad than Tom ever even hoped to be. It's not like we were close before all this happened anyway, you know. You were always my favorite parent."

We both giggled after that.

I knew she was still hurting even if she didn't want to admit it. It would take her time to cope with this new trauma that Tom had given both of us, but I would be there to help her through it.

She had climbed into bed with me after that and we cuddled while she told me how much she liked Heath and Reid.

"They really are the best. I don't think I've ever seen such devotion from anyone," she admitted. "I'll forever be grateful that they're in our lives. I hate to think about what would have happened if you hadn't ever met them." She nuzzled my shoulder.

I smiled as I brushed her hair down in a soothing motion. "Me too," I whispered

She grinned up at me. "I'm just happy to see you finally be treated the way you should have been all these years." I had to agree with her on that point.

My boys had showered me with flowers and everything that I could have asked for. They waited on me hand and foot this whole time without so much as a grumble of a complaint. If I so much as tried to do anything by myself, Heath would force me back into bed with a strong reprimand.

They were so gentle with me and at first, I'd needed their gentle touch. But now, almost two weeks later, I was craving something different. As hard as I tried to get them to fool around with me, they wouldn't budge. Both of them claimed I was still too fragile. All I could get from them was kisses, and it was driving me crazy.

I looked back up at my doctor and waited for him to finish. "When you hit your head, your brain started to bleed immediately. That coupled with the fact that you were shot, should have killed you within minutes. Luckily, we were able to get your brain bleed under control, but you will be sporting that little bald spot for a while. Thankfully, the bullet didn't do too much damage. We did have to remove your gallbladder and repair some of your liver, but you should be fully healed within the next couple of weeks."

I smiled up at him as I used both my hands to grab my men. "Does that mean I get to go home today?" I was practically vibrating with excitement.

He smiled back at me, showing me that lady-killer smile. "Yes, Ms. Hart, you get to go home today."

I started to bounce slightly with my excitement until my stitches reminded me not to do that. "Okay, now on to the serious question. When do I get to have sex again?" I asked, not even a bit ashamed. A near-death experience would remove a lot of a person's shame, I'd found.

Reid busted up laughing as he gripped my arm, and I heard Heath choke on the sip of water he'd been taking. I smiled with wide eyes as I stared at my doctor. He was trying his hardest not to laugh but failing miserably.

"Well, you need to wait until we take your stitches out so it will probably be another two weeks before you can engage in any sexual activities," he said as he cleared his throat. He was smiling ear to ear now while I was left with a frown. This was going to be the longest two weeks of my life, I feared.

I looked at Reid with a pout, and he started laughing loudly again. Frowning, I turned to Heath who was grinning at me. "It'll be okay, sweetheart, we have waited this long, we can wait another two weeks," he said around a chuckle. I didn't know why they thought this was so funny. I wasn't laughing. I was horny, dammit.

I watched as Dr. Young turned to leave my room, nearly knocking into Lindsey and Emily. He grabbed Lyns by the shoulders to steady her. She was carrying a huge bouquet of flowers that she could hardly see over. She was apologizing profusely, still not able to see who she had run into.

Ian took the flowers from her and set them on my bedside table before turning back to face her. Lindsey immediately flushed, and Emily's jaw dropped when they looked up at the doctor. Ian looked taken aback for a moment as he looked at my daughter.

Emily covered her mouth to smother a giggle as Lyns stuttered and rubbed her hands down her thighs. "I-

I am so sorry about that. I shouldn't have gotten a bouquet that was bigger than me." She laughed nervously. I could tell that she was almost struck dumb by how handsome my doctor was.

Ian shook his head as he regarded her. "No, it's okay, I should have been watching where I was going." His smile was swoon-worthy.

Emily gave me a knowing smile before looking back at the exchange happening in front of us. As if they both remembered there were other people in the room, Lindsey looked toward me and cleared her throat. Dr. Young blinked and faced me again. "All right, you are free to go, be careful with those stitches, and I will see you in a couple of weeks."

I gave him a flamboyant salute as he turned and walked out the door with one more glance at Lyns. When she turned to me, she widened her eyes. Emily rushed past her, fanning herself while mouthing the words *Oh, my God*.

I nodded at her. "I know, he's hot, isn't he?" I said and we both dissolved into giggles. Reid huffed beside me, and I turned to him. "Not as hot as you, babe," I said with a reassuring wink.

He looked at me with a wicked smile. "I think your tally is up to thirty-five now, bunny. Are you trying to get to forty before the day's up?"

My eyes widened as I looked back at Emily. "Hey, girl! So good to see you!" I said loudly, switching the subject. Heath and Reid both started laughing after that.

A couple of hours later, Heath was pushing my wheelchair down the hallway on our way to the truck. I was finally on my way home. It was no longer the boys' apartment. It was our home, but not for long. According to the boys, we would be looking for a new home soon.

The lease would be up in three months, and they weren't joking when they said they weren't going to renew it.

They promised after I was all healed up, we would go look for houses together. The prospect of buying a home with the two men I loved made me happier than I could even try to explain.

Heath refused to let me try to climb in the truck as he picked me up, cradling me, and plopped me in the passenger seat. I caught him with my legs, bringing him closer to me before he could walk away.

I grabbed his shirt and pulled him in for a panty-melting kiss. When he pulled up for air, he looked at Reid as I leaned forward to kiss his neck. "We have created a monster, Reid," was all he said as I got a shiver out of him. I grinned against his neck. They had no idea.

## Chapter Twenty-Seven

*Three months later*

"We can just set that box in the kitchen," I told Jill as we lugged boxes full of my dishes through the front door of our new home.

The house had been absolutely perfect when we had looked at it three months ago. It was a cottage-style home with three bedrooms and two bathrooms. One of them was a huge master suite that included a big clawfoot tub I couldn't wait to soak into.

We had spent the last month renovating certain parts of the house to meet our needs. Like upgrading the shower in the master bath so we could all fit into it comfortably. The spare room we had made into my office. I was officially a published author with Brookes Publishing. I was currently on my second book in the series, with my first book currently climbing the best sellers list.

After my stint in the hospital, my life had fallen into a peaceful rhythm. I was up and walking without anyone hovering within my first week home. We had found this house fairly quickly after. Once we purchased it, the boys started the renovation while I sat back and watched.

They treated me like a porcelain doll for way longer than I wanted them to. I had finally had enough after three weeks of their delicate treatment when I decided I needed to take the reins and show that I wasn't going to break.

I still giggled when I thought of their faces as they woke up to me riding Heath. It hadn't taken very much to convince Reid to join in after he saw what I was doing to his friend.

Once they realized that I was obviously up to par, they frequently took advantage. Reid made good on his promise of an erotic spanking as he had me tied to the bed and they took turns doling out the punishment. I would be lying if I said I hadn't enjoyed every bit of it.

They had taken advantage of my tied-up state that night when they told me that I was going to marry one of them. It wasn't a question. Neither one of them liked the feeling of almost being kicked out of the hospital because they technically weren't family. Reid had also told me that he didn't like the fact that I shared a last name with "that fucker" as he put it.

When I first moved here, the idea of getting married again left a bad taste in my mouth. But now, when I thought of being married to them, I went all soft and mushy inside. I couldn't imagine my life without them. I couldn't think of anything better than being their wife.

Since I could only legally marry one of them, the boys had to flip a coin for the honor. Reid pouted his way into a sympathy blow-job when he lost. Although I was technically married to Heath now, they were both my husbands. I wore both of their rings, they both wore mine, and we all changed our last names to Gillup-Hudson.

We'd watched Tom's court proceedings safely from the comfort of our living room. Apparently, all of the drama that had gone down between us was enough to get the local news station's attention. They ran a story on what had happened as well as the trial. Tom was going to be going away for a long, long time.

Jill's lawyer proved to be everything and more as she helped the state try him for multiple counts of fraud, stalking, and two counts of attempted murder. I had tried to find some sympathy for the man I once loved as the judge read the verdict of fifty years, but I couldn't.

Today was finally moving day, and I was ecstatic to finally be getting my fresh start. I had liked to say that I'd gotten my new beginning when I moved to Florida, but that was a lie. My new life hadn't started until I had finally accepted myself. It hadn't started until I met these two amazing men who opened my eyes to so much more. No matter how long I lived, I would never be able to repay them for what they had done for me.

"All right, that's all of it." Reid grunted as he and Heath moved our bed into our bedroom. They laid it down on the floor with a huff. I smiled as I walked up to Reid and put my arms around his neck.

"Hello, my bunny," he said with a grin as he brought his lips to mine.

"Hello, my Viking," I murmured against his lips. He grunted as he brought his hands down to my ass, squeezing me. I twisted around as I felt Heath come up behind me, caressing my ribs.

"My turn," he mumbled as he brought our bodies flush together. I could feel his hand leave my side to pull Reid in closer to us. Trapping me between them just the way I like. I sighed as he brought his lips down to mine.

I could hear Jill from the kitchen. "All right, I am out of here, Kate. I'll talk to you tomorrow. Use protection," she yelled.

I pulled away from Heath's mouth long enough to giggle and tell her goodbye. Before she had the front door shut, they were tossing me on the bed. I stared up at my husbands as they started to strip their clothes.

I had a ridiculous grin that cracked across my face as I looked at them. In no time, they were fully stripped, and so was I. Heath was the first to lie on top of me, drugging me with his kisses.

He spread my legs with his hand as he went

exploring. "Always so wet for us, sweetheart." He groaned as he ran his fingers through my labia.

They seemed to be in a hurry to get inside of me today. One second, Heath was driving me crazy with his fingers, and the next, he was dragging me on top of him, reverse cowgirl style. Reid stood in front of me as Heath pushed his way into my pussy with a deep groan.

I gasped at the intrusion, and Reid pushed his cock into my open mouth. Reid held my head still as he fucked my mouth. Heath was thrusting up into me as his fingers played with my asshole. I could tell quickly where this was going as he made a grab for the lube in one of the moving boxes.

Reid kept up his deep thrusts as Heath pushed me up and forward to prepare me for what was about to happen. He lubed himself up and was leading me back onto him within seconds. I made small passes on top of Heath, burying him deeper and deeper in my ass as I went.

Reid pulled himself out of my mouth and started to stroke himself. My breaths came out in short puffs as I managed to take Heath all the way.

Now it was Reid's turn. They gently laid me down until my back was fully against Heath's front. Heath bent his knees, taking my legs with him. He used his advantage over me to spread me wide, making room for Reid.

When he had me where he wanted me, he snaked his arm around my torso, finding my swollen clitoris. He started to rub me in short circles as Reid came into my view, looking down at me with hooded eyes.

"You are so fucking beautiful, Kate," Reid said. Heath started to move beneath me. Fucking my ass in long, deep strokes.

Reid leaned down, and suddenly his mouth took

the place of Heath's fingers. He sucked my clit into his mouth and flicked his tongue fast. Heath picked up speed as he fucked me harder.

I was breathing heavily as I felt my orgasm build higher and higher. "Oh, God! I am going to come," I screamed right as Heath grabbed both of my breasts, rolling my puckered nipples. I felt my eyes roll back as I exploded, clamping down on Heath. He groaned long and hard into my ear at the feeling.

Before I completely came down from my orgasm, Reid was shoving his way into my pussy. I gasped and looked up at him as he gave me little time to adjust. This position put him at the perfect height to hit my G-Spot, and I came again with a long moan as he raked his cock across it.

"Fuck yes!" Reid growled as he looked down at where we were all connected. Heath's hands continued to play with my breasts as they both fucked me with rapid strokes.

I could feel Heath's breath against my cheek as he panted. "I'm going to fill you up, sweetheart. You are going to be so full of my cum, you'll be able to taste it," he grumbled as he reached back down and pinched my clit. I screamed again as I came for the third time, bringing them over the edge with me with long groans.

Reid collapsed on top of me, not losing his place inside of me. We all lay there for a good while catching our breath. Heath's hands were rubbing up and down my sides.

Reid finally pushed up onto his hands to look down at me with a lazy smile. When he kissed me, I started to move my hips between them. Their hands tightened on me as I felt them starting to harden again. I felt Reid chuckle as he looked down at me. "Aren't you satisfied, bunny?" he asked.

I turned my head to kiss Heath as I churned my hips. Looking between them with a smile on my lips, I said, "I'm just getting started."

****

*Jill*

It was getting late, and all I wanted to do was get home and take a nice long bath. I'd spent the whole day helping Kate move into her new home. I was so happy for my best friend. She had been through hell for most of her life and she deserved to be happy. I was only a little bit jealous of her.

I knew I shouldn't think like that. The only reason I didn't do relationships was my own fault. Ever since the incident in college, I'd made a point not to do relationships. I also never put myself in a situation where I wasn't completely in control either. I hadn't even found myself wanting anything more until recently. Watching Kate find her new life was just bringing up too many feelings that I needed to put a lid on. The last thing I needed was another person to make happy.

I pulled into my dark driveway and parked my car. Turning it off, I sat in the dark trying to decompress for a moment. For the last three months, I felt like my control was slowly slipping away from me. My nerves were shot and my anxiety was at an all-time high. I stayed up later than normal now because I didn't want to sleep. I wouldn't ever tell Kate this, but I'd been having some very disturbing nightmares ever since I got shot.

My dreams were always the same. Kate and I running for our lives and then exploding pain across my shoulder. In the dream, I would be on my back looking up at Tom as he leveled the pistol at me. Just before he would pull the trigger again, his face would morph into Jason's. The wood floor I was lying on would turn into a stale-smelling bed. I would wake up screaming as he started to descend on top of me.

Just thinking about the dream had me sweating and gripping the steering wheel with white-knuckled force. I shook myself and stepped out of my car. I needed to put that shit behind me. I was almost thirty-five years old and still having nightmares about shit that happened back in college. My therapist would have a field day with me.

After walking up my sidewalk, I unlocked the front door and pushed my way into my house. Fiona came running for me, and I lovingly picked up the white feline. "Hey, baby, you're always happy to see me aren't you." I crooned.

Stroking the cat's soft head, I looked around my home. I bought this place shortly after my publishing firm took off. It was sleek and modern. Everything had a place in this house. I would be lying if I said that I wasn't a little OCD with my organizational habits. Most people would call me anal, but I never cared what most people said. I needed control in my life, and I had to find it however I could.

Sighing, I turned to put my keys on the table next to my door. I had just dropped my keys in the bowl when I felt a breeze graze over my knuckles.

Looking back toward my door, I saw something that made panic slither down my spine. The small window next to my door handle was broken in. Looking down, I saw the evidence all over the floor. There was glass everywhere. Fear gripped my chest as I looked around for any sign that someone was in my home. I grabbed my keys again and slammed out my front door, running back to my car.

I tossed Fiona in the passenger seat and locked my doors. My breath left me in short, labored puffs as I dug through my purse and found my phone. Unlocking it with shaking fingers, I called the only person I could think of who would know what to do.

He answered on the first ring. "Detective Santos," came his clipped voice over the line. I was hyperventilating as I tried to tell him what was happening.

"Jill? You need to calm down, Red. I can't understand you. Where are you?"

I could hear the roar of an engine starting in the background.

"I-I'm—my house. P-lease," was all I managed.

I was having a full-blown panic attack now as I struggled to breathe. My lips had gone tingly, and I couldn't feel my fingers anymore as my vision blurred at the edges. I could barely hear Damon's voice as I faded out.

"Stay on the line with me, Red. I'm on my way. Jill? Jill!"

I dropped my phone as I gasped for one last breath before everything went black.

**The End**

**EVERNIGHT PUBLISHING ®**

www.evernightpublishing.com